ONE NIGHT TO BE SINFUL

"I'm coming," Abigail called even as the fingers of her free hand closed around the door handle.

Dim light from the wall sconces in the hall flickered across the hard angles of Calvin's face and the muscles clearly defined between the folds of his opened shirt. Abigail felt an odd tingling run up her scalp as she stared at the broad expanse of dark skin exposed before her, than a hot blush stain her cheeks when she realized she was staring.

Her wide eyes lifted quickly to the face of the man before her. He did not appear to be too concerned with her ogling. As a matter of fact, he appeared totally unaware of where her attention was directed, as his had also drifted. Abigail felt the heat of his gaze like a physical caress as it ran along the exposed skin of her neck then lower to her bare shoulders and the upper curves of her breasts. Abigail had not donned her robe in coming to the door and felt ridiculously exposed in only her thin nightgown with lace straps in lieu of sleeves.

His gaze had been on her bare flesh for perhaps seconds, but they had passed like hours for Abigail. When Calvin's eyes finally lifted to hers, she noted that they had gone to an almost smoky shade of blue. His attention dropped again, and she felt her mouth go dry . . .

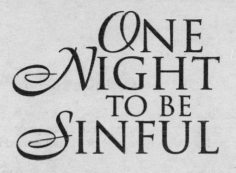

ONE NIGHT TO BE SINFUL

SAMANTHA GARVER

ZEBRA BOOKS
KENSINGTON PUBLISHING CORP.
www.kensingtonbooks.com

ZEBRA BOOKS are published by

Kensington Publishing Corp.
850 Third Avenue
New York, NY 10022

All Kensington titles, imprints, and distributed lines are available at special quantity discounts for bulk purchases for sales
promotion, premiums, fund-raising, educational, or institu-
tional use.

Special book excerpts or customized printings can also be
created to fit specific needs. For details, write or phone the
office of the Kensington Special Sales Manager: Attn. Special
Sales Department. Kensington Publishing Corp., 850 Third
Avenue, New York, NY 10022. Phone: 1-800-221-2647.

ISBN 0-8217-7942-7

First Printing: September 2005
10 9 8 7 6 5 4 3 2 1

Printed in the United States of America

Prologue

It happened in a rush, the crack of the whip and the startling snap of the reins in two. She saw the smile abruptly disappear from Patrick's face, and the sudden advent of uninhibited understanding made his features as handsome as they'd been the day they first met. The horses screamed, a god-awful sound of abject understanding. One of the rear wheels ruptured under the strain of its burden. The phaeton tipped to one side, screeching against the wooden rail of the bridge as it barreled forward.

When the railing splintered, all went painfully silent. She looked to her left and saw Patrick tumbling backward out of his seat. No, not tumbling: throwing himself out of the doomed conveyance. Her heart lurched into her stomach as the phaeton plummeted off the bridge. She came up off her cushioned seat, her bonnet flying away, never to be found again, and her hair exploding around her like a living thing. Her skirts billowed open like a silk umbrella, then pressed rippling against her legs as she fell.

The river water was like ice, and she gave a great, open-mouthed gasp as she hit its surface. There was no time to register the pain of her back and shoulders making contact with the hard rocks beneath the water; her wide eyes were focused on the phaeton as it crashed down beside her. Her lashes fluttered as water sprayed across her face and lowered with grim understanding as the vehicle began to tumble onto its side.

She did not scream—could not because her lungs had emptied in a silent rush of unfathomable pain as the carriage rolled over and across her. On her remaining breath, her nostrils flared in a whimper.

The sound of breaking bone managed to be heard above the splash of the phaeton finally settling in the water.

The star-speckled sky was a blur beyond her tear-filled eyes, but as her gaze shifted to the edge of the bridge, she thought there stood the shape of a man. The familiar figure looked down at her for a long time before turning away.

The bliss of painless oblivion beckoned like the warm hold of a lover. Her gown was now soaked—later she would realize it was more with blood than river water—and her hair was floating around her. Her skin was as pale as the moon above, her lips already turning blue. When she let her eyes slip closed, stars were reflected in the tears that seeped down her cheeks.

Chapter 1

From behind an abandoned crate against the wall, greedy little eyes peered at the newcomer. He was much like the others who often visited the alleyway, those who looked very much out of place in one of London's seedier districts. The stranger's eyes gleamed in the moonlight as he paused at the entrance, doing a quick once-over of the damp brick walls and littered ground. As with the others at odds with the homeless and the aged prostitutes who frequented the alley, he honed in on the door painted a brilliant shade of red in the depths of the dark passage.

The footpad seriously considered the man making his way farther into the alley, licking his chapped lips as he took in the other's fine garments and the gold chain dangling from his watch fob. A moment's glance, however, as the stranger passed, was all the thief needed to see he was outdone. The newcomer was more than twice his size, and the expression

on his face as he evenly met the stare of the footpad almost dared the other man to make a move.

Once he was certain the grimy little man hiding
beside the crate had settled back against the wall,
the marquis made the last few steps that took him
to the starkly red door so specifically described in
the note. He did not knock but simply pushed the
door inward and stepped inside.

"Take your coat, my lord?"

The young boy appeared out of nowhere the moment he was over the threshold, unsmiling with arms
outstretched. While removing his hat and greatcoat, Calvin Garrett did a quick survey of Justin's.
It was not, he noticed immediately, as crowded as
most gentlemen's clubs; the lights were dimmer and
the atmosphere more relaxed. The only youngster
present was the boy now taking his gloves, the rest
of the gentlemen beyond the age of indolent frivo-
lity. Most of the men were in small groups around
the lacquered tables; only one sat alone. Calvin recognized the man who had called him here.

The young lord looked up from his glass as Calvin
closed in on his table. Thomas Wolcott's normally
benign countenance was visibly angst-ridden, though
some of the furrows in his brow relaxed when he
caught sight of the other man. He rose to his feet,
his face looking orange under the weight of the
lantern light and a wealth of freckles.

"You found the place well enough?"

Calvin accepted the hand the other man produced, shook it familiarly. "I had my doubts when I
began to follow your directions. I thought there
had been an error."

"I have heard some say that you can gauge the
strength of the men who frequent Justin's by their

valor in getting to the place," Wolcott said as he re-seated himself. "I took the liberty of ordering you a brandy."

Calvin regarded his longtime friend over the rim of the glass before swallowing. "Would you care to explain why you brought me here tonight?"

Wolcott sighed, running a hand through his thick hair. "I apologize if my request took you from a prior engagement. But I fear that if I do not act now, something unfortunate might happen."

"Are you in some sort of trouble?" Calvin frowned.

"No, not I." The other man shook his head. "It is my sister I am worried about."

"Jeanette?"

"Abigail."

Whereas a picture flashed to life in Calvin's mind of a petite and rather comely young woman at the mention of the first sister, no image came to mind of the second. Though he recalled Thomas mentioning the other woman—older than Jeanette but younger than Thomas—on a few occasions, Calvin had never met her.

"She hasn't lived with Jeanette and I for years now. She left Town about three years ago and makes her home in North Rutherford—a few hours away. We have a small estate just outside the village. My grandparents spent most of their lives there, and it was maintained by a small staff in the years follow-ing their deaths."

"Your sister lives there alone?"

Wolcott's ears turned pink. "I know it sounds unusual, but Abigail is the most intelligent of fe-males. Since her return to North Rutherford, the estate has gone from near-ruin to an exemplary upkeep. It seems like I abandoned her to her own devices, but she is sensible. An independent thing, really—"

"You need not take the defensive with me, Thomas," Calvin interrupted. "I just thought it interesting that the woman lives without family supervision."

"Well, as I said, I always thought Abigail to be remarkably independent." Wolcott broke eye contact as he was brought another drink. He looked down into his glass as he said, "I am beginning to doubt myself, however. Perhaps I simply feel guilty now that I am putting so much effort in Jeanette's coming-out and contriving a list of adequate suitors for her. After Abigail's engagement ended, she showed no interest in returning to the marriage market. This, along with other circumstances, kept me from pressuring her into another match."

"So now you wish to find her a husband?" Calvin could vaguely recollect Wolcott mentioning his sister's engagement, if not its end.

Wolcott made a face at his companion's words. "I'm afraid it's a bit late for that. Her increasing age, inclination toward self-reliance, and . . . other conditions have secluded her from new courtships. I hate to admit it, but Abigail is well on her way to becoming a spinster." He inclined his head. "I must say, for all accounts and purposes, she seems content."

"If she is happy"—Calvin lifted a single brow—"then why all this sudden worry about her?"

"It's not one thing, really, so much as a few oddities in the past several months."

"And they are?" Calvin was genuinely curious. Wolcott had made his sister out to be a true original. More than he was interested in what was worrying his friend so, however, he wanted to know why Thomas was telling him all this.

"As of late, Abigail has begun sharing company with a group of women whom I have never before met. One of whom I believe to be Emily Paxton. She, if you didn't already know, is currently pleading a case for divorce before the courts."

Calvin shrugged. "It is not uncommon for individuals of shared interests to become friends. Paxton must have the same tendency toward independence as your sister."

Wolcott rested his elbows on the table to lean forward. "For the past two months, Abby has been removing considerable sums of money from her account. Our man of affairs tells me she refuses to explain where the money has gone."

"It is her account to work with as she wishes, is it not?"

"That's not all. Three weeks ago I received a letter of complaint from Lord Raleigh, whose property borders the estate in North Rutherford. He believes a member of our household has stolen one of his best horses."

"Why would your sister steal a horse?"

"She wouldn't." Wolcott waved the idea off. "That's ludicrous. But listen to this." He reached into his coat pocket and removed a folded letter. "Three days ago I received this from family friends who were passing through North Rutherford. It inquires as to how well my sister fared after the awful fire that almost burned down the stables."

"What fire?" Calvin scowled.

"Bloody hell, man, I have no idea what they are talking about. Abby sent no word to me of any fire." Wolcott slapped the letter down on the table.

"I paid my sister a visit, in due haste. She told me there was no fire, but I could have sworn there were sections of the stable newer than the rest, as if they had been rebuilt."

Calvin watched his friend shove all his fingers through his wild hair, and then calmly inquired, "Did you happen to notice a new horse in the stables?"

It took a moment, but Wolcott laughed.

"I can imagine what I sound like. It worries me, though. Abigail is no liar, most especially not to me."

"You sound like a concerned brother, Thomas." Calvin downed the last of his brandy and set the glass on the table. "I must admit, I don't understand why you're telling me this."

For the first time that evening, Thomas Wolcott smiled. It was a decidedly discomforting smile to the man seated across from him.

The marquis lifted a black-as-soot brow and waited.

"You know you are my best friend, Calvin. You are the only one I would share this with. The only one I would trust with my sister's well-being."

"You'd have me, a veritable stranger to the woman, encroach upon her private life?"

"It's a somewhat trickier matter than that." Wolcott was thoughtful before saying, "As I said, Abigail is independent and incredibly solitary. She loathes large crowds, and as far as I know, the originals of which I spoke have been her first friends in quite some time. The end of her engagement three years ago created quite a stir in the ton. Ever since, she has remained excruciatingly private."

"Let me make myself clearer, Thomas." Calvin's tone lowered as a group of men passed the table.

"I do not understand how you propose I should intrude upon your isolated sister's life."

Wolcott took a deep breath. "I'd like you to take on a position as part of the house staff."

"I beg your pardon?"

"In my visit with my sister, it was made known to me that she lost a member of her staff. Tuttleton, I believe his name was. An excellent old chap who supervised the servants and maintained the upkeep of the land."

"You want me to pose as a servant?" Calvin's voice lowered even more.

"It won't be for more than a few weeks, I assure you, Calvin. Just long enough to poke around the estate a bit and tell me what Abigail is truly about."

"I don't think my . . . disposition is suitable for such a job," the other man said carefully.

"Quite the contrary, Calvin."

The marquis gazed silently at the other man, waiting.

"My sister is an excellent judge of character."

"And you believe she will look at me and see a member of the lower class?"

"Forgive me for being so blunt, Calvin"—Wolcott winced even as he said it—"but you were born a member of the lower class."

Though the true words hit him with the force of a blow, Calvin didn't flinch. He negligently leaned back in his chair.

"I'm sorry," Thomas said. "Sorry." He sighed. "I need your help, man. I would never forgive myself if something happened to Abigail, and she has gone ungoverned for so long it is impossible for me to try to control her now. I just need to know . . . I need to be certain she is in no danger."

Chapter 2

It took some effort, but Abby managed to hold down her breakfast. She stared for a full minute at the polished surface of her desk, shifted her gaze to the clock set atop the mantle in the far wall, then returned her attention to the top of her desk. Anything was preferable to watching the veritable fossil seated across from her forcefully relocating fluid from deep in his throat to the yellowed handkerchief he produced. Because it would be rude—though she was certain the man gagging before her had no use for such charms—to cup both hands over her ears, Abby ran a finger over the list of names she had begun to pen earlier in the week. With her free hand, she dipped her quill into the inkwell.

Beside each name on her sheet of foolscap, she had been making notes to herself. Printed rather elegantly beside the first name on her list she had written *kind, courteous*, and then—after finding the silver teapot that had been left outside her study

door missing following the applicant's departure—
THIEF. These comments seemed to set the prece-
dent for the next five gentlemen to apply for the
butler position. One man had no past work history
because he had spent most of his adult life in
prison; another almost made Abby inebriated by
the smell coming from his pores. Beside the name
above that of the man now seated before her, Abby
had penned, *Stares at front of bodice instead of into
eyes.*

She was thoughtful as she gazed at the name of
Harold Lloyd, the man who was noisily pocketing
a thick portion of mucus into his hanky across from
her. Then she wrote very precisely, *Consumption?*

"Now," Lloyd spoke, his voice like stones gur-
gling in his throat, "where was we?"

"I had asked"—Abby looked up and winced when
she caught the older gentleman shrewdly inspecting his most recent handkerchief deposit—"if there
were any chores you thought you might not be
able to handle?"

"Well"—he sucked a deep, wet breath through
his nose—"I don't wash windows or anything else
for that matter. Women's work, it is. I can't be carrying stuff up and down no stairs. Bad back, ye know.
I'm deaf in me right ear, so visitors will have to let
themselves in most of the time." He coughed, then
made a growling sound deep in his throat.

"Thank you for your time, Mr. Lloyd," Abby said
quickly, before he could hawk up another one of
his lungs. "Margot will see you out."

"Eh"—Lloyd heaved himself out of his chair and
scowled down at Abby over his veined nose—"where
is the man of the house?"

"This is my home, Mr. Lloyd," Abby clarified.

"No, I mean"—the old man carefully folded his handkerchief into his pocket—"where's the chap who runs this place? Your husband or whatnot?"

"Margot!"

"I'm here." The woman appeared breathless in the doorway. A knight in dusty apron, her bright orange hair curled out from her round face like the rays of the sun. She took one look at Abby's expression, then moved quickly forward to take Lloyd's bony arm. "I'll show you out, sir." She shuffled him quickly toward the doorway, glancing back over her shoulder to say apologetically, "Could hardly hear you in the kitchen, love."

"It's all right, Margot." Abby saw the other woman's bright eyebrows lift in question and quickly shook her head.

"Sorry, miss." She whispered, though the younger woman doubted Harold Lloyd could have heard if she shouted. "You'll find someone."

Abby smiled in return until the study door fell closed. She took a deep breath, filling her cheeks like a chipmunk, and then let the sigh escape her in time with the sinking of her heart. Over her neatly penned descriptions of the men who had applied for the butler position she made a large X.

Tuttleton had been like a grandfather to her, and his only requirement before taking the position in her home had been that he would be able to bring his son to live with him. She found it hard to believe, however, that the loyalty and work ethic she had appreciated in him had been a creation of her love for the man. She hated to think that when her unfailingly polite butler had left this world to find his place in heaven, he had taken with him the last of the loyal and hardworking men.

It was not difficult to believe, however, given her recent interviews for the position he had left vacant. She didn't expect anyone to talk to as she had been able to do so easily with Tuttleton, didn't expect anyone to fill her heart as he had. But was it too much to hope for an employee who didn't offer lewd glances or steal one's silver?

Abby sat back in her chair, reaching absently to rub at her leg through the material of her plum-colored gown and wondering how Margot would fare at controlling more than just the dusting and linens, when the woman again appeared. She popped her head around the small opening she had made at the door to peer at Abby. There was a peculiar glint to her eye.

"Were you expecting another gent to apply for the position today, miss?"

"No." Abby frowned. "Why?"

"Because there is one here." Margot stepped aside and let the door swing completely open.

Abby did a quick survey of the man who almost filled the doorway, eyes widening as they moved back to Margot. The other woman shrugged.

"My apologies," the stranger said and stepped into the room. "I know I come unannounced. I thought perhaps you would be so kind as to take a moment for an interview."

Margot shrugged again, and Abby slowly let her attention move back to the man. She had a feeling she and her maid had shared the thought: *This is a butler?*

The man was the youngest yet to apply for the position. Which didn't exactly say much, being that the youngest before him might have walked with the dinosaurs.

His hair was dark as a starless night, the skin across his broad forehead and cheeks taut and colored from the sun. He was lithe, but his shoulders filled his worn brown coat to the point the seams strained. His fingers were long, their nails clean and clipped. In one hand he held the hat he must have doffed upon entering her home.

"You are Lady Wolcott, are you not?"

Abby blinked and prayed she hadn't been silent for as long as she thought. "Yes. I am Abigail Wolcott."

"My name is Calvin Garrett." The man crossed the space between the door and Abby's desk in three long strides. He held out a hand, and when Abby tentatively offered hers, he took it in his and bowed.

Over the straight line of Calvin Garrett's back, Abby saw Margot's cheeks sink inward with her smile. She stepped back into the hall and let the door close.

Abby did not rise and, for the first time since beginning her interviews, felt ill-mannered because of it.

"Please, have a seat, Mr. Garrett," she said as he straightened. She watched as he folded himself into the chair she had set before her desk earlier. She thought, in the time it took for him to find his seat, he did his own survey of her.

His eyes were blue, not like the sky, but the ocean at sunset. Abby felt slightly self-conscious of the tendrils of hair that had lost their place in her chignon and now fell down at her neck and temples. Not unlike an applicant that had come before him, Calvin Garrett's gaze drifted across the front of her bodice, but for only a heartbeat. Just long enough for Abby to register none of the lewdness that wafted off the other applicant like cologne.

She wondered where the man had heard about her position. Abby had made some inquiries of a placement agency in Town, but they sent her the names of the men they were sending to her for an interview. She was positive she would have remembered this name.

"Lord Wolcott directed me here."

Abby winced as if the man had physically poked in her mind before registering his words. "Thomas?"

Garrett reached into his coat and produced a folded piece of foolscap. "Yes. He gave me a reference."

"Oh?" Abby unfolded the letter and found the almost-illegible male script warmly familiar.

Abby,
Forgive me for interfering in your search for a suitable butler to replace your last. It just so happened that Mr. Garrett, who has been under my employ for the past year, has decided he wishes to leave Town. I thought you might be able to give him a position there.
Garrett has always proved a trustworthy and tireless worker. He tends to seem a bit arrogant, but is a decent man at heart. I would not have directed him there did I think anything less.

Thomas

Abby's gaze lifted from the letter. Garrett met her eye evenly, but she wouldn't call his look arrogant.

"Have you ever overseen an estate before, Mr. Garrett?"

"Yes."

Abby waited and, when he did not go into detail, mentally found the list of inquiries she had made for her applicants. "Can you safely maneuver a carriage or like conveyance on stone as well as dirt paths?"

"Yes."

"Do you have any objection to having a female overseeing your work?"

It took him a moment, Garrett holding her stare the entire time before answering, "I have never had a woman oversee my work before." Abby thought she saw his right eye twitch slightly. "I should think not."

"Can you lift large amounts of weight?" Though it hadn't occurred when she had asked the question of prior applicants, Abby began to feel uncomfortable. "Say, ten stones?"

"Yes," he returned rather thoughtfully, his gaze taking on a questioning gleam.

"So, sir." Abby felt her neck and cheeks warm. "If need be, you could bear the weight of a full-grown woman like myself?"

His gaze flashed over her again. Though she was only visible from the waist up, Abby felt like she was being inspected from head to toe. There was a slight curl to Garrett's mouth when he replied, "Easily."

Abby cleared her throat and lifted her chin. "Do you have any objections to answering doors?"

"No."

"Helping in the stables if need be?"

"No."

"Going up and down the stairs several times in one day?"

"No."

"Helping the house staff"—it sounded more impressive than simply saying Margot—"with rudimentary cleaning if need be?"

There was that brief eye twitch again. "No."

"Well, then," Abby said, because she had run out of questions. She looked down at the list of near-riffraff on her desk. Her eyes moved to the creased letter from her brother in London, then back up to Garrett. He was quietly, patiently, watching her.

"I suppose that is all there is, Mr. Garrett." She folded her hands together atop her now-unnecessary list. "The butler position is yours, if you'll have it."

Now Garrett blinked at her as if surprised. He quickly recovered to nod.

"I'll just have Margot—"

"Yes?" The door swung open the moment Abby said her name.

She gazed at the woman knowingly. "Please show Mr. Garrett the room that is to be his." Abby turned back to the man now rising. "Feel free to collect your things and tidy up any loose ends that may need it. I'd appreciate it if you could be back by the end of the week."

"I have my things." Garrett looked down at her. "In the hall by the door. I can begin now."

"Oh?" Abby nodded. "Oh. Well, then, Margot will just show you your room. I'll let you settle in and be by directly to give you a brief tour before it gets too dark. I hope you are comfortable here, Mr. Garrett."

"I'm sure I will be, madam." In his tone, Abby

was vaguely reminded of a term her brother had used for the man in his reference. He halted at the door, glanced back over one broad shoulder. "And it's Calvin."

Abby lifted her brows at the closed door.

Chapter 3

Calvin had decided, upon agreeing to his best friend's plot, that he would not even attempt to imagine the conditions he would be forced to endure. Despite his efforts not to do so, however, two grim ideas had forged their way into his thoughts. The second had been his certainty that he would be in a small square room with low ceilings, cold floors, and a cot for a bed, perhaps located in the lower floor of the house or in the stables.

The bedchamber to which the maid with the painfully orange hair led him was large, almost as much so as that in his home in London. There was a large rug directly before the door with a full-length settee and two leather chairs. Calvin deposited the single valise he had brought in one of the latter as he moved across the room.

The chamber was fully illuminated with afternoon sunlight from two open windows, but several lanterns and a hearth in the wall insured he would have an equal amount of light at sunset. There was a writing table in one corner, and in the opposite angle a ceramic washbasin and water pitcher. A bed covered with a well-worn but distinctly inviting coverlet took up a good deal of the room. Across from it was a table laden with decanters. Calvin went to the table, removed the heavy stopper from one of the crystal decanters, and inhaled.

When the knock sounded from the bedchamber door, he quickly assumed the maid, Margot, had returned to rectify her mistake of putting a butler in a room filled with niceties and liquors no servant could afford.

The maid was, in fact, there in the hall when he opened the door. She looked up at him, her smile neither sheepish nor apologetic. "Abby—" She shook her head, pale face turning pink. "Lady Wolcott will show you around now."

Calvin stepped past Margot and directly to his right, where the carpeted stairs reached the second floor of the house. From here he could see down the stairs and the silhouette of Abigail Wolcott as she tugged a wide-brimmed bonnet over her hair. In his mind, Calvin replayed his first encounter with Thomas's sister and silently conceded that he had been incorrect in not only his second preconceived notion concerning his stay at the country estate. His first had been Lady Abigail—Abby to her maid—Wolcott.

It only stood to reason that, after the description offered by the woman's brother, she would be old . . . or at least older. There was no gray in her hair, as Calvin had fully expected, not even hints at the temples or brow. The vaguely shimmering stuff was dark with the faintest touch of red. The peach-colored skin of her face was unlined and, whereas

Thomas's face was a mosaic of freckles, only a few scattered across the bridge of his sister's nose and the tops of her cheeks. Her eyes were unusual compared to those of her brother and sister, Jeanette. While her siblings had pale green eyes, hers came from the opposite end of the color spectrum. An interesting shade of bay, they gleamed with intelligence and genuine congeniality.

As he neared her, moving silently down the staircase, Calvin also noted that she did not dress like he had anticipated. The idea of a lonely spinster brought to mind dark gowns of black and gray. Abigail's gown was white with a plum print. The coat she had donned, for what he suspected to be a tour of the grounds, was the palest of violets. Calvin also observed, as his boot heel hit the last step, that both the gown and the coat were cut shorter than most. He could clearly see the laces of her walking boots.

He blinked then, when he caught the gleam of steel wrapped about one.

"Have you seen Harry?" Abigail asked absently, not looking up from her gloves.

"Who is Harry?" Calvin returned and immediately realized the woman had not expected him so quickly.

She jerked, a slight jump that would have affected her little was she not precariously balanced on that bit of metal wrapped around her right boot and disappearing up under her skirts. Abigail's head shot upward, eyes wide with surprise then horrified understanding as she tipped backward. She tried to catch herself on her good leg, frantically reaching for something that had been set in the shadows against the hall table. The wooden forearm crutch clattered to the floor at the same time her left leg gave out under the sudden weight put upon it.

She gasped, but before she toppled to the floor, Calvin reached for her.

He caught her elbow in one hand, crushing the soft material of her coat in his grip, and put another steadying arm around her back. Under the pressure of his forearm, Abigail's weight shifted forward and she fell into the wall of his chest. There was something about the soft press of her breasts against him that further corrupted his idea of a matronly old spinster.

Even as Calvin was trying to steady her back on her feet, Abigail had grasped the edge of the hall table for extra support.

"Excuse me," she said quickly. She was not looking at him, but fixed her gaze on the crutch lying on the floor. In the shadows of the hall, Calvin still caught the slightly upward tilt of her chin.

Calvin knelt, his gaze inadvertently moving to the heavy metal bracketing her ankle, and reached for the crutch.

"I thought you were Margot." Abigail accepted the crutch the moment it was offered, slipping her arm into the wooden cup and wrapping her fingers about the grip.

"I didn't know," he said almost to himself. Not responding to Abby's comment, but speaking of a different matter entirely.

Abigail's gaze slowly lifted to meet his. She was standing so close, her breath fanned his neck. Calvin felt a curious stirring inside him.

"I am not an invalid, Mr. Garrett."

Her barely audible words brushed his skin like a caress, and Calvin had to struggle beyond the feeling of every hair on his scalp lifting to register her words. His brows drew slowly together as he watched her take a step backward. He ignored the desire to again cross the space between them as he met her russet gaze. Void of the warmth it had maintained even when he arrived unannounced on her doorstep, it was filled with determination and more than a hint of defensiveness.

"It has been two months since Tuttleton passed on. There was nothing I could not attend to. Margot, Cook, and I managed fine." Her tone implied they could easily manage fine again.

"I am certain you did, Lady Abigail," Calvin said, for lack of a better reply. He wasn't certain what she was looking for as she continued to gaze up at him in the shadows of the foyer.

"Now, Mr. Garrett"—she took a deep breath and turned on her bracketed leg for the door, resting between steps on her crutch—"let us be on with the tour."

"Lady Wolcott?"

She was forced to look back over a shoulder when he didn't follow her. "Yes?"

He rubbed a hand through his hair, where the vague tingling sensation at the touch of her breath had subsided. "Calvin. Call me Calvin."

He tried not to wonder, as he was led down the path from the house to the stables, about the slightly uneven gait of Abigail Wolcott. Calvin couldn't imagine why her brother hadn't told him, unless—

he reflected on the inflexible lift of Abby's chin when she stumbled in the hall—he feared the same amount of prejudice that his sister was so defiant toward. For the first time since sharing a table with the man at Justin's, he recalled Thomas talking of an engagement and considered the idea that Lady Abigail's defensiveness had to do with its ending. Walking not far behind her, able to see the woman's gentle profile from the corner of his eye, his brows drew slightly together.

His thoughts were brought to an abrupt halt when he realized Abigail had stopped walking. He caught himself, as she lifted one hand to the closed door of the stables, before he crashed into the straight line of her back.

"We have only a few horses." Abby glanced back over her shoulder and frowned a little when she had to look up to meet his eye. "I have but one man who cares for them."

He met her gaze evenly before stepping to the side. Calvin lifted a hand to press at the wood over hers and aided her in a shove. He caught her brows snap together before she faced forward again. As the stable door swung inward and his guide stepped inside, he internally noted he would have to be careful if he wanted to remain at Lady Abigail's home. Then he realized, for the first time since taking on the role of her secret guardian, that the idea of staying did not strike him as unpleasant.

"How many?" He finally focused on the stable they had entered, and his eyes widened.

"Three. Two geldings and a mare." Abigail had moved on ahead, her steps fluid despite the crutch she used.

Only three horses, Calvin thought as he surveyed his surroundings, *and the stable is larger than many of the townhouses in London.* It was a remarkable structure, really. Long, with rectangular windows running the length of the walls near the ceiling, the stable was bright, with only the vaguest scent of hay and oats. The straw that lightly carpeted the floor was clean, as if it had just been laid out.

"Tuttleton did an excellent job of rebuilding the place." Abigail's voice was touched with a slight sadness, and Calvin imagined there were few in the gentry that would speak longingly of a deceased servant. "He didn't do it alone, of course. Mainly oversaw the work of some carpenters we obtained from the village."

Calvin turned toward Abby and found that while he inspected the stables, she had moved to one of the horses that had poked his head out of a stall at her arrival. She ran an open palm up and down the animal's broad nose with such deliberate lingering that the man watching her started to feel a tightening in his lower body. He looked away.

"Your butler designed this place?"

"No, he handled all the labor. I made the design."

"You?" One of Calvin's brows lifted before he thought about the insult he may have mistakenly conveyed.

Abby didn't appear affronted in the least, however; her eyes gazed steadily into eyes of a darker hue, as if she shared some form of silent communication with the horse. She said absently, "The skeleton of the building was there already. I just made a few modifications."

Calvin was impressed. He had never met a woman who would rather devise architectural designs than gossip with her friends or sit comfortably in her parlor reading the latest ton-approved novel. Then again, he decided as he watched Abigail whisper something to her horse then grin when he bumped her beneath the chin with his muzzle, the woman had already begun to strike him as unusual. Something in his eyes must have said as much, because when Abigail turned to face him, she smiled sheepishly.

"Achilles." She gave the horse one last pat before heading for the opened doors at the rear of the stable. "I've had him for three years now, as long as I've lived here."

"He seems to be in excellent condition." Calvin followed her to the brilliant light cast by the setting sun.

"Oh, he is." Abigail nodded as she took to a second path that curved from the stables to the rear of the estate. The delicate violet flowers of the ivy that streamed along the gray stones of the house caught the sunlight like small stars. "He is very smart, and I have never seen him spooked. Even when we ride late at night."

"Why"—Calvin scanned the lush carpet of grass that spread out around them and the great trees that dotted the property—"at night?"

Abby came to a halt, not looking at Calvin as she dusted away some blades of grass that clung to her coat. "I just prefer to ride then," she said absently.

Calvin watched as she squinted, still careful not to meet his eye, and did her own survey of the land about them. Even under the golden glow of the sun, he saw the color run from her face before her lips pressed tightly together. Her gaze darkened as she focused on a point in the far distance. Calvin's lashes drew slightly together as he followed her stare.

He had not noticed them before. The other estate was surrounded by trees and more than a furlong away. The two riders, he was certain, had not been present when they had made their way to the stables from the house. Though they were far enough away that he could make out little of their features, he knew they were a man and a woman, the latter with long hair that billowed out behind her like a cape. Their horses were fixed between where he and Abigail stood and the house behind them.

"Lord Raleigh's property," Abby said, "begins where you see the downed tree."

Calvin's gaze moved to the oak that looked as if it had taken the brunt of several bolts of lightning then back to the two not far from it. On the wave of a breeze, he thought he detected female laughter.

"Calvin." The fact she used his name caught his attention, as did the seriousness of Abigail's tone. "I'd like to believe I do not make harsh requests of those individuals who work in my home. So I will kindly ask that you do not involve yourself with my neighbors or any of their . . . goings on."

Abigail did not wait for his agreement but turned away to continue toward the house. Gazing at the taut line of her back beneath the tapered material of her coat, Calvin lifted a brow.

He watched with cold eyes, his features impassive, as the object of his attention turned back to her home. From so far away, Raleigh noticed, her disfigurement was indistinguishable. She did not look like one of the weak, open to prey, but just another unimpressive member of the female herd.

"Well, what have we here?"

Raleigh knew the attention of the woman at his side was not focused on Lady Wolcott, but the man who walked a step behind. He peered at Katrina from the corner of his eye, noting the interest that gleamed in her beautiful blue eyes as they inspected the man from head to toe. A smile curled her full, pouting lips.

"The lady has taken a lover, perhaps?" Raleigh said.

His cousin laughed aloud at that. "Really, Edmund, you go too far. Her face might be deemed comely in the vaguest sense of the word, but that limp of hers is quite unattractive. Rather like a lame horse." Katrina brushed a thick tendril of dark hair behind her shoulder. "What man would take a lame horse into his bed?"

"Men don't bed slow animals, they shoot them." Raleigh's fingers tightened on the reins of his horse. "When was the last time I sent Dobbs to pay Lady Wolcott a visit, do you recall?"

Katrina's fine brows drew together, her gaze moving only momentarily to the man at her side. "Surely several weeks ago."

Raleigh nodded, the setting sun highlighting the silver at his temples. His thin lips curled. "It's about time he paid her another visit, wouldn't you think? Just so the lady of the house doesn't forget her mistake in meddling with her neighbor's affairs." He glanced at his cousin. "And why don't you find out who that man is?"

"It would be my pleasure, my lord."

Raleigh could not say his emotions at that time rivaled his cousin's. Turning back to gaze at the man who, in fact, appeared to be looking directly at him, he could say his feelings bordered on disturbed.

Chapter 4

"I'm not certain"—Abigail ignored the rush of blood to her head as she frowned under the settee—"if Mr. Garrett will make a suitable addition to our household."

Margot threw back the curtains of the last parlor window so the room was fully illuminated with morning sunlight. Ignoring the lovely scenery, rolling hills of grass dotted with budding trees, she peered behind the length of the curtains. "Why ever not?"

Abigail sat up, blowing a tendril of hair off her brow. The movements gave her a moment to compose her words carefully. "He is not much like Tuttleton."

"True." Margot paused to fist her hands on her hips and offered thoughtfully, "Mr. Tuttleton was an excellent man."

"Yes." Abigail smiled. An image of the older man with snow white whiskers and bare scalp flitted across her mind.

"And Mr. Garrett is surely much younger and—no insult to our dear Tuttleton—a great deal more handsome."

Abby's smile disappeared when her mental picture of her departed butler was replaced with the features of Calvin Garrett, eyes so blue they were almost black gleaming in the light of the setting sun. "I hadn't noticed," she lied and reached for the crutch lying against the settee beside her.

Margot's orange brows lifted, but she said nothing as she went to a table in the corner and looked beneath the embroidered cloth that covered it.

Abigail lifted herself off the soft cushions of the settee and moved toward the tall chiffonier against the far wall. One might have suspected the odds were highly against Harry being able to open one of the cabinet drawers, but once Abby had found him slumbering comfortably at the bottom of a valise in her dressing room. She put nothing past the small beast anymore.

"What is it you see unfit with Mr. Garrett?" Margot inquired all too casually from across the room.

Abigail had pushed away the mental image of the man and didn't particularly appreciate the other woman bringing it back. She remembered the very up-close view she had when she all but collapsed in his arms. The hair at her nape rose at the thought.

"There is the fact that he is a lot younger than Tuttleton was."

"Only a few years older than you, I'd imagine."

"Even worse," Abigail muttered as she nudged the drawer she had just opened closed with the toe of her half boot. Her encumbered leg moved stiffly as she let it settle back on the floor.

She had once fallen in front of Tuttleton. It had been a bad tumble from six steps up the staircase after she inadvertently let the hem of her gown get caught beneath her crutch. She had landed in a daze at her butler's feet. *"Awright, m'lady?"* Tuttleton simply grasped her beneath her arms and stood her on her feet. The stumble had been embarrassing, but not as much so as the one she had taken before Calvin Garrett.

Abby had always prided herself on her ability to carry on with ordinary tasks just as well as the next woman despite her encumbered appendage. It was difficult, she learned soon after taking her first venture out of rehabilitation, to convince others of her capability. It would be even harder, she decided the moment she almost hit the floor before Calvin, to convince her new butler of the fact.

She ignored the nagging tune that surfaced at the back of her head every time she thought of the encounter. When Calvin had caught her before her fall, and late that night, as she lay awake in bed, dreading the nightmares to come, the music returned. The song was from a play she went to see with her dear friend, Augusta. As was the other woman's custom, she chose a romantic story of a love beyond anything Abby had ever experienced in her nine and twenty years. Not even with Patrick. In the play that she could almost hum the song to, there was a scene where the main character—a lovely young woman with golden hair and a perfect stride—was captured in the arms of her hero. Her breasts had been crushed against the hard wall of his chest as his hands pressed into her back, not unlike the way Abigail and her new butler had stood in her foyer after he stopped her fall. Abby had dug her hands into the material of his coat sleeves, just as the heroine had her hero's. The lovers' mouths had been a hairsbreadth apart, much the same way as Abby and Calvin's had been.

For a moment there in the foyer of her home, with her heart pounding in her ears and her legs shaking, Abby wondered what would happen were Calvin to kiss her just as the handsome actor had kissed the actress.

"Abby?"

She blinked, finally focusing on the rows of shimmering silver cutlery she had exposed in the next chiffonier drawer.

"I said"—Margot's voice was touched with concern—"Mr. Garrett isn't much older than you."

"I should think men, especially those of his age, judge a woman a great deal on her physical qualities," Abigail said, sliding the last drawer closed. "The fact that his sole supervisor will not only be a woman, but one who is somewhat lacking in the physical qualities he is accustomed to, might be more than he can bear."

She heard the rustle of Margot's skirts before the woman touched her lightly on the back. "Just because a man is young like Lord Valmonte," she said gently, "and almost as handsome, it does not mean he will share the same character. I wish I could make you understand. Then maybe you would not be so contented with this solitary life you've chosen."

Abigail's head lifted, something hitting painfully close to her heart at her maid's words.

"Bloody hell, woman! Get out of my room!"

"What on earth . . . ?" Abby turned away from Margot at the gruff male shout.

"Oh no," Margot said.

"What is it?"

"When Mr. Garrett did not show for breakfast, Mrs. Poole appeared very irritated. She mentioned something about not letting the man believe his post would consist of his rousing when he felt like it and slacking on his chores."

"Oh no." Abby matched the maid's worried tone exactly as she made for the parlor door.

The dream he'd been having disturbed him, and the face he opened his eyes to in the midst of it was even more disturbing.

It had begun as a nightmare. He had been alone again, in the workhouse of his youth. The stale odor of sweat was vivid in his nostrils as he stood gazing into the long room with its small, evenly spaced beds and walls covered with block lettering about a God who would never step foot in the hell that was the house. The cold was unbearable and his uniform insufficient. His heart pounded in his ears as he stumbled backward then spun away from the childhood prison.

Instead of nightmare trickery as he fully expected—turning into the same hall over and over again until he woke up screaming, perhaps—Calvin stepped into the golden warmth of an unfamiliar room. The chamber was all flickering shadows save for the small circle of light cast by the hearth onto the bed. Amidst the mussed bedclothes was a woman, naked—at least from where he could see her bare back to where the white sheet wrapped about her hips. Her dark hair was a stark contrast to the pale flesh exposed, the curves of her shoulders elegant where the firelight kissed them. Calvin seemed to watch himself as he moved toward the bed and ran his fingertips along her spine. The woman sighed, the sound soft and sultry. Calvin smiled, his gaze lifting from his fingers to the crutch propped against the far wall.

"Here now, we'll have none of that idleness round here!"

Calvin's eyes opened wide to a badly wrinkled face well suited to the ugly voice that had pierced his dream. The old woman's nose nearly touched his as she glared at him.

"Get up, I say!"

"Who the hell are you?" Calvin's own voice was less than alarming, muffled by sleep and his pillow.

"I'm the cook."

Then Calvin suddenly remembered where he was and who he was supposed to be. He sat up abruptly, ignoring the old woman's gasp at his naked torso as he focused first on the sun pressing into his window and then the clock atop his hearth.

"Damnation," he hissed under his breath.

"I'll not allow," Lady Abigail's cook was going on, the hands on her hips fisted so tight every vein was exposed, "ye to go about as if yer role as the lady's manservant is of no importance. She pays a tidy sum to have ye up in time to get to work on yer daily chores. Ye'll not be lazy or—"

"*Bloody hell, woman.*" Calvin had thrown his legs over the side of the bed. "*Get out of my room!*"

The woman gasped again, her lips nearly disappearing as she pressed them together. "No," she hissed then, reaching for the blankets that covered him, "ye get up!"

A stunned silence filled the room the moment the cook yanked away the blankets. Her eyes went round, the wrinkled skin around them going into deep grooves, as Calvin rose naked to his feet.

"Good Lord," the woman whispered.

Calvin lifted a brow. "I'll take that as a compliment."

He savored the quiet that followed the door slamming closed for only a moment before moving to the bag he had yet to unpack from the day before. As he slipped into the clothes he had procured from one of the men who cared for his grounds in Town—the legs of the breeches a little short and the shirtsleeves too tight—he heard a commotion from the hall beyond his door. He dimly wondered what the old crone was saying about him.

The rap at his bedchamber door was soft, tentative. "Mr. Garrett?"

At her voice, he felt the tension of putting his first full day at her estate to a wrong start fade. He looked up from his boots and smiled. "It's Calvin, Lady Abigail. Calvin."

The silence stretched before she spoke again through the door. "I apologize for Cook's behavior."

"Don't ye apologize, m'lady." The waspish voice followed hers from a distance, as if the woman was moving down the stairs. "He should have been up for ye."

"Thank you, Mrs. Poole." Abigail's tone became exasperated, but not unkind. "That will be all."

"She is right," Calvin called as he grabbed his coat and headed for the door. "I should have been awake already. You have my apologies, madam."

He swung the door open on the last word, apparently surprising the woman who stood on the other side. Whereas he hadn't yet brushed his hair and was in need of a shave, Abigail looked fresh and new. Her hair was drawn back from her clean face, and she wore a pale pink gown. The soft swells of her breasts above her bodice, he noticed before forcing himself to meet her eye, were the same pale hue as her naked back had been in his dream. Once meeting her gaze, he realized she was wearing a peculiar expression. One of her brows was raised, and her lips were curled only at one corner.

He heard Mrs. Poole call from the end of the stairs, "He talks funny."

Calvin abruptly wondered if the cook was speaking of the reason his employer was gazing at him so oddly. He tried to remember how his own manservant spoke.

"It's all right, Mr.——" Abigail's eyes squeezed closed then opened again, and in the shadows they gleamed like dark jewels. "Calvin. I imagine you had a long journey to get here and were quite exhausted. I saw it was past midnight once the light went out beneath your door."

Calvin looked at the woman before him anew. He wondered briefly if she was keeping a tally on his sleeping habit as what might suit a servant.

She flushed pink as if reading his thoughts. "I am usually up quite late."

"You have a hard time sleeping, my lady?"

"It's not the falling asleep that troubles me."

She looked down before turning toward the stairs. "It's where I fall once I am there."

Calvin thought about her words, slipping into his coat before moving toward the stairs. Abigail moved slowly down, carefully steadying her crutch with practiced ease before lowering her stiff leg. "Would you like my arm, Lady Abigail?"

There was that look. A brief flash before she looked down at the steps again. The defiant and slightly angered expression passed through her gaze. "I do not need your help," she said stiffly. "Thank you."

Light filtered in through the foyer, hitting the end of the staircase the moment Abigail reached it. Calvin saw her look down the hall toward the opened doorway and then frown.

"Timothy, what is the matter?"

Calvin came off the last step to glance between his employer and the man who stood in the opened doorway. He was tall and slim, with dark hair that hung over his brow as he bowed his head, which he did the moment he caught sight of the stranger beside Abigail.

"The stables, Lady Abby."

"Oh Lord." Margot, who had appeared from the parlor, bore an expression of worried awareness.

"They were wrecked again, Timothy, is that it?" Abigail's expression remained composed, Calvin saw, though as she moved toward the young man, her mouth drew downward.

"No, my lady." Timothy shook his head at his feet, then offered the woman a brief and sorrowful gaze of dark brown. "Worse. I cannot say it."

Chapter 5

Heedless of the dew that painted the grass and dampened the hem of her morning gown, Abby chose to forgo the path that led to the stables, cutting through the lush greenery in a faster route. Without asking, Timothy had offered his elbow, and she wrapped her fingers around the thick material of his coat. Margot was on her opposite side, murmuring to herself and twisting her fingers in the linen of her apron. Yet Abby was more aware of the man trailing silently behind than she was of either of them, her employees for as long as she had lived in the country.

He had looked rather grim when he threw open the door of his bedchamber, the lower half of his face covered with a day's growth of beard and his hair tangled. His clothes were wrinkled, as if they had spent the night in the bottom of his valise and had not been folded neatly in his armoire. The day before, she had seen him always in his coat; today, however, he had opened the door in only his shirt and breeches. Abby had briefly wondered if he had had the clothes since his earlier years; the muscles of his arms and shoulders pressed into the shirtsleeves enough to pull the fabric to its breaking point.

As the stables came into view, she quickly shook away the memory. She noted Timothy's arm tensing beneath her fingertips and gave the young man a gentle squeeze. She saw him glance at her from the corner of his eye before quickly looking back down at his feet. He was agitated; Abby could make out that much in her taciturn stableman, despite his efforts not to show it. She couldn't imagine what could have come about in the stables—worse than what had happened before—that would unsettle him so.

"For heaven's sake!" Margot caught it immediately, and her exclamation, a mixture of anger and shock, brought Abby's gaze into focus.

"Hell." She heard the brief and guttural grunt from the man who stood behind her.

Abby was thoughtful. "Who'd have thought it was possible to spell *bitch* incorrectly?"

The words were painted in large, red letters. The paint still dripped down the wall of the stable like fresh blood. The correlation made Abigail wince and look away. Her gaze moved immediately to the man who had come to stand beside her— who was, in fact, looking down into her face.

"Do you know who did this?" Calvin's eyes were a fierce blue in the morning sunlight, his features drawn.

Suddenly, Abby was more self-conscious of the slander misspelled across her stable than she had been before. She couldn't imagine what her new butler thought of it or what he thought of her because of it.

"I have an idea." She looked away.

"Scoundrel," Margot hissed. "I imagine he didn't even do it himself. Probably sent that filthy little toady, Dobbs, to perform the task."

"Margot," Abby said to quickly prevent the woman from saying too much in front of the veritable stranger beside her, "would you please get word to Emily that I will be unable to meet with her today? Ask if we can postpone our plans until tomorrow."

"Of course." Margot snapped to the task like a member of the militia.

"Timothy, please prepare the carriage for Margot. Timothy?" She turned, and though he was the same age as Abby, he gazed at her like a broken-hearted child.

"I'm sorry," he said softly, looking down into her eyes, then lower still. "I didn't hear him this time. I should have stopped him."

Her own heart sinking, Abigail stepped nearer to pat the man on the back. "Remember what I said last time? If you hear anything, I don't want you going near that awful man at all. You are to come to the house directly."

"But I scared him away last time."

"Still"—Abby shook her head vehemently—"I'll not take the chance again. I would be very upset if anything happened to you, Timothy." She smiled, propping her free hand on her hip, politely ignoring her stableman's embarrassment. "Besides, it's only paint. Only words, and misspelled at that."

"Come on, Timothy!" Margot called from where she had disappeared inside the stable.

He looked up at Abigail from beneath the thick

mass of his dark bangs. "I don't like to leave you alone now."

"She won't be."

Abigail watched Calvin as he walked toward Timothy. She felt her hackles rise, having seen other men treat him in a most impolite manner. The slightly older man, however, lifted a hand to the other.

"Calvin Garrett," he said. "I'm now under the lady's employ. I'll keep an eye on her while you are gone."

One of Abigail's brows lifted at Calvin's rather possessive tone. She thought about pointing out that she needed him to take care of her like she needed a hole in the head. Then she saw Timothy give his hand a brief shake, though he refused to meet Calvin's gaze.

"Timothy Tuttleton," he offered, giving the other man a cautious once-over. "She's tough," he said, making Abigail's heart lift, "but not as tough as she thinks."

Abigail scowled.

"I thought as much." Calvin nodded, the corners of his mouth twitching.

"You won't go anywhere?" Timothy pressed.

Before the two could continue with their man-to-man banter, as if she were not even there, Abigail interrupted, "You may rest assured, Mr. Garrett will be busy here for most of the day. He does have the wall to repaint." She ignored Calvin's pointed look until Timothy turned to make his way inside the stable. Then she lifted her chin and met his eye. "There is paint," she said, "left over in the storage room." She pressed her crutch into the earth as she moved to walk away.

A startled gasp escaped her; the firm hold on her arm was so unexpected. Calvin's fingers, just above her elbow, fit all the way around her arm and then some. His touch was strong and warm through the material of her muslin sleeve.

Calvin's face, when she looked back at him, showed no apology. His gaze seemed to have gone dark with concern. "Lord Raleigh sent a gentleman to do this to you?"

Before she could think about it, she recalled the brief glimpse she had viewed of Mr. Dobbs from her window, scurrying away from her stables less than a month before. "There is nothing gentlemanly about Mr. Dobbs, I assure you."

"Why?"

Calvin's tone was so intent that the whole story almost escaped her before she remembered he was little more than a stranger. Not to mention the fact he was under her employ and had no right to be making demands. Her lips pursed as she glared down at the fingers wrapped about her arm. After a long moment, when she felt heat rise up her neck, and a hint of worry, he released her. "That is really none of your concern, sir."

While Calvin applied the first coat of paint to the stable wall, the sun rose to directly above his workplace. As that first coat dried, he had taken a brief break—Timothy had brought two plates from the house, each laden with buttered bread, potatoes, and thin slices of pork. The butler and stableman had shared their meal in communal silence after Calvin had debated then dismissed the idea of interrogating the younger man for information on Lord Raleigh and his disliking for their employer. After the meal, he had helped Margot carry some rugs from the house and assisted her in beating them until not a single grain of dust exploded from their depths. He saw Abigail only once, standing at the window of her study as he performed the task. When he paused to wipe at the sweat dotting his brow and dampening his hair, he caught sight of her. The moment his head turned in her direction, however, she quickly left the window.

It was close to the time when the sun was to begin its descent upon the horizon when he went to work on the second coat of paint. He was almost finished, pressing down the grass near the wall with his boot as he brushed the bottom corner, when a shadow blocked the sun over him. He glanced over his shoulder to see Thomas Wolcott, immaculately attired, with a broad grin taking up most of his face and not even a single drop of sweat upon his brow.

"You got the position."

"How very astute of you to notice." Calvin straightened and winced at the dull ache in the lower part of his back.

"How are you doing?" In the sun, Thomas's freckles merged to make his face an interesting shade of orange.

"How do I look like I'm doing?" Calvin lifted a brow.

Thomas had stopped grinning, but the corners of his lips twitched. "Like you fit in rather well, my friend. I'm glad I asked for your help."

"Wonderful." The other man moved to the pail of water he had put to the side. He sank the bristles of his paintbrush inside, making the water an interesting shade of blue-gray. Without looking up, he said, "You neglected to tell me a few facts about your sister."

"Nothing of import," the other man returned quickly, his chin lifting in what appeared to be a hereditary gesture.

"Has she always been in that brace?"

"No. It happened three years ago."

"How?"

"A carriage accident, but I don't see why that is significant to the matter at hand."

"I would just like to know"—Calvin shook out his brush and laid it on the edge of the pail—"how long she has been building that wall around herself."

"You have to understand what Abby has gone through, Calvin." All hint of humor was gone from his friend's face now. His eyes were touched with sympathy and, the other man thought, guilt. "It took a long time for her to heal. She had broken her leg in several areas. In one place"—Thomas swallowed—"the bone tore through the skin."

"I don't need to hear this, Thomas," Calvin said, trying to ignore the vivid rush of unnameable emotion at the thought of the woman with her bay-colored eyes filled with misery and pain.

"I think you do, Calvin." Thomas ran his fingers through his hair. "Her first surgeon said he didn't think she'd be able to walk again unless he removed the leg entirely. We found another man right away, but Abby had a lot to go through to get back on her feet and manage independently. Then, after having gone through all that, she had to deal with the stares and whispers behind her back. What bothers her most, I think, is the fact that people believe her incapable of functioning on her own simply because of a slight limp."

"I'll have to agree." Calvin remembered her cold glare when he had offered to help her down the stairs just that morning.

"There are other things." Thomas shook his head. "Things I feel I am not at liberty to share without her consent, that make what happened to her even worse."

"Her engagement ended around that time"— Calvin recalled their conversation at Justin's—"did it not?"

"If you only knew the half of it, my friend." The other man's smile was bitter, angry. He took a deep breath and some of the hardness left his expression. "Is it too soon to inquire about your progress on the matter that brought you here?"

"You brought me here," Calvin reminded him. "I never had the desire to interfere in Abigail's personal life." In truth, he hadn't at the time Thomas had asked him to play his spy game. Now, however, something inside him was very interested in finding out what was going on at Lady Abigail's estate. Besides that, there was a part of him that wanted simply to learn about the woman herself.

"Of course, of course." Thomas accepted the blame with a slight glint in his eye.

Calvin put his hands on his hips, looking out past the stables where Wolcott land ended. "Lord Raleigh does have something against your sister, but I have yet to deduce what fuels his prejudice. I believe he had something to do with the fire you mentioned. He sends another to do his dirty work." A man named Dobbs. He nodded toward the fresh-

ly painted stable. "You're looking at the latest re-
covery from his attention."

"What was it?" Thomas frowned.

"A slanderous word was painted on the side of
the building."

"Bloody hell."

"Incorrectly spelled, I might add." Calvin said
for the first time what he had been thinking about
while at work. "This Dobbs character bothers me
even more so than Raleigh. The viscount doesn't
want to get his hands dirty, but his man has no
qualms with setting about frightening a woman
alone. He's stupid, if his spelling is any indication,
and that makes him dangerous."

"Do you think he will harm Abby?" Thomas's
tone hinted at worry and undiluted love.

"I've no idea what Raleigh and Dobbs's plans
are." Calvin caught movement over Thomas's shoulder and focused on the house behind him. The
woman in question was moving toward them slowly
but steadily. She had not changed from her gown
of earlier, and a few tendrils of hair had escaped
the braids pinned to the back of her head, yet she
looked as fresh as she had that morning. Her
cheeks and nose were slightly pink beneath a scattering of freckles. When her eyes fell on her brother,
they filled with recognition and she smiled.

"You may rest assured," Calvin said, "she will
come to no harm while I am here."

He ignored Thomas's curious expression as he
tried to understand the earnestness of his own
tone.

Chapter 6

"Thomas!" Abby wrapped one arm about her brother's shoulders as he squeezed her with enough force to lift her off the ground. "What are you doing here?"

"I was just passing by, love," he said as he set her on her feet. "Going to a friend's in Sheffield to help him survey some land on which he plans to build a home for himself and his new wife."

"Well, that sounds interesting," Abby lied. There was something peculiar about the way in which her brother had systematically rambled off his plans. She looked around his arm to where Calvin leaned against the fence. "Dinner will be served in a few minutes, sir, if you'd like to wash up." She turned back to Thomas. "Will you stay?"

"I cannot, I'm afraid. I wish to make it to Sheffield before nightfall. I am to help my friend survey some land—"

"For a new home for his new bride, yes."

Abby was as surprised by Calvin's interruption

as she was by the odd flicker in his eye and tone of voice.

Thomas released a dry laugh. "I see you offered Mr. Garrett a place here." Then, as if the man wasn't standing no more than a few feet away, "How well is he working out?"

Abby blinked, her gaze inadvertently moving to the man. His hair was damp at his nape and just above his ears, and his thin shirt stuck to his shoulders with sweat. She had noticed, when catching sight of him assisting Margot with the rugs from her study window, the lawn material clung to him like a second skin when wet. It clearly defined the lines of muscle corded around his arms and the details of sinew in his broad back as he worked. Abby quickly looked away. "He appears to do a fine job."

Thomas made a peculiar coughing sound behind his hand. "Well, Abby," he said once he cleared his throat, "that is good to hear. By the bye, love, why on earth are you repainting the stables? They looked to be in excellent condition when I last visited."

Abigail slowly shifted her gaze from her brother's open, smiling features to the wall, which now showed not a hint of the crude defamation that had been there that morn. "Better to do it now than wait for the paint to chip so other coats would be uneven." The lie hung heavily about her as her attention moved to the man who still leaned against the fence. His face was devoid of any emotion as he met her eye.

*   *   *

Less than an hour later, as she stared unseeing at the plate set before her, the weight of the second lie she had given her brother in less than a month sat heavily on her heart. "I saw no reason to make him worry."

"Understandable, m'lady," Mrs. Poole offered generously as she spooned a portion of red mullet on her plate.

"He has enough on his mind with Jeanette's coming-out."

"Certainly." Margot nodded from her seat diagonal to Abigail's.

"Not to mention"—Abby frowned slightly—"I do not want him to think I have gotten myself into trouble."

"But you did," Margot said from around a bite of fish, and then caught herself. She looked up at her employer and friend, smiling. "Not without good cause."

"Speaking of trouble"—Mrs. Poole scowled as she stacked a considerable amount of fish on the plate before one of the empty chairs at the table—"where is Garrett?"

"I thought he had gone to wash up." Abby looked at the empty chair her cook had put across from her, then turned to Timothy. He sat at the end of the table, waiting silently as he always did, for Abby to take her first bite.

Timothy met her gaze before his shifted to the door that separated the dining room from the kitchen.

Picking up her crutch from where she had laid it against her chair, Abigail rose and made her way around the table.

"Tell him," Mrs. Poole called after her, "I only serve at one table. He'll get no personal attendants here."

"I'll be sure to do that." Abigail chuckled at the old woman's indignant tone.

Before the door to the kitchen swung closed behind her, she thought she heard the cook say to those that remained at the table, "Did I tell ye I saw him naked?"

Her brows had drawn together at that, and there they remained when she saw the man who sat at the scarred table in the middle of the crowded kitchen. He rose quickly from his chair when she entered, and she saw he had donned a clean shirt and a different coat. His face was cleanly shaven and his hair combed back from his forehead. Abby wasn't certain if she liked this man or the one who had borne a sheen of sweat across his taut muscles better.

She scowled, wondering where *that* thought had surfaced from.

"Sir," she said, the irritation in her tone aimed at herself, "dinner is being served."

"I was waiting for Mrs. Poole," he said, "to tell me what was expected of me."

Suddenly it hit Abigail that her new butler might not be accustomed to the informal dining arrangements they practiced in her home. Servants, in most estates, ate on their own time and only entered the dining room to wait on their employers. Abby had always found the idea of sitting alone at her large dining-room table while others hovered about waiting to refill her sherry glass ludicrous.

Her tone was gentle when she said, "You are expected to eat, Calvin." She ignored the slight skip of her heart when the man's gaze—almost black in the shadowy kitchen—dropped to the curve of her smile. "Come along, sir."

"You found him," Margot said when Abby returned to the dining room. She wondered if her maid's uneven smile had anything to do with Mrs. Poole's turn of conversation before Abigail had gone.

"I hope you like fish, sir." Abby moved around the table and to her seat. She didn't realize Calvin had followed her until he tugged her chair away from the table. He gazed at her steadily, as if daring her to refuse the nicety, until she lowered herself in the cushioned seat. She was very aware of his fingertips brushing her back before he removed them from the chair. "You will after you've tasted Mrs. Poole's mullet with Cardinal sauce," she said absently.

"He liked his midday meal well enough," Mrs. Poole said as she filled her own plate and sat beside Abigail. "The plates Timothy brought back were clean. The pork was from last night's dinner."

"If remnants of your meals are so delicious"— Calvin sat, then offered the woman he had cursed only that morning a smile—"then I imagine the meal at the moment it is prepared is extraordinary."

From the corner of her eye, Abby thought she saw the old woman's wrinkled cheeks shade. The corners of her mouth twitched as her gaze moved back to the man who sat across from her. The glow of the tapers set at the center of the table made his skin golden and the flash of his teeth white when he grinned at her. Abby quickly sank her fork into her vegetables.

"Any sightings of Harry, Lady Abby?" Margot had no idea the amount of relief she brought her employer when she began the conversation.

Abigail swallowed, shook her head. "I think I might try the attic following dinner."

"You might not have to search that far up, m'lady." Mrs. Poole spoke over a mouthful of fish. "Either we have a very large rat, or he's been in my pantry sampling everything from the turnips to a sack of wheat flour."

"Did he leave footprints?" Abigail's heart lifted at the thought that she might be able to track down the missing animal.

"Paw prints, dear," Margot chuckled.

"Not that I saw." Mrs. Poole sank her teeth into a roll.

Abigail sighed.

"What"—Calvin spoke for the first time since beginning the meal, setting his fork down as he did—"exactly is Harry, might I ask?"

"A rabbit."

"Unusual animal to keep for a pet."

"Abby saved his life, she did." Margot was eager to tell the story.

Calvin lifted a brow at Abby. "Did she?"

Abigail felt suddenly self-conscious, her lips closing around her forkful of fish.

"His mother had been caught in a trap, was already dead when Abby found them. Poor little fellow had curled up beside her on the cold ground. He was just a tiny thing when she brought him here. Had to make him eat and everything."

"You keep traps?" Calvin directed the question at Abigail.

"No." Her answer came swift and disgusted.

"One of Lord Raleigh's." Mrs. Poole reached for the platter of fish, her plate already empty.

"He accidentally put it on your land?" Calvin's tone was curious, almost testing.

"It was no accident, I am certain." Abby had lost her appetite at the remembered sight of the beautiful rabbit almost decapitated by the steel claws of the trap and the nonexistent weight of her kit when Abby carefully cupped him in her palm. Since that day, she and Tuttleton had begun to take rides about the property, searching for instruments of death.

"Lady Abigail—"

Whatever Calvin was about to say in a rather earnest tone of voice was brought to a halt when Abby released a startled cry. The sharp crack of sound pierced through the walls and a sudden flash of light burst through the dining-room window.

"Thunder." Timothy eyed his employer worriedly from beneath his bangs.

Margot said quickly, unnecessarily, "The storm has been brewing for some time."

Abby nodded, ignoring the interested gaze of the man sitting across from her as she reached for her sherry. As she lifted the glass to her lips, her hand trembled.

It was going to be a long night.

He was looking for the rabbit. Though the hour was late, he had been unable to sleep. He lay in bed, staring at the flickering bursts of light across the ceiling as the storm reached its crescendo. By the time the thunder was rumbling off to the west, he had climbed from under the bedclothes and was slipping into his boots. Calvin's attempt to find the ever-ellusive Harry was genuine. He had first searched the library and then the kitchen, where the animal had last made his presence known.

He was still looking for the rabbit, he told himself staunchly as he opened the door to Abigail's study. A nagging sense of his real intent sat at the pit of his belly.

The room had not changed since his interview there, save that the chair in which he'd sat was repositioned near the wall. Calvin set his taper on the desk and moved around the room. As he peeked behind the curtains, he wondered about making some call to the rabbit then realized he had no idea what sort of noise would beckon a rabbit the way a whistle might a dog. He got down on all fours to look beneath Abigail's desk, and as he straightened, his gaze moved with intent he didn't attempt to hide over the items littered across its top.

Taking up most of the desk—weighted down by pieces of charcoal in various states of use, a ruler, and compass—was a drawing. No, not a drawing, Calvin decided as he moved around the table, but what appeared to be some sort of design. Though he was interested in the nature of the detailed drawing, Calvin had more pressing matters on his mind. His gaze moved to two leather-bound ledgers set atop each other at the corner of the desk.

He lifted the corner of the first book to neatly penned script. He flipped through a few of the pages, finding mostly to-do lists and a few mismatched notes, one of which said simply, *ASK EMILY ABOUT S. BLACK.* The last penned page was a list of men's names and beside each a few words that, Calvin presumed, referred to their character. He suddenly realized this had been Abby's list of applicants for her butler's position. He chuckled as he read a note about a gentleman who stared at her breasts for an indecently long amount of time, then decided that if one had to stare at something, the front of Abby's bodice could be pleasing.

Calvin carefully moved the notebook to the side and reached for the one beneath it. It was Abigail's account book; that much was clear from the moment he opened it. He ran a finger down the even lines of print and monetary figures, his brows lifting when he saw how much was put out for the wages of Abigail's servants. Each value posted was explainable, going out for food toward the horses or the house; a great deal was spent on books and soaps, add-ons to the renovation of the stable that Calvin assumed had been after the fire. There were two postings, however, of a withdrawal from her accounts that went well over one hundred pounds each. The only description of the funds spent came in the initials, *P.V.*

Calvin frowned, doing a second quick survey of the registry, then returned the book to the desk. He made sure to place the other leather-bound ledger atop it before reaching for the taper he had brought with him. He closed the study door, deciding upon the best method of getting a note to Thomas to ask him if the initials meant anything to him. He had reached the end of the staircase, lost in his thoughts, when he heard her scream.

Though he had no reason to be so certain, Calvin knew the cry had come from Abigail's room upstairs. He took the steps two at a time, his taper flickering wildly then going out as he reached the upper landing. Tension coiled down his spine as he moved quickly to the door of the woman's chamber. Then the door beside it swung open.

"Don't, lad." The old woman's words were no more than a whisper, but they stopped Calvin in his tracks. "She'll be all right."

Calvin scowled at Mrs. Poole in her frothy white nightgown and untied sleeping cap. He was irritated that the woman appeared so calm when something unnameable clawed at his insides. Worry, he finally realized, such as he had never felt for another human being since he had been born on the streets of London.

He lifted a fist to knock on the door.

The cook's hand was cold when she caught his wrist. "Ye'll embarrass her." When Calvin blinked, she released her hold on him. "It's the storm. Whenever it comes, you may be certain that m'lady will have one of her dreams."

"Dreams?"

"A nightmare"—Poole waved her hand dismissively as she turned back to her room—"memory— what have you." Her point made, she closed her bedchamber door.

Calvin stared at the door of Abigail's chamber as if he could see through it. He finally registered the old woman's choice of words. "Memory," he whispered into the darkened hall and frowned when he heard a muted thud . . . the distinct sound of Abby's crutch hitting the hard floor as she walked.

Chapter 7

"Funny," the woman in the bleak gray gown said without a hint of humor touching her dark gaze. "I thought I was the bitch."

"You are, Emily." Harriet Mosley was one of only four women not intimidated by the other. She smiled. "Abby is a *betch*. Your title is still intact."

"Good to know," Emily Paxton said without emotion.

The other two women in the library burst into laughter. In the gleam of the early afternoon sunlight, Abby even thought she detected a soft glint in Emily's eye. She was glad her friends had come, she decided then, though she had doubted her mood when they arrived an hour before. She hadn't slept well, and the fact was evident in the shadows beneath her eyes and her somewhat lacking disposition. As with the days that often followed her nightmares, she had kept herself removed from most of the individuals in the house.

"So this is why you did not come into the village

yesterday?" Emily was saying from where she stood near the empty hearth.

"I'm afraid so." Abby moved toward her desk. "I have started a tally, so to speak, of my grievances against Lord Raleigh. The next time I do venture into the village, I will pay the magistrate a visit and make a formal complaint."

Harriet frowned. "Did you say you thought you saw the magistrate hunting with Raleigh the last time the viscount had one of his parties?"

Abby's nose wrinkled. "Yes, but Mr. Kingsly must take my complaint whether he is a friend of Raleigh's or not. That is his job." She chose to ignore the dubious glance her friends shared as she dropped her gaze to the top of her desk and frowned.

"If you like, Abby, I might be able to assist you in this matter," Emily offered.

"Pray tell." Harriet's eyes rolled. "Do you have plans of accosting Lord Raleigh as you did Lord Black?"

"That, Harriet, was a totally unrelated matter. I was mistaken in my judgment of Black's character. I have no doubt that Raleigh is a scoundrel." A muscle flexed in Emily's jaw. "Exactly the sort of man I know how to deal with."

Blinking, certain that everything was in its place atop her desk despite the sudden feeling of unease that had hit her, Abby looked up. "I think I have the matter under control for now, thank you."

"Where exactly was the slander put, Abby?" Harriet rose to her full and considerable height, walking to the window where it looked out over the stables. "I did not see it when we rode up, and there's no sign of it on this side of the building either."

Abby sat in her chair, preparing to share her designs with the other women. "It was on this side," she said, then smiled with appreciation, "but Calvin did an excellent job of repainting the wall."

"Calvin?"

Abigail looked up and saw that both women— one still standing at the fireplace and the other returning to her seat—were watching her.

"Mr. Garrett," she explained. "He has taken over, as much as anyone can, Tuttleton's old position."

"I see." Harriet dragged her chair nearer the desk, looking over Abby's designs. "These are your new blueprints for the shop?"

"Yes." Abby nodded. "There are a few final touches to be made. That's why I needed a second opinion."

"We are ready to help you, Abby." Emily walked to the desk, her back rod-straight as she gazed at the plans. "I cannot imagine we would come up with anything that surpasses your ideas."

Abigail grinned, the remnants of her poor night— the echoing screams of horses and her own frightened whimpers—finally gone. "I'm so glad you came."

Emily's lips were twitching dangerously upward when she met Abby's eye. Then the knock at the study door diverted her attention.

"Come in," Abby called, expecting Margot with tea.

The newcomer bore a silver tray laden with cups and an engraved serving pot, but it was not her maid.

"Margot went to chase after a shadow she thought looked like Harry," Calvin said. He looked distinctly uncomfortable standing in the doorway that his wide shoulders almost filled, bearing the brunt of two intrigued stares. He had awoken late again. His hard jaw was unshaven and his black hair looked as if its only combing had come from his fingers. "I brought your tea."

"Thank you." Abigail considered the overall look of uneasiness her butler wore as he walked stiffly to her desk. She wondered briefly if he had never served tea before.

He set the tray on the edge of her table, meeting the gazes of her friends evenly, as if daring them to slander his serving.

"These are two of my best friends, Calvin," Abigail said. "Emily Paxton and Harriet Mosley."

"Mr. Garrett." The women nodded in unison.

"Ladies." He straightened, turning his attention back to Abby. His lips barely moved as he asked in a rather dour tone, "Do I serve you?"

Abby felt like laughing. The picture that had formed in her mind of the man doing such a thing tickled her. "I think we can manage, thank you."

She thought she heard Calvin sigh before turning back to the door and leaving the room a lot faster than he had come.

"Your new butler?" Harriet did not look at Abby.

"Mr. Garrett."

"Emily?" Harriet said.

"Yes?" The other was staring at the closed door like Harriet, but whereas the other woman's eye gleamed with unveiled interest, hers was rather thoughtful.

"Remind me, when we get back to the shop, that I would like to look up what buttlering exactly entails."

* * *

He stood on the edge of the field, hands folded on his hips with the wind pressing his too-small shirt against his chest, the ends of his jacket against his thighs. His eyes gleamed dark blue where they did not reflect the cacophony of colors spread out before him. It was obvious some sort of harmony needed to be made of the jumble of plants if it was to look anything like the gardens impressing the ton.

"Where the hell do I begin?"

Calvin's focus on the seemingly insurmountable task at hand was diverted by a rhythmic cadence carried through the earth below his feet. His attention moved from the overgrowth of shrubbery, his head slowly turning so that he might watch the horse approach. Its rider was a woman sitting sidesaddle. The ribbon of her jaunty hat trailed out behind her, the skirts of her matching riding gown rippling against the mare's side.

Calvin's brows drew together. The woman had come from the property bordering Lady Abigail's. He was dimly certain it was she who had ridden beside Raleigh on the only occasion he saw the man. Despite the genuine, slightly sultry smile that curled her full lips, Calvin had only one thought when the woman brought her mount to a halt no more than four feet away.

Trouble.

"Greetings, sir," the woman said breathlessly. Her breathing made her full breasts rise against the opened buttons at the top of her velvet coat. Lying within the crevice made between each full globe was a large diamond set in a string of pearls.

"Good afternoon." Calvin kept his voice emotionless. He did a quick survey of the woman's face. She was beautiful, with high cheekbones, a small nose, and pale skin. The self-assured gleam in her emerald green eyes suggested she was not unaware of her physical attributes.

"I am Lady Katrina Raleigh." Though she had time to rest, her voice remained breathless.

"Lord Raleigh's wife?"

"Heavens, no." She laughed, and Calvin found the artificial sound grating on the nerves. "He is my cousin."

Calvin continued to watch the woman, silent and waiting.

Katrina Raleigh blinked, as if surprised that he had not read her mind. "And you are?"

"Garrett." It was all he dared to offer. He did not recall ever having met the viscount but wanted to take no chances that the man would recognize his name. Calvin was still unsettled about the intent gaze of Emily Paxton earlier in Abigail's study.

Lady Raleigh did not ask him if he was a friend or relative of Abigail's. Something about the way in which her perfect gaze traced his dirty breeches and shirt—pausing a little too obviously at his hips and shoulders—expressed that she already understood his place.

"The name sounds familiar," she said, and Calvin felt the hair at his nape rise. Then her black brows lifted. "Do you have family that may have worked for the viscount?"

"I couldn't say." Oddly enough, it was the truth.

"Well," the woman gave Calvin a final, languid once-over before looking at him through her thick lashes, "I just thought I would introduce myself."

She tugged on the reins of her mount but had only turned a little away before she met Calvin's gaze again and sank her teeth into her bottom lip. "Perhaps we shall meet again, Mr. Garrett."

"Perhaps." Calvin inclined his head, but a bitter taste filled his mouth as he watched Lady Raleigh trot away. She reminded him of a woman he had known several years before, and the comparison wasn't flattering.

Releasing in one deep breath the tension that had settled in him the moment the woman made her approach, Calvin turned back to his earlier task. His jaw setting grimly, he knelt and began to yank at the overgrown weeds crowding around his feet. He was on his third handful of thick stalks and fiercely green leaves when he heard the shout.

"Mr. Garrett!" Then, more loudly and filled with what sounded a lot like horror, "*Calvin! Stop!*"

He turned in the direction of the cry and decided that Abigail moved quite fluidly despite her braced leg. She came from the back of the house, her gait eating up the space between them in haste and her normally tranquil features clearly exposing her surprised unease.

"What," she gasped, "what are you about, sir?" She was breathing as rapidly as Lady Katrina had when she approached. Her chest heaved, but only the slightest glimpse of her soft breasts pressed up above the lace border of her striped bodice.

Calvin, unimpressed with the bounty put on display by the other woman, found himself having to draw his gaze away from below Abigail's neck to focus on her face. Her cheeks were pink and her lips set ever so slightly apart, the latter striking him as even more interesting than the careful smile

Raleigh's cousin had worn. He was reminded of only two days prior, when he had held Abigail in his arms—much to the woman's dismay. Her lips had been parted then, and something as vaguely wicked as the emotion curling about his spine at that time rushed into his lower body.

"I've finished polishing the silver"—he had to clear his throat when his voice came out coarse—"and sweeping the floors. I helped Timothy with the horses. For want of anything else in need of my attention, I thought I'd work on your garden." He glanced down at the sunflowers that almost reached her hips. "Forgive my bluntness, Lady Abigail, but it is sorely in need of care."

"Forgive mine, Calvin," Abigail countered quickly. "But you will touch my flowers over my dead body."

His attention lifted again, and he saw the woman's chin lift. "Excuse me?"

"It has taken me three years to get my garden as I've always wished it to be. Tuttleton broke his back sowing all the seeds then assisting myself in keeping them watered. I'll not have you ruin all the hard work we put into it."

"You want it to look like this?" Calvin couldn't mask his disbelief.

"Yes, sir, I do." Abigail's gaze softened as a delicate breeze set the flowers surrounding them into motion. Daffodils and vibrantly hued bluebells rustled against the ends of her skirts. "I know it leaves a lot to be desired among those with more . . . linear tastes."

"Many in Town have gardens in various shapes, all set around one focal point." Calvin felt something tug in the depths of his chest as he watched the wind press Abigail's skirts against her legs, highlighting the shape of her hips and swell of her bottom. Several tendrils of hair had escaped her untied bonnet, their dark tips tickling the corners of her mouth as she smiled.

"My garden does have a focal point, Calvin," she said gently and pointed to the nearby estate. "Both my bedchamber and study windows look out onto it. When I am standing at either of those windows, all I can see is flowers."

When she faced him again, Calvin wondered at what Abigail had seen in his features that made her smile fade and her eyes quickly move away.

Chapter 8

Well after the sun had begun its descent, when the sky was interesting shades of pink and purple, the stable door slid open on silent hinges. The silhouette created on the hay-strewn floor was that of a rather rounded man, but the individual who came to a halt at the first stall was a woman.

"Achilles." Abigail whispered a loving greeting for the horse that had been waiting expectantly. The gray's muscles, elegantly detailed beneath the taut flesh of his flanks and shoulders, were tense. Trembling, almost, in eagerness.

Abigail released the latch that kept the stall closed. As the door swung open, the animal moved forward. He nudged his rider gently in the space between her shoulder and jaw. She pressed her forehead against the smoothness of his long cheek and reached for his reins. Achilles already bore her saddle and the folded blanket that gave Abigail's leg added comfort.

"Come." Abby guided the gray to the rear opening of the stable. Once outside, a slim figure approached her on silent feet.

"Thank you for getting him saddled, Timothy."

Timothy only nodded, focusing most of his attention on accepting then holding to his chest the crutch she offered. He waited until Abigail hefted herself up and onto the horse's steady back to speak. "Have a safe ride, Lady Abby."

Abigail smiled down at Timothy's bowed head then gave Achilles the slight nudge with her knees that set him into motion. The steady cadence that took them out of the fenced area and into the approaching night was only a beginning. Before they returned to the stables, Abigail planned to have the wind rushing through Achilles' soft mane and pounding at her cheeks and throat. It was a familiar ritual, an exorcism of the demons that hounded her dreams. A vindication to herself; she would not allow the memories of the past to haunt her future.

Within the space of an hour that passed like only minutes they reached the end of their much-traveled trail. Just as it did every time Achilles brought her there, the small clearing at the path's end served as an almost instantaneous balm to the burning that had filled her lungs at her rapid breathing. The horse moved familiarly to the large oak that sat where damp soil gave way to the slope leading down into the pond. Using a jutting branch from the tree and the gray's massive back for support, Abigail lowered herself to the ground. She held herself against the tree as Achilles lumbered away and toward the pond. His front hooves were immersed in the water before he lowered his head to drink.

The horse's movements made circular ripples

in the water that had, until that time, appeared to be smooth black glass reflecting the tiny pinpoints of stars above. Abigail rested most of her weight on her left leg, leaning against the oak as she watched Achilles drink. If the abrupt sound of a twig snapping underfoot not far behind hadn't warned her, the way in which the gray's head abruptly lifted would have.

Abigail had time only to frown before she sensed the intruder. Her head slowly turned, and she struggled to keep a firm hold on her sudden alarm at finding the man standing in the shadows of the night. The moon glowed faintly across his crooked and yellow teeth as he smiled.

He woke once again to the old wrinkled face peering down at him. Once again out of the dream of the firelit bedchamber. Instead of from the desolate trenches of the workhouse, however, he turned into the room from a window that overlooked an acre of flowers.

"Not again," Calvin said into the plump softness of his pillow. He opened one eye then let it slip back closed on a wince. Mrs. Poole's nose fairly touched his.

"Get up, lad." Her hand was cold on his bare shoulder as she gave it a shove.

"Please, Calvin," said Margot. "It's important."

"Damnation." Calvin let both eyes open now, focusing on both the aged cook and the fiery-haired woman who had sidled up close behind her. "Have you women no notion of the meaning of privacy? Do you barge into everyone's rooms late at night without knocking?"

"Mr. Tuttleton didn't mind," Margot said.

Calvin growled low in his throat.

"We are worried, lad." Mrs. Poole stuck to the matter that had brought her there. "About Lady Abby."

Calvin frowned and sat up, the remnants of sleep fading fast. "Another nightmare?"

"No, sir." Margot shook her head, her eyes wide and focused on his bare chest. "She is not here."

"The lady goes riding late in the day." Mrs. Poole moved away from the bed on bare feet. She opened the armoire and removed a shirt, then retrieved Calvin's jacket from where he had left it across a chair. "Returns in the evening, not too late."

"Not this late." Margot's tone was hollow, worried.

Calvin threw back the bedclothes and got to his feet. He chose to ignore the younger woman's startled gasp, then her disappointed frown as she saw the breeches he wore.

"Where does she ride?" He did not look up from buttoning his shirt.

"There's a trail"—Mrs. Poole held his jacket open for him—"just outside the stables. It goes to a pond at the end of the property."

"Abby usually stops there to rest." Margot dropped his boots at his feet.

"She may very well have been thrown," Calvin said grimly, not caring for the mental image the thought brought to mind.

"No," Mrs. Poole countered in a tone that brooked no argument. "Achilles would never do such a thing to her."

"I'd like to think she may have simply fallen

asleep while relaxing at the pond," Margot said with a forced cheerfulness.

"Has she ever fallen asleep before?" Calvin looked up once he had finished with his boots.

Margot's face went pale as she shook her head.

"Timothy has a horse ready for ye, Calvin," Mrs. Poole said. "Hurry."

He heard the last from where he was striding quickly to the stairs.

"Mr. Dobbs." Abigail felt it was important to speak before he had the chance. She kept her tone cool, hinting at none of her distress at being caught alone with the man.

"Did ye get me message?" His lips were thin and black in the darkness, like wet leeches moving atop each other.

"Oh." She let her brows lift. "Was that you?"

"Ye know bloody well it was." Dobbs's shoes crunched down on dried leaves as he stepped nearer. "Lord Raleigh doesn't want ye to forget about him."

"Forgive me for saying so, sir"—Abigail kept her tone controlled and light—"but you'd do well to not come out and tell me it is Raleigh who employs your . . . shall we say, unusual services? It takes away some of the surprise."

Dobbs blinked, his cold black eyes filled to the brim with meanness—leaving little room for intelligence. He smiled. "He knows what yer hiding. He knows that spindly manservant of yers took his horse."

"You mean the same manservant who sent you running from my stables?" Abigail almost smiled at the memory. "I do miss Tuttleton." She gasped then, for the round man moved surprisingly fast.

Dobbs closed in on her until they were toe-to-toe. His breath, smelling strongly of onion and rot, fanned her face. Abigail swallowed, her fingers sinking into the bark of the aged tree that was the only thing holding her upright.

"Despite yer meddling in his business, the viscount has a proposition for ye," Dobbs said, a fine spray of spittle landing across Abigail's cheeks and eyelashes.

For the first time since she could remember having her accident, Abby wished she had her crutch handy. Not to keep her standing upright, but for the satisfaction she knew it would induce if she were to bash this ruffian over the skull with it. "And that is?" she breathed, her fear rising at the unbearable proximity of the man.

"He wants yer land. Will pay ye, Lady Wolcott, to get the hell away from him."

"No." The word came from the pit of her stomach, before she even thought about forming it.

"Think before ye answer, lady." Dobbs was unsurprised by her refusal. "Lord Raleigh doesn't mind waiting, and I don't mind helping ye make up yer mind."

An icy grip closed around Abigail's heart at the cruel intent that radiated from Dobbs's large body. Then her heart stopped beating entirely when the man leaned closer still, until his pockmarked cheek touched hers. Just above her ear, he sniffed her like a dog.

"Ye smell good."

Abigail gasped, her arms shaking with the urge to shove at Dobbs's chest. She held herself steady, however, painfully aware that such a movement would send her tumbling to the ground. She stopped her teeth from chattering by pressing them together, then said through them, "Get away from me, you filthy pig."

Dobbs actually backed away, blinking that stupid blink of his.

"You tell Lord Raleigh"—her voice was loud, near shouting, to hide her terror—"I'll die before I'll let him have my home."

Dobbs's gaze flashed as if he were insulted. As if he expected her to swoon over his snorting in her ear. "Be careful what ye say." His attention dropped to Abigail's legs, one of which had begun to tremble under the long minutes of bearing her weight. "I know ye can't run."

Chapter 9

He did not find Abigail at the pond, but an unknown man. Before he and the brown and white gelding Timothy had given him broke into the clearing, Calvin stopped and watched the stranger through a growth of saplings.

He stood at the very edge of the pond, nothing more than a dark shadow holding what appeared to be a long twig against his leg, with his free arm draped over his horse's back. The man's forehead was pressed to the animal's side, and from where Calvin stood he was vividly aware of what a lonely figure the stranger made.

He lowered himself from his gelding, tying the reins to one of the slim trunks of the saplings, and moved into the clearing on silent feet. As Calvin drew nearer to the motionless man, he quickly scanned his shape. He did not know where Abigail was and wasn't certain if the stranger had anything to do with her absence at the place her servants were certain she'd be. He had spent the first seventeen years of his life on the streets of London or fighting over a stained bunk in the house, and if there was one thing he had learned, it was that it was better to think of everyone you didn't know as someone you might not like.

The man did not make an intimidating figure. His shoulders were slight, his arms thin under the form-fitting shirt he wore. The hem of the shirt reached just below the waist of his long pants, where the stranger's hips flared. Calvin frowned, his gaze going lower. Something uncomfortable nagged at the back of his skull as he focused on the other's legs. One was bent slightly, and the other was stiff.

A bolt of understanding slammed into Calvin. When his head lifted, he saw Abigail's lift too. Before he could even realize her intent, the woman swung around with the stick she had been holding raised. Calvin saw the grim intent in her gaze and thought— in the faint moonlight—he caught a glint of fear before he ducked. He felt the wind from the insufficient blow stir the hair across his scalp and, without thinking, rushed the woman.

Abigail screamed as he wrapped his arms around her waist, her hands digging into the shoulders of his coat as her instrument of destruction fell to the ground. Her horse—Achilles, Calvin now remembered—offered a disgruntled snort but did not move from where he stood.

"Abigail," he shouted above her thrashing, "it's me!"

"Get off!" Her command was so razor-sharp that he immediately obeyed. Abigail remained on her feet for a full second before her eyes went round and she collapsed back into the thick plants that surrounded the water.

"Son of a—" Calvin's jaw went tense as he held back the most vivid part of the curse. "What the hell are you about, riding out in the middle of the night? What can you be thinking?" He edged nearer, was reaching for her when he recalled her vehement refusal of his hold a moment before.

"Do not yell at me." Abigail pointedly ignored him, reaching for the reins of her gray.

"I'm not—" He stopped and lowered his voice. "I'm not yelling." He said through his teeth, "I would just like to know what you think you are doing."

"At the moment, I am trying to get away from this water." She glared at Calvin through a shining mass of hair that had escaped the simple braid she wore. "Now, if you will kindly step aside. . . ."

"Give me your hand." Calvin stepped forward, holding out his.

"No!" She released the reins with only one hand to wave off his, but it sorely dislodged her perilous balance. She tumbled back to the ground, her open palms going back to catch her and sinking into mud.

"You damn fool," Calvin hissed. Ignoring the anger that surrounded her like a shield, he reached out and captured Abigail beneath her shoulders. "Let me get you out of here." She gasped, her dirty hands settling on his arms as he lifted her from the ground and off her feet.

As he wrapped a steadying arm about her back, Calvin was abruptly aware of the slightness of the woman despite her acrid tongue. The pressure of his arm on the back of her shirt drew the material taut against her front. She had left the first few buttons open, and the skin of her throat was pale, lovely in the moonlight. Her breasts rose with her stuttering breaths, small and soft and clearly defined under the shirt. Calvin's gaze lifted and focused on her parted lips. He refused to meet her eyes, refused the warning bells that went off in his head, and gave in to the hot coil of interest that closed tighter and tighter around his insides as he looked at her.

His head bowed, and he covered her parted lips with his own.

Abigail's thoughts did not turn to mush the moment Calvin kissed her, as they did for the characters of the love stories she used to read before the conclusion of her engagement. She was very aware of the ramifications of the contact of his mouth on hers. He was her manservant, he had just called her some unflattering names, and he was a veritable stranger. And despite all this, she could no more not receive his kiss than she could make herself walk unfettered again.

She had wondered what it would be like to be kissed by this man, and now she knew. Never, she thought then—despite what might come of the extremely inappropriate embrace—would she again be so pleased with giving in to temptation. Though her thoughts didn't muddle, her heart beat erratically and a slow burning began low in the pit of her belly. Her muddied fingers dug into Calvin's coat sleeves, and the arm around her back tightened, pulling her against the rigid wall of his chest. Something fluttered against her ribs when she felt the beat of his heart through her shirt, uneven as her own.

Then his moist breath touched the insides of her lips, and his tongue slowly slipped into the cavern of her mouth. That was when Abigail's thoughts evaporated into senselessness. A not-unpleasant heat rose to her breasts. She was suddenly oblivious to the pain that had been nagging at her leg since before her fall and remembering things she thought she had left behind three years before.

Abigail lifted her own tongue to lightly trace the underside of Calvin's and felt him shiver. Then she brought her teeth, so lightly it might have been imagined, across him. He groaned into her mouth. Finally, Abby pressed his tongue between hers and the roof of her mouth and drew on it.

Calvin's mouth tore away from hers. "*God.*" His hoarse whisper brushed her damp lips.

Abigail blushed, not meeting his eyes. She felt suddenly exposed and more than a little at a loss for proprieties. She also, Abby acknowledged with a small, inward smile, felt rather amazing. Her lashes lifted and she met his gaze only briefly, saw his eyes burned like the blue flames inside a fire, and quickly lowered her head again. She had no idea what to say.

Calvin saved her in a most unsuspected way. He returned to his earlier condemnation. "You should not ride out alone, Lady Abigail."

She sighed, her grip loosening on the taut muscles of his arms. Abby reached for Achilles, steadying herself by gripping the saddle. "I must," she said without looking at Calvin. "It is more comfortable for me to ride in men's attire; in light of day, the risks are greater that someone might see and condemn me."

"If not for yourself, for your mount." She felt his gaze on the side of her face as he spoke. "In the darkness, it is almost impossible for a horse to see a hole in the ground. He could break a leg."

"No." Abby shook her head, holding steady with one hand and using the other to pat one of Achilles' large shoulders. "Timothy walks the trail daily, looking for ruts in the sand."

"And does Timothy take the trail with you?" Calvin's irritation appeared to grow with her every sensible answer. "Have you no idea how dangerous it is for a woman to travel alone in the dark? You might be approached by any kind of miscreant."

Abigail felt an icy shiver slip down her spine, suddenly remembering the foul stench of Mr. Dobbs as his cheek touched hers. She reached for the reins.

"Why are you shaking?" The voice of the man much too close behind her was low, knowing. "What happened out here tonight, Lady Abigail?"

"It's none of your concern." Her hands tightened into fists in an effort to stop their trembling.

"Like hell." One of Calvin's hands reached out, rough and warm and very large, and wrapped around hers. "You came at me with that stick like you'd gladly take my head off. Someone came after you? Raleigh?"

"No. Lord Raleigh would never leave the comfort of his home for anything other than the hunt."

"Dobbs, then." Calvin's fingers tightened almost painfully, his breath fanning the hair at her temples as he snapped, "Dammit, woman, stop evading the subject. What did the man do to you?"

"He gave me a fright, if you must know." Abigail's head turned, going silent for a moment as she realized they were as close as they had been before he kissed her. "He cornered me and said that Lord Raleigh wishes to have my property and left little doubt that he would go to great lengths to see he gets it."

"Bloody hell, why didn't you say something sooner?"

"Why should I, sir? I took care of the matter at the time."

"Lady Abigail, I hate to spell it out for you, but a stern talking-to will have little effect on a hired ruffian."

Abigail glared at the man a full head taller than her, the heated intimacy they shared minutes before long forgotten. "What bothers you the most about me, Calvin? My independence despite being a woman or despite the fact I am lame?" Without waiting for his response, she lifted her good leg to the stirrup and hefted her full weight, with a fluidity that pleased even her, into the saddle.

Chapter 10

Abigail took a deep breath and rapped lightly on the door. There was perhaps nothing more difficult, she mused as she stood patiently awaiting a response, than having to be the one to speak first after an argument. Though she wouldn't exactly call her . . . interaction with Calvin Garrett the night before an argument. Their words had become heated, certainly, but they had remained silent for the journey from the pond back to the estate. Not that Abigail had encouraged conversation, remaining a yard ahead of the man for the ride back. She had felt the impact of his stare between her shoulder blades like a physical thing, but had refused to look back.

In the upstairs hall of her home, the door before her still closed and silent, Abigail frowned slightly. She knocked again. "Calvin?"

She couldn't imagine the man was deliberately ignoring her. This was his post, after all.

"Did you need me, Lady Abigail?"

She jerked at the sound from the top of the staircase. Abigail lifted a hand to her breast as she turned to face Calvin. "I had thought you were still abed as before."

One of his dark brows lifted, his expression difficult to read in the shadows. "I believe I am now adjusted to rising early in the morn." His gaze flickered, and Abigail could have sworn he was looking at the bodice of her gown. "Going somewhere?"

He was looking at her gloved hand.

"Yes." Abigail nodded, moving toward the staircase. "I must make a call in the village." She glanced at Calvin from the corner of her eye as she stepped past him, hoping she would not have to ask.

"I shall accompany you, then?" He turned to follow a step behind.

"Please."

"Before we go, my lady, I should like to speak with you about last night."

It was highly improbable, but she could have sworn she felt his breath tickle her nape. Then his words registered. Suddenly a picture of herself in his arms flashed to mind, her breasts pressed into the hard wall of his chest and his lips parting over hers.

She stopped halfway down the steps. "Oh?"

"What is it exactly"—Calvin spoke calmly enough to the back of her head—"that Lord Raleigh has against you?"

"Oh, that." Abigail winced at the high pitch of her laugh.

"I know you think it none of my concern, but as I now live in this house and have seen the unsubtle threats of Raleigh's man, I would very much like to know what is going on. I'd like you to tell me." His tone suggested that he could hear the tale from someone else but preferred his employer's account.

Abigail imagined there were plenty of individuals, most if not all from the estate bordering hers, willing to tell the story.

"I have, since coming to live here in North Rutherford, been unmoved with the viscount's mode of living. He is very wealthy, and in the manner of some men with too much wealth, he indulges himself incessantly. During the season, he throws parties every night of the week, and something about the individuals he invites to these gatherings hints at impropriety." She peered over her shoulder at Calvin, who wore a look of quiet interest. "On the morning after one of these parties, Tuttleton had to remove two still-inebriated men and a partially nude woman from my garden."

"Charming." Calvin's expression hinted at sarcasm not present in the word's meaning.

"Indeed." Abigail nodded. "But that is not the only reason I do not care for Lord Raleigh, not even the greatest." Her tone was filled with distaste as she continued. "The viscount likes to think himself a great huntsman. I am somewhat unimpressed with his skills at the gruesome sport, however, in that he raises the animals he hunts on his grounds like sheep. The slaughter of these poor creatures comes at the end of the barrel. He even sends out his servants the night before a hunt to put up nets so that pheasants cannot fly away. The servants also run through the fields to frighten the animals out into the open. Beaters, I believe they are called."

The fingers of her free hand curled into a fist. "And that is not even the worst of it. There are times when Raleigh and his cohorts are well into their cups, and the things they do to those poor animals before they die make death a pleasant future."

"You've seen this?"

A bitter taste filled Abigail's mouth as a heavy weight settled at the back of her eyes. She nodded.

"I'm sorry, Lady Abigail." Calvin's tone curled about her eardrums and lifted the hair on her nape. "You strike me as a woman who has little tolerance for cruelty."

"It is unbearable." She met his eye for only a moment, something in his intent gaze tugging at long-forgotten feelings deep within. Abigail turned and continued down the stairs. "He was even so bold as to put traps on my land for small game. That was when Tuttleton and Timothy began to search the property. They were good enough to return the blasted traps to Lord Raleigh's property in a heap. I thought it made an excellent point."

"Raleigh didn't take it so kindly, I presume." Margot had put Abigail's coat on the table in the hall, and Calvin stepped forward to retrieve it before she had a chance.

Her movements were awkward as she lifted her arms to the open sleeves. She was certain her heart stopped when Calvin's hand moved to straighten the collar of the long, navy-colored coat. Abigail told herself it was an accident when his knuckles brushed the underside of her jaw—though the contact was almost lingering—even as she decided that the velvet material of the coat was the same color as his eyes.

"No." Abby struggled to focus on the conversation. "That was when all this trouble began, I'm afraid."

"What about the horse he claims you stole?"

"There is no horse," Abigail said with fluid ease. Her brows drew together. "How did you know about the horse?"

Calvin's back was to her as he reached twice to get hold of the door handle. "I think Margot mentioned something about it after Mr. Dobbs debased your stable wall." He held open the door, and Abigail immediately found the outside air heavy with the promise of rain.

She sighed.

"After you, Lady Abigail." The movement stiff, Calvin bowed.

She stepped over the threshold, before leaning on her crutch to glance back at the man again.

He lifted his brows in question.

"It's Abby."

Calvin would have liked to tell himself he didn't know why a smile was curling at the corners of his mouth as he followed his employer to the carriage in the drive. But he did. It was more than the dusting of freckles across her cheeks and the soft gleam in her russet eyes as she glanced back and corrected him.

Abby.

It was absurd, but he felt like he had just won a small battle.

"Timothy will drive the carriage if I must make a brief trip, mostly to a friend's home. He gets uncomfortable around large crowds and other vehicles, and I hate to ask him to take me to the village."

Before Calvin could think to do what was in all

probability part of his post, Abigail reached up to open the cab door. The vehicle was simple and well maintained, the inside seat heavily cushioned.

"I'd have thought you would rather a phaeton, Abby." He used the familiarity because he could. "They would serve you more open air and be less—"

"I do not care for phaetons."

Her words were so abrupt and cold, he could not help but ask, "Why?"

She was looking down at the tops of her slippers, one hand still on the carriage door and the other tightly wrapped about the handle of her crutch. "I was in an accident with one." She looked up, meeting Calvin's gaze, and smiled. Her eyes suggested she was sharing a joke, but the bittersweet curve of her lips struck him as humorless.

Abigail shifted, her hand moving to hold herself steady as she lifted the wooden crutch. "If you would be so kind as to put this inside for me. On the floor."

Calvin quickly complied and lifted a steadying hand to her elbow. He wasn't certain how he was to go about assisting Abigail into the carriage. His own footman did nothing more than open his carriage door and then close it once he was inside. He had never paid any attention to the etiquette for assisting ladies into carriages and was sure that—if he had—it wouldn't serve in his situation with Abby. He was again struck by the awkwardness of his post and his unsuitableness for it.

Then Abigail looked back over her shoulder at him.

For lack of a better idea, he slid one hand beneath her arm and knelt slightly to put his arm against her knees. She gasped, her hands moving quickly to grip the lapels of his coat as he lifted her into his arms. She was soft against him, the curve of her hip and her thigh tangible even through the material of her coat and dress. He noted that the leg brace she wore stopped at the knee, where his hand was pressed to the bulk.

"Calvin. . . ." Whatever she was about to say died off as her chin lifted until her lips were barely an inch away from his.

He wondered if she was recalling their shared embrace of the night before. As he did so now, he felt flames curl against his loins. The same fire that had kept him awake for most of the night and then carried him into an increasingly familiar dream and an acute state of discomfort when he woke.

When he had found Abigail at the door to his bedchamber not more than minutes ago, he had been sure it was to ask him to take leave of his post. He was more than a little irritated that she acted as if the kiss had not happened. Especially when the touch of her lips on his, not to mention that incredible thing she had done to his tongue, had affected him like none other.

There, standing with her in his arms beside the open door of her carriage, he was sorely tempted to kiss her again. Just to be sure he hadn't imagined her response.

"Lady Abby!" Margot barreled out of the house with her unbound hair trailing out behind her. She came to an abrupt halt in between the door and the carriage when she caught sight of Calvin and the woman in his arms. She blinked with curiosity, the rolled paper she had just been waving almost touching the ground in her limp hand.

"Calvin was just helping me into the carriage, Margot."

Abigail's voice, as she turned away from him to her speechless housekeeper, reminded Calvin of her brother's as he had lied. It suggested, then, that her thoughts had been drifting to a place she felt she had to proclaim they were not. Calvin felt the urge to smile again.

"Ah, well . . ." Margot started toward them again, this time letting her gaze move from her employer's features to Calvin's face. He scowled when she grinned. "You left your papers."

"Oh!" Abigail's interest sounded forced as she released one of Calvin's lapels to take the rolled paper. "I very nearly forgot."

"Have a safe ride." Margot continued to grin, not moving other than to let her eyes move between Abigail and Calvin.

"I hope I am assisting you correctly, Lady Abigail," Calvin said as he turned her back to the carriage.

Abigail wouldn't meet his eye. "This isn't how Mr. Tuttleton did it."

Calvin said through clenched teeth, "What did he do, lie facedown on the mud and let you walk on his back?"

"No, he held my arm and gave a little boost," Abigail said simply, totally unaware of his aggravated tone.

Chapter 11

There was a sign in neatly penned female script that read CLOSED FOR RENOVATIONS set against one of the shop windows. It was the only spot in the two large windows that bracketed the door which was not blocked by unfolded sheets of the *Post*. Even the wooden sign that dangled from the overhang had been taken down to be repainted. Not for the first time, Abigail hoped she and Emily had not been incorrect in their belief that a renovation would improve their bookshop. As it were, business couldn't get any worse.

There was a soft, welcoming jingle from the bell above when she opened the door.

The two women who had been carrying books from a shelf to one of the many crates that lined the floor looked up together and smiled.

"We weren't expecting you today, Abby," Augusta Merryweather said.

"Emily said she and Harriet saw your designs yesterday." Isabel Scott produced a white handkerchief to wipe her hands. "I should think that would have saved you the trip here."

Abigail let the door close behind her, not unaware of the man who was leaning patiently against the carriage outside. "I wanted to be certain everyone liked the new plans."

Dimples appeared in Augusta's cheeks. "They're perfect. We know it."

"You cannot be certain without looking."

"We are certain"—Isabel had gone on to polish her spectacles—"because you created them."

"Would you please"—Abigail feigned frustration as she sighed—"just give them a quick onceover?"

Isabel and Augusta exchanged a look before the latter reached for the designs. Both women's faces disappeared as they opened the blueprints and held them up for inspection.

"Excellent, excellent." Isabel's tone was even more controlled than usual.

"I love what she's done with the shelves," Augusta said.

"Moving the counter . . . simply ingenious."

"The reading nook in the corner is a brilliant notion."

"Indeed."

"And what's this she's done with the floor?"

"Rugs, I believe."

"Ahhh."

Abigail folded down the top half of the designs so that she could see her friends' faces. Isabel gazed up at her innocently over the rims of her specs; Augusta was fighting to hold back a smile.

"I wanted an honest judgment, unfettered by loyalties."

"Loyalty is one thing." Isabel neatly rolled the documents. "Knowing that your friend is a genius at architectural designs is another."

"Thank you both." Abigail let her gaze travel the skeleton of the shop. "There is one more person I should like to share them with. Has Bernice returned from the buying trip?"

"Not yet." Augusta was back at the bookshelf along the far wall, stacking various titles in the crook of one elbow.

"I am under the impression"—Isabel lifted her chin—"that she has run off with Black."

"I think the immodesty of that phrase is slightly hindered by the fact the man is her husband." Augusta rolled her eyes toward Abigail. "I received word from her at last. Bernice said she has found more than enough books to fill up our new shelves. She also mentioned that the countryside they passed in reaching the book dealer was quite intoxicating."

"There is no reason for a woman to lock herself up in a country inn with the man who is her husband." Isabel countered. "It borders on impropriety."

"Sounds romantic to me." Augusta shrugged, and Abigail was certain she was the only one who saw her smile falter.

"Speaking of romance," Abigail said before she could lose her nerve. She felt painfully on the spot when both women's gazes suddenly focused on her anew. "I must confess, your opinions of my sketches were not my only reason for coming here today."

"Oh?" Augusta leaned back against the counter, her expression more than a little interested.

Isabel eyed a wooden chair suspiciously before carefully laying her handkerchief atop it then sitting. "Go on, Abby."

"I was hoping you both would be here today"— Abby began to work the rolled paper between her hands—"so that I could have the benefit of two varied opinions on another matter entirely."

"And what is that?" Augusta asked.

"Did Emily happen to mention that I have found a man to fill the post Tuttleton left in his passing?"

"No." Isabel folded her hands on her lap. "Harriet did."

"She said," Augusta added, "he is handsome."

Abigail winced.

"Did he bring you here today, Abby?"

"Yes. He's waiting outside."

Without further ado, Augusta pushed off from the counter and moved to the clean glass pane that took up a good portion of the shop door.

"Gus, come away from there!" Isabel whispered, as if the man beyond could hear.

"He is not unattractive," Augusta mused aloud. She giggled softly. "Is it that his coat is too small or his shoulders are too big?"

"Most of his clothes are a bit"—Abigail chose the word carefully—"snug."

Augusta glanced back over her shoulder to clarify for the woman who could not bring herself to take a peek. "They are too short, much like Harriet's."

Isabel pushed her specs up higher on her nose. "Perhaps he wears hand-me-downs also."

"Perhaps," Abigail said.

"But that is neither here nor there. What else was it you wanted our opinions on?"

"Your butler?" Augusta was still gazing out the window.

"Yes."

"You do not like him?"

Abigail felt her cheeks burn as she stared down at her gloved hands, which had gone tighter over her designs. "I kissed him."

Isabel gasped at the same moment Augusta spun away from the door.

"Actually," Abigail corrected herself, "he initiated the kiss, but I was a willing participant."

"You kissed him back?" Isabel's tone bordered on horrified.

"Yes." Abigail squeezed her eyes closed. "Very much so."

"Was it a nice kiss?" Augusta inquired politely. "Like in love stories?"

"*Was it*—Augusta, what on earth are you about, asking such things?" Isabel came up off her chair as if it had caught fire. "Of course it was not a nice kiss. The man took advantage of Abby."

Abigail opened a single eye. "I don't believe so."

Augusta shook her head. "If he was hurting her, I should think Abby would not have kissed him back."

Isabel's eyes widened, as if the fact had only just registered. "Abby, forgive me for being so blunt, but a virtuous woman cannot go about kissing the men who are under her employ."

"He *is* rather handsome."

"No matter how handsome he is." Isabel shot the unconcerned Augusta a quelling glance. "What if one of the other servants happened upon you?"

"We were outside." Abigail was aware of the lameness of her argument even as she said it.

"Even worse." Isabel began to pace. "Who knows what might have happened if you had been seen by someone who lacked the devotion those who work for you possess? One of the greatest gossips in all of England lives in North Rutherford. Marcella Rueben would love nothing more than to rise up the chain of scandalmongers again."

"She was placed low on the list of legitimate gossips by the ton after her inadequate description of Lord Black," Augusta agreed.

"I cannot imagine the kind of things someone like her would say, the rumors she would spread. A lady cannot do such things as kiss a man whom she also pays for various services. It is . . . well, it borders on indecent."

"You're right," Abigail sighed, a cold sense of loss closing around her heart. "I should not have let him kiss me. I definitely should not have kissed him back. I am no green girl lacking awareness in the ways of the world."

"It is over and done with, however." Augusta reached out to lightly touch her elbow. She sent Isabel a pointed look. "No use in brooding over the past, especially when it was only a shared kiss."

"Yes." Isabel took a deep breath. "Yes. There is nothing that will change what happened."

"I must be careful it does not happen again." Abigail turned toward the door.

The vise around her heart tightened even further. When she had been in Calvin's arms, she had felt . . . something unexplainable. It reminded her of the bliss she had briefly enjoyed in the first few weeks of her engagement. It reminded her of being loved. There was a difference in Calvin's embrace and that of Patrick Valmonte, however. Calvin's had felt better.

"Abby?"

She stopped to glance back over her shoulder when Isabel spoke from where she had ceased pacing.

"I didn't mean to make such a fuss. I know you came as a friend seeking help, and I—"

"Gave me the honesty I much needed." Abigail made herself smile.

"I would not like to see you abused. Or hurt."

Isabel didn't say the word, but its presence was evident in the air between them.

Again.

"Abby?" Augusta's smile was gentle. "You never answered my question."

Abigail swung open the shop door and offered with complete honesty, "The kiss was very much like those in the love stories, Gus."

The chiming sound of a bell that accompanied Abigail's exit from the nameless shop alerted the man gazing calmly about his surroundings outside to her departure. He straightened from where he was leaning against the carriage as she met his eye. Abigail offered him only a brief inclination of the head before she turned and moved on down the packed-earth road. Calvin wasn't sure what had happened inside the building, but she had left it without the smile she had worn on entering and appeared a bit pale around the cheeks.

"Abby." He had to jog to catch up with her, noting she was a bit startled by his approach.

"I have to pay a call at the magistrate's office." Her gait did not lessen, and she hardly looked at Calvin as she spoke. "I will be back shortly."

"I'd like to go with you." He regulated his stride so he could walk beside her.

She appeared to speed up, her crutch hitting the white soil below with heavy thuds. "There's no need."

"I am a witness, Abby"—he stopped when she did, just outside a building with a solid maple door—"to what was painted on your stable."

"You think Mr. Kingsly will find the report of a woman lacking?" Abigail's brows snapped together under the shadow of her bonnet.

Calvin frowned, not certain what had occurred to change the easy camaraderie they had shared less than two hours before. "No," he said carefully. "I thought you could use a friend."

Abigail blinked as if she only just realized the chill of her attitude. "Thank you, Calvin. You may come inside with me," she said, "but I shall have to ask you not to interfere."

"I would not embarrass you before others, Abby."

She looked away quickly, and Calvin opened the door.

"I was wondering how long the two of you were going to stand out there!"

The magistrate was younger than Calvin had expected, perhaps no more than a few years older than himself. His hair was dark, most of it brushed forward as if in an effort to hide his considerable forehead. His mustache—near blond, oddly enough—ended in two small points that aimed up toward his earlobes.

"Mr. Kingsly." Abigail's tone remained serious,

though the magistrate's had been almost exuberant. "I was hoping you might have a moment to speak with me."

"I always have time for my townspeople." He smiled to expose small teeth shaped like perfect squares. "Especially the pretty ones." He shot Calvin a wink.

Calvin ignored the gesture, watching the woman beside him from the corner of his eye. She had missed the byplay and, perhaps, everything the man had said. Her attention was focused on the hearth that took up one wall of the cramped building— or, more to the point, on the large deer head that peered sightlessly out from the wall above it. When she turned back to the magistrate, her expression reflected some of the doubt Calvin suddenly felt.

Abigail shifted, stepping nearer to the desk behind which Kingsly stood. At the sound of her brace making contact with the wooden floor, the magistrate's gaze dropped to her legs.

"Why don't you have a seat, Lady Wolcott?" he said without looking up.

"No, thank you."

"Are you certain?" The magistrate finally let his gaze lift, his smile like that one would offer a feeble old woman. "I don't want you to overexert yourself and fall."

Calvin's hands clenched into fists at his sides.

Abigail's jaw flexed. "I am certain."

"How about this fine gentleman with you?" Kingsly's attention moved to Calvin. By the time he had done a quick survey and had to lift his chin to see the other's face, his smile had dimmed somewhat.

"This is Mr. Garrett," Abigail said.

"Ah, the fellow who took up Tuttleton's old post." He did not appear concerned with the way the other two individuals in the room lifted their brows at his knowledge. "An interesting character, your predecessor. Old as dirt, if he was a day. It was his time to go, really."

Calvin heard a crackling sound and didn't have to look to know it was the blueprints in Abigail's hands.

"I should like to make a complaint, sir," she said stiffly, "about a neighbor."

"Duncan Simmons?" Kingsly propped his hands on his hips and shook his head. "What has that old codger done?"

"Nothing. Mr. Simmons, his good wife, and I get on well. It is of the owner whose land borders mine on the west that I speak."

"Lord Raleigh?"

"The same."

Kingsly lowered himself into his chair and folded his hands to make a pyramid beneath his chin. "What would be your complaint, dear?"

"Some of his employees have trespassed upon my land, as well as friends of the viscount's in a less than sober state."

"Ah, well, mistakes do happen." The ring on the magistrate's slim pinky winked in the light of the taper upon his desk.

The reflection of the gem within caught Calvin's eye.

"I am certain that some of these intrusions were no accident." Abigail spoke in a crisp tone that brooked no interruption. "I have made my opinions on the subject known to the viscount. Since then, these trespasses have only worsened. I believe Lord Raleigh is deliberately setting out to frighten me."

"Has he harmed your person in any way?" Kingsly's gaze ran down the length of Abigail's form, pausing once over the crutch she leaned against and again at the delicate curves of her hips.

Calvin kept his promise to Abigail. He said nothing, only coughed. The magistrate's attention moved to him only briefly, catching Calvin's single lifted brow then moving away.

"No, not directly," Abby was saying. "But the man who threatened me harm is employed by the viscount."

"He told you Raleigh pays him to threaten you?"

"His wording left no doubt in my mind."

"But he did not come out and say it?"

A wave of understanding hit Calvin. He had to press his teeth together to keep from calling the other man a rather choice name. Kingsly was playing Abigail for a fool, downplaying her every comment. Attempting, in short, to make her seem like she was overreacting.

His intent did not appear to be lost on Abigail. Calvin could see little of her face beyond her bonnet, but her back had gone rigid and her words were clipped when she again spoke.

"No, sir, he did not say it."

"I know the viscount, Lady Abigail." He smiled again and continued in a tone that was best suited for a child's ear. "He was the only landholder, only gentry that helped me obtain my position as magistrate. We have been acquainted for almost two years. He has never struck me as the sort of man who would attack a defenseless woman."

"I told you, Raleigh himself did not—"

"Lady Wolcott, your brother does not live with you at the estate, does he?"

"No."

"And you have no husband, correct?"

Son of a bitch, Calvin thought.

"I do not see what that has to do with this," Abigail snapped.

"A woman alone and lonely can imagine all sort of things in a given situation. I'm not saying you were not accosted, Lady Abigail, but mayhap your fear enhanced the tale afterward. Dramatized it, if you will."

"I beg your pardon?" Abigail's rage was palpable.

Kingsly offered Calvin a second man-to-man look. "Take her home, Mr. Garrett. See to it she gets some rest, and be so kind as to watch the shadows for this man who is trying to harm her."

Calvin couldn't stop the words. "You do not tell me what to do."

Kingsly blanched.

Calvin turned to the woman who was his employer—so to speak. She slowly faced him and then moved to the door.

"Have a good day, Lady Wolcott."

"Go to hell," Abigail said.

Calvin looked back at the gape-mouthed magistrate and smiled.

Good girl, he thought.

Chapter 12

The night sky had disappeared behind a heavy blanket of mottled storm clouds. The ominous folds of blue-gray shifted and swelled above like a brooding thing, like the anger that continued to fester inside Abigail. Her crutch hit the bed of straw silently before she took a tight grip on the bridle and swung herself atop Achilles' back. The massive gray's tail flicked upward, and he let out a sharp snort, as if he sensed his mistress's emotions and was eager to help her be rid of them.

The horse's shadow floated between the hanging lanterns on either side of the stable as the animal trotted impatiently to the exit then halted abruptly just beyond the opened doors. Abigail wasn't sure if Achilles was as surprised as she or simply reacting to her sudden tenseness. She was certain, however, hers were not the only eyes fixed on the rider who stood in their path.

She felt a moment's fear until, in the dim light from the stables, she saw the man on the horse was not stocky, with mean black eyes. He sat tall in the saddle, his shoulders broad and his waist compact. The horse he rode was one of Abigail's own.

"What are you doing?" Abigail hissed, directing her anger at the man who, for a second time, was intruding upon the solitude of her ride.

"You shouldn't be out at all," Calvin said, his voice calm despite her irritation. Abigail could make out nothing of his features, only the dark shadow of his head tilting toward the sky. "It's going to rain."

"We shall be fine." A slight nudge, and Achilles was moving again. Abigail did not look in the direction of the other on horseback as they passed him.

"I thought you would say that. I am going with you."

Abigail scowled, not liking the close proximity of his voice or the beat of hooves following after her. "That is unnecessary."

"I disagree."

Undisturbed, Achilles continued in his easy canter as the woman on his back turned at the waist to glare at the large shadow following them. "What is it about you, Calvin Garrett? Why must you go to such pains to annoy me? Especially now, when I should very much like to be alone."

"I do not want you to get hurt." The words came out in a low timbre.

Sudden, unwelcome sensation sizzled down Abigail's spine then spread outward to her limbs. She faced forward again. "I will return before the rain comes."

"I am aware you are an intelligent-enough female to get out of the rain."

"Big of you."

"It is your stubborn refusal to worry about your own safety in regard to those that may be lurking in the dark that concerns me."

As they left the cleared land for the tree-lined trail that reached to the ends of her property, Abigail understood. "I can take care of myself today just as well as I did yesterday. I do not need to be taken care of."

"Do not speak to me like you do those who judge you because of a minor physical flaw, Abby. I see you as a damned stubborn woman whose focus on independence borders on lunacy," Calvin said. "Not a cripple."

Abigail brought her mount to a stop. The one behind her shifted slightly to the side then forward until, in the dull glow of the moon behind clouds, she could see Calvin's eyes. So blue they were almost black, they met and held hers. At the brief contact, Abigail was abruptly aware her anger at the worthless magistrate back in the village had disappeared.

"Calvin?"

"Yes, Abby?"

"I believe that is the nicest thing anyone's ever said to me." She saw him blink, taken aback, and laughed. Achilles stepped into motion again.

"You make it hard, you know." Calvin kept his horse in step with hers. "You have built up a wall around yourself that prevents all the ignorant insults and sympathy from coming in."

"As well I should." Abigail's jaw tensed as she continued to stare straight ahead. Her smile disappeared. "You cannot imagine how bothersome it is to have people smiling at you with such pity in their eyes that you begin to wonder if it is really as bad as they think. To hear them whisper behind your back, as if you were not only lame but also deaf, about how terribly tragic it all is. Telling their friends that the poor dear used to love to dance and that she was abandoned by the man who was supposed to have loved her more than any—" She took a deep breath, horrified that she had shared so much with this man she hardly knew at all. Abigail said simply, "You do not understand."

"I understand," Calvin said, apparently less than traumatized by her rant, "that there are individuals with whom you need not put up your protective armor. As it is, you make it difficult for a man to know what to do around you."

"Rest assured, Calvin." She tried to keep her tone impersonal. "As my employee, I shall tell you what I need."

"Will you?"

His tone caught her off guard. He had completely ignored her effort to draw a line between them and set new boundaries. Calvin's words came out from low in his throat, and his amusement was audible. She knew she shouldn't, but she couldn't help but glance at him from the corner of her eye. His gaze was rising from the swell of her breasts against the old material of her shirt to her mouth. Without thinking, Abigail let her tongue slip out to dampen her suddenly dry lips, and his gaze flared upward to meet hers.

Abigail's head snapped forward and she surreptitiously guided Achilles into a faster pace. "You ride well, sir." She turned her head again. "Did you grow up in the country?"

The rumble of his chuckle worried her, mostly

because of the hair it made rise at her nape. He answered her amiably enough, however.

"Quite the opposite. I was born in London."

"Whereabouts?" Abigail, too, was born in Town.

"I don't know." Calvin's voice was devoid of the humor it once bore. "My first memory is of the parish where I lived before I went to the workhouse. I spent most of my youth in the latter."

Abigail looked at Calvin when the remnant flash from a bolt of lightning illuminated the night. Much as she had when discussing her past, he was facing forward, his spine rod-straight and his hands curled tightly about the reins.

"Some," Abby offered cautiously, "would say you were lucky to have had a roof over your head and food, when others were starving on the street."

"Some have no idea what it's like in the house," Calvin returned grimly. "There are many times when going hungry and cold outside its shelter seemed like a dream."

"You never knew your mother?" Abigail asked, anxious to change the topic.

"She died in childbirth."

Abigail frowned. "Have you no family at all, Calvin?"

She sensed him looking at her when he said, "My father was alive until I was seventeen years old, but I never knew until circumstances after his death made him known to me."

"I'm sorry," Abigail said softly.

"Don't be. How can I miss what I have never known? In truth, being alone for almost half my life has served me well. I have learned that you really don't need anyone."

"Perhaps that is why. . . ." Abigail let her words

die off, not certain she wanted the man to know that thoughts of his demeanor—of him—took up her time.

"Why what, Abigail?"

She did not look at him. "Since you came here, you've never actually struck me as the kind of man who accepts orders from others."

"I'm not." A rumble of thunder echoed through the night. "I wasn't," Calvin said then, "until I met your brother." Without warning, he maneuvered his horse until it was turned in the opposite direction and reached for Achilles' bridle.

The horse let out an indignant snort, but came to a halt. Abigail frowned, curious.

"Now that I have answered all your questions, my lady," he said, "perhaps you will answer one of mine."

Abigail felt her heart sink, but she offered a brief nod. "Ask."

He was silent for a long time. Then: "Why did you choose to move yourself out into the country all alone?"

She blinked; it was not the question she had been expecting. Not the carefully worded one that always came when people first met her. Yet, Abigail was certain, there was little about this man that had struck her comparable to anyone else in the world. She smiled.

"Actually, I have always liked the country. My grandparents lived here when I was small, and I can remember visiting them, riding with my grandfather and sitting with my grandmother as she read. Mrs. Poole already had her post at the estate; she was my age now."

"That cannot be right," Calvin said. "That would

only put her in her forties now. She must be older than that."

"Either poor Mrs. Poole hasn't aged well at all," Abigail chuckled, not displeased, "or you have a misconstrued idea of my age."

"So you wished to live here all along?"

Abigail nodded. "I was forced to live with my parents when I was a child. Then my brother and sister and I took care of each other when they passed. I was kept in London after I turned eighteen for other reasons."

"The engagement you mentioned?" Calvin's tone suggested he was interested in that detail but would not ask.

"Yes. Once that ended, I saw no reason to keep myself in Town. It's very peaceful here"—Abigail smiled wryly—"or at least it had been until the trouble with the viscount began. London's not so far away that I cannot see my family and friends after less than a few hours' ride. One of my best friends, Bernice, lives here in Rutherford."

She tried to explain. "There's something very nice about returning to a place that always brought you happiness in your childhood, you know?"

"No."

Abigail blushed.

Calvin appeared unconcerned with her thoughtless words. "Do you not miss the goings-on of polite society? The parties and danc—" He cut himself short.

"I miss it sometimes," she answered with an honesty she had never even shared with her friends. "I miss the dancing most of all. You may not believe it to look at me now, Calvin Garrett, but I used to be a wonderful dancer."

"I believe you."

She felt heat steal up her cheeks at his words. "The worst of it is, I think I could still maneuver about the floor if given the chance and a slow waltz."

"Then why don't you?"

Abigail's gaze dropped, as it always did, to her leg sitting stiff in its stirrup. "No one asks anymore."

Calvin shifted, and she was suddenly aware that he was much closer than he had been before. While she had talked, he had moved his horse until their knees—his left and her left—were almost touching. Abby could see his chest rising and falling in time with her own breathing.

"I would have liked to see you dance, Abby."

A burst of lightning flared above, clearly illuminating the blunt lines of Calvin's cheekbones, his hard jaw, and the unnameable emotion that filled his dark eyes. He lifted a hand.

"We should go back now," Abigail said quickly. Achilles moved fluidly, turning around on the path without pause then breaking into a gallop in the direction of the estate.

Behind them, she could have sworn she heard a familiar chuckle.

Storm clouds heaved across the sky. A violent crack of thunder pierced the night, as the water became something foul. It clung to her like a black mud, weighing down her limbs and sinking into the material of her gown to chill the skin beneath.

The phaeton was a living thing: she saw it first from the corner of her eye and managed to turn her head from the congealing liquid in which she lay only with the greatest effort. The vehicle closed in on her, cutting through the mire like it was water. There were no horses drawing it along; the phaeton moved of its own accord, picking up speed as it closed in on her.

Her eyes widened in horrified understanding, and the vehicle came barreling toward her. Her heart threatened to burst from her chest as she struggled in vain against the sticky ooze that held her in place. The wheels of the phaeton would crush her skull—she knew it as surely as she knew they had crushed her leg years before—and she did now what she hadn't been able to do then. Abigail screamed.

The sound of her own cry echoed in the dark of the bedchamber as she sat up amidst the tangled sheets. Her unbound hair clung to her cheeks, and she brushed away both the dark tendrils and the remnants of her tears as she concentrated on steadying the ragged beat of her heart. Memories of the nightmare settled at the base of her spine, where her skin was chilled from sweat and the cool night breeze. A brief flicker of lightning brought her surroundings to light, and she caught her own reflection in the mirror on the far wall.

Her hair was damp, her skin pale, and her eyes haunted. Abigail sighed. Dark spirits disturbed her dreams on stormy nights, yet she looked like the ghost. She saw the mirror image of herself jerk abruptly at the sudden banging on her chamber door.

She pressed the back of a hand to her heated cheek. "I'm all right!"

Abigail was not surprised when the knock was repeated. Her voice sounded weak and wobbly to her own ears. Despite her frequent dismissals of their offered comfort, she reasoned silently that perhaps she did need one of Margot's warm hugs or Mrs. Poole's stiff drinks this night.

With the ease of someone who had performed the task for a long time, Abigail reached for the crutch she kept against one of the bedposts without having to look. She favored her left leg even more than usual, not simply because she had not donned her leg brace but because the chill in the air made her joints ache abysmally. There was a third, more insistent knock by the time she was halfway to the door.

"I'm coming," she called even as the fingers of her free hand closed around the door handle. She let the door swing inward under the complete certainty she would find Mrs. Poole in her ruffled, round cap or Margot with her hair sprouting about at odd angles on the other side. Later, she would be loath to imagine what her face looked like when she found Calvin at the opened door.

Dim light from the wall sconces in the hall flickered across the hard angles of his face and the muscles clearly defined between the folds of his opened shirt. Abigail felt an odd tingling run up her scalp as she stared at the broad expanse of dark skin exposed before her, then a hot blush stain her cheeks when she realized that she was staring.

Her wide eyes lifted quickly to the face of the man before her. He did not appear too concerned with her ogling. As a matter of fact, he appeared totally unaware of where her attention was directed, as his had also drifted. Abigail felt the heat of his gaze like a physical caress as it ran along the exposed skin of her neck then lower to her bare shoulders and the upper curves of her breasts.

Abigail had not donned her robe in coming to the door and felt ridiculously exposed in only her thin nightgown with lace straps in lieu of sleeves.

His gaze had been on her bare flesh for perhaps seconds, but they had passed like hours for Abigail. When Calvin's eyes finally lifted to hers, she noted that they had gone to an almost smoky shade of blue. She swallowed.

His attention dropped again, watching her throat work, and she felt her mouth go dry.

"I'm sorry if I woke you." Her whisper sounded loud and, she thought, a little unsteady.

Calvin ignored her apology. "I have something for you." His words were low and gravelly, hinting at things she could only imagine.

"Oh?" Abigail's voice cracked. Her heart stopped when Calvin's gaze dropped until he appeared to be looking down the length of himself.

"He was under my bed."

Abigail blinked, and her own gaze lowered. In noting the man's almost-naked chest, she had quickly diverted her eyes before allowing them to travel any lower than the plane of his stomach and the delineations of sinew set therein. Now she focused on the hands he had cupped just beneath his belly. In his large palms, the bundle of brown and gray fur looked as tiny as he had been when Abby had first brought him home.

"Harry!" Her mouth curved in a smile, and shimmering black eyes peered up at her from behind thick lashes.

"Where shall I put him?"

Abigail blinked at the roughness in Calvin's voice, her smile dimming only a little when she saw he was watching her lips.

"I'll take him." She maneuvered back from the door and held open her free palm.

Calvin eyed her arm and then the rabbit that was nearly three times its width.

Abby chuckled when he lifted a brow and slipped her fingers between Harry's belly and Calvin's palm. She made herself ignore the rough skin of the man's hand and concentrate on the rabbit's soft fur as she lifted him. Her leg shook warningly.

"I have to sit." She did not look up as she cuddled Harry to her breast and moved toward the nearest available place to position herself. On the edge of the mattress where she sat, she settled the rabbit down beside her. Harry sniffed the sheets worriedly before the familiar scent of the woman who raised him and the gentle stroking of her fingertips behind his ears calmed him. He lay down with his nose bobbing against her hip.

"Thank you," Abigail said.

"You called out."

She felt suddenly embarrassed, more so than she had been at the thought of being caught gaping at him, and managed a crooked smile. She doubted he could see her, however, in the shadowed bedchamber. "I have nightmares." She repeated, "I'm sorry if I woke you."

"I was awake." Calvin stepped into the room.

Abigail's heart stopped.

"What was your nightmare about?"

His gall at both invading her private domain and sleeping thoughts should have angered her. She should have insisted he leave her room.

"My accident," she said.

"Would you like to talk about it?" The offering came stiffly.

Abigail couldn't help it. There was something about his discomfort that was amusing. She chuckled in the dark, and the brittle laugh changed directions, aimed at her own actions. "There's a storm and an accident. I fall into a stream, and my phaeton comes down after me."

"Not just a nightmare, then."

A cold shiver snaked down Abigail's spine. She wasn't sure if it was memories of the past or the sudden closeness of the man that affected her. "No," she said. She peered up at Calvin, nothing more than a large shadow looming over her in the dark. "If you'll excuse me, I should put Harry in his hutch and myself back to bed."

He stood for so long she wondered if he was deliberately ignoring her, then said, "All right." He turned and took two steps away before coming to a halt.

Abigail's fingers stilled in Harry's fur.

Calvin came back to her and in one fluid move reached out. She gasped when his hand almost brushed her cheek then dropped to her shoulder. She hadn't even realized the strap of her gown had fallen until he carefully lifted the scrap of lace back in place. The door closed heavily behind him, and Abigail continued to sit wide-eyed atop her bed. Her skin burned where his fingers had touched it . . . where they had lingered.

Chapter 13

The parchment made a satisfying crackling sound as Calvin crushed it within his fist. Remnants of the rain that had stopped only a few hours before dripped off the roof of the stable and onto the brim of his hat. It felt like an icy drop of rainwater had found its way inside the collar of his coat and shirt, trickling slowly down his spine. The chill was not that of cold water, however, but harsh awareness.

The initials P.V. bring to mind only one name.

The note had come early that morning; Mrs. Poole had given it to him along with his breakfast of sausage and tomatoes. Calvin had recognized Thomas Wolcott's wax seal instantly and silently hoped the cook did not. So much had happened in the short space of time since he had sent Thomas the brief query, he had forgotten to expect a reply. The one he had received had been more than unexpected, in fact. Upon reading the response,

Calvin had felt an unwelcome rush of emotions, one of which was rage.

He could still see her face each time he closed his eyes. Her dark hair unbound and cascading down her shoulders like a shimmering cape. Her face soft and white, save for the few freckles scattered across her nose and cheeks. As if it had been moments and not almost twelve hours before, he saw her bay-colored gaze lift from beneath lashes damp with tears as she opened the bedchamber door.

Not the gaze of a woman who appeared either stupid or suffering the pain of a broken heart.

Calvin couldn't understand what the hell she was doing.

Patrick Valmonte, the scoundrel to whom Abigail was engaged three years ago.

Calvin jammed the crumpled letter into his coat pocket, glaring into the sun as it broke through the lingering clouds above and stole under the brim of his hat.

The man, as far as he understood it, had abandoned Abigail when she needed him the most. Whether it was because Valmonte couldn't handle the horror of what had happened to her or the disfigurement it entailed, Calvin didn't know. He was certain, however, that the man he had never met before was nothing short of a bastard.

"So why," he breathed low in his throat, "in God's name is she giving him money?"

It was like as not a question he would never get an answer to. He had invaded her privacy, Abigail's personal accounts, to obtain the little he now knew. To confront her with his knowledge would be to expose himself for what he was and why he was really there. He was certain, once she knew the truth of his and her brother's scheme, she would be enraged with them both and might very well banish Calvin from her life forever.

It was a risk, Calvin admitted to himself while standing alone outside her home with tentacles of jealousy and anger curling around his heart, he did not want to take. He couldn't explain it and, in truth, didn't even try to exhaust himself doing so. He was well aware he had found out everything Thomas had wanted to know about his sister. Knew what was going on between her and Lord Raleigh and actually believed the rather peculiar women who were her friends added quality to her life. That she was sharing funds with Patrick Valmonte was a mystery in itself, but nothing Thomas could not confront her with himself.

Yet Calvin had sent no word to the other man that their investigation need not continue. In truth, he had a bad feeling about what Raleigh was trying to do, which had only been magnified upon watching Abby's encounter with the magistrate. Abigail was alone, and too stubborn, Calvin believed, to accept her brother's help no matter the circumstances. Whether she knew it or not, she needed her new butler for reasons only he was aware of. And reasons he had stopped trying to tell himself only concerned the safety of his best friend's sister prevented Calvin from even conceiving of taking his leave now.

Reasons that had a lot to do with her smile the night before, undeniably innocent and unknowingly seductive as the strap of her nightgown slipped quietly off her shoulder. Calvin only hoped when this farce was over, Thomas wouldn't be calling him out onto the dueling field and Abby did not hate him.

The gleam of sunlight on steel caught his eye, and he lifted his gaze to the open field. It stretched from Abigail's land to the fallen oak and beyond. Just at the singed tree, there stood two men. The first Calvin recognized as Lord Raleigh; the other was more broadly built. The man standing in the shadows of the stables muttered a dark curse as his gaze followed the beam of the sun to the guns both men carried.

Harry calmly approached the rug where Abigail sat, left leg stretched out beneath the designs she was scrutinizing. He sniffed the charcoal and the stained fingers in which the chunk of black rock lay, then shifted his survey to the thin paper unfolded on Abigail's lap.

She frowned, losing her focus on the bookshelves that took up most of the library wall. "Would you kindly stop that?"

Harry did not pause in nibbling the corner of her designs.

"Quit." Abby put a clean fingertip to the rabbit's nose and gave a gentle nudge.

Harry gave her a brief sniff, snuck his head under her hand, and continued to consume her paper.

Despite her poor mood, Abigail could not bring herself to yell at her found pet. She carefully rerolled the papers she had been reviewing for the bookshop and put them atop the settee beside her. As she used both the sofa and her crutch to rise first to her good knee and then her feet, she cursed the nightmare that had ruined her sleep the night before. Then she cursed herself for not admitting that it had not been the nightmare but what had occurred afterward that kept her tossing and turning for the rest of the night.

Once on her feet, her gaze traveled back to her bookshelves. On a sigh, she moved to the farthest column to her right. The books on these shelves, Abby was certain, had not been touched in three years. Her charcoal-stained fingertips ran across the well-worn spines and remembered titles. When she found one of her old favorites, she carefully tugged it from the rest.

"I thought you didn't read those anymore."

Abigail turned to face the woman who stood in the doorway. The coat she wore, her gown, even the barrettes in her hair, were new, suggesting she was a woman of considerable means. The fact that the coat was brown, the walking gown was pale green, and one of her barrettes was slightly askew clarified that—despite the fact she had gone from rather meager beginnings to marry a notorious earl—she would always be Bernice.

"I'm growing rather worried with all the books Harriet suggests," Abigail said. "All those stories about the avenging souls of murdered persons and restless spirits cannot be good for one's constitution."

"It makes you wonder. . . ."

"About ghosts?"

"About Harriet." Bernice grinned. As she stepped in the room, her bronze gaze flashed behind her spectacles, inspecting Abigail's eyes and the shadows the other woman knew were beneath. "I hear tell it has been storming a lot. Are you all right?"

"No worse than usual."

In a way, Abigail was aware she and her friend had something in common. Remarkable things had occurred to them both on separate nights when the sky had gone gray with thunderclouds and the wind howled like a pack of wolves. On Bernice's blustery night, she had been attacked by two blackguards then rescued by the man who would love her for the rest of her life. On hers, the man she believed loved her had left Abby to die.

She shook off the memory to ask the other woman, "Shall we go for a walk?"

Bernice nodded, linking her arm through Abigail's as they moved from the room. "I should think I managed to acquire enough books to fill the new shelving arrangement you have planned." She held open the front door, squinting a bit in the sunlight that had broken through the clouds. "The book dealer gave me an excellent discount."

"The one Rosabelle Desiree told us about?" As they began down the path from the door, Abigail found herself scanning the grounds for a familiar figure in a too-small coat. She squeezed her eyes shut when she realized what she was doing.

"Yes," Bernice said. "I believe it was because of his . . . relationship with Rose that he offered us such a deal."

Abigail smiled, her lashes lifting. Since becoming friends with the well-known courtesan, they had come up with some very interesting terms in referring to the woman's line of work.

"I heard you and Sebastian took your time in returning home from your trip." She turned her head in time to see Bernice's eyes gleam.

"It was lovely countryside." The other woman's gaze lowered; then she peered at Abigail from beneath her lashes. "Or so it seemed from our window at the inn."

Abby made out the strange sound through their shared laughter. It snapped through the air abruptly, like the crack of a whip. She gasped at the sudden pain against her right ear, lifting her fingertips to where her skin stung.

"What was that?" Bernice was frowning.

"I'm not certain. But I think I was just stung by a—" Abigail's words died in her throat as she looked at the hand she had placed against her ear and found it wet with blood.

"My God, Abby," Bernice breathed, producing an embroidered handkerchief from her coat pocket. Remembered horror haunted her gaze as it met the other woman's. "That was a gunshot."

"Terribly sorry!"

Cold awareness flared to life inside Abigail as she let Bernice press the small square of cloth to her injured ear. Her gaze slowly moved to where she heard the sound of his voice. His damnably familiar voice.

"Touchy trigger, you know." He stood so close to the invisible line that separated their properties that Abigail could see every line on the viscount's face and the less-than-apologetic gleam in his eyes.

Lord Raleigh held his hunting rifle against his broad chest. It was Dobbs—a smirk curling his full lips—who held his gun with one hand at the trigger and the barrel aimed toward the ground. Abigail was certain it was he who had fired the bullet that grazed her ear.

"Abby." Bernice's voice came from far away, as did the dull pain in her ear. "Abby, who is that?"

Abigail felt frozen in place, certain her heart had stopped. She did not blink, too scared she would release the tears that pressed against the backs of her eyes before the monsters waiting hungrily for her reaction. Had she moved just an inch to her right, had she not been happily watching her friend's blissful smile, the bullet would have torn through her cheek.

"Abby?"

"That"—her lips barely moved as she spoke—"is Lord Raleigh and his man."

"I know the viscount." Bernice lifted a trembling hand to point, not at the men in the field but to the side of them. "I meant the other man."

Though her head did not, Abigail's gaze shifted. He was moving away from the shadows of the stable, his even gait intent as he stepped through the opening in the horse pen and over her property line. His broad shoulders were hunched as if an invisible wind were beating at his back—or, perhaps, his insides—and his wide-brimmed hat cast his features into shadow.

"Calvin?" Abigail whispered. Then, when she realized his intent, "Calvin!"

Raleigh saw him first. Dobbs hadn't realized the other man approached until his gun was wrenched from his limp fingers. His expression was slow in displaying his surprise, but his pain was evident the moment Calvin slammed the butt of the rifle into his stomach.

Abigail gasped, her lashes fluttering wildly as she tried to tell herself she wasn't really seeing this. She started across the lawn and toward the man who appeared to be eager to come to blows.

"Now see here!" Lord Raleigh reached for Calvin's arm, but something in the other man's face stilled him.

"He could have killed her."

Calvin's voice, as Abby approached, made the hair stand up on her nape. It was dark and gravelly, filled with foreboding. His knuckles had gone white, his grip fierce over the gun he still held. His gaze moved slowly, near black in rage, between the viscount and the man who was doubled over.

"Calvin." She was breathless.

"It was an accident," Raleigh said to him. Something passed between the two men as their gazes clashed, something that terrified the woman who had stepped toward them. The viscount's eye broke away first as he did a slow survey of the man opposite him. "A gentleman of rank would understand that."

"I understand what is going on, Raleigh," Calvin returned, totally unconcerned with the judgment that laced the other's words. "And I can assure you, it is not about to continue while I am here."

"Calvin," Abigail hissed as her gaze darted between the viscount in his tailor-made suit and tilted hat to the other man in the coat too tight across the shoulders and a hat that appeared rather battered.

"Who do you think you are?" Raleigh said through his too-white teeth.

"Not a hirable henchman." Calvin glared down at Dobbs and back. "Not a crooked magistrate you can put in your pocket. I take care of Lady Abigail."

A whole new kind of anger burst to life inside Abby. Her jaw clenched and her eyes narrowed as she focused on Calvin anew.

"Come, Dobbs." Raleigh nudged his toady none too gently as he began to turn away. "The lack of culture this close to the edge of my property is tiresome."

"You take your friend and you go, Raleigh—"

"Calvin, stop this at once," Abigail ordered.

"Don't either one of you come anywhere near the lady's home again. For the next man to threaten her, there will be hell to pay."

"I said stop!" She couldn't be positive that it was her tone and not the fact the viscount had finally left that made Calvin turn in her direction.

It was breathtaking, actually, how quickly his gaze could go from being pitch black with anger to brilliant blue with concern. It met her own gaze only briefly before turning to her injured ear. He lifted a hand. "You are hurt."

Without compunction, Abigail slapped his hand away. "What do you think you are doing?"

She saw the moment understanding hit Calvin, when he realized that she was infuriated with him. A muscle ticked in his jaw as he said very slowly, "What was I supposed to do? Let him go on with his scare tactics?"

"You are to let me handle this, Calvin." Abigail shook her head. "This is my home, my affair. In fact, it is none of your concern at all." She sucked in a deep breath when he stepped closer.

"Like hell it isn't."

Her free hand clenching into a fist, the other tightening around her crutch, Abigail held her ground. "Who do you think you are, sir? Have you forgotten that you are under my employ?" She scowled up at the man twice her size and a full head taller than she.

"They could have killed you, Abigail." Calvin stared at her as if she were insane.

"I am beginning to think it is you who will get me killed. I was handling everything on my own. You cannot imagine how you may have made this worse for me. What happens when you are no longer here to fight my battles? Then what can I possibly do after you have enraged them so?"

A small, alarmed sound escaped Abigail when Calvin's hand shot out fast as lightning, closing around her upper arm like a vise and drawing her near. He lowered his head until their noses almost touched and their lips were a heartbeat apart.

"I would not leave you to them," Calvin said. "I will be here to watch over you."

Despite his intoxicating nearness—the clean scent of his soap and an altogether too disconcerting smell that was pure maleness—his words cut through her like knives. She heard not his true intent but the weakness in herself his words implied. A moment before his lips touched hers, she said, "Not if I do not want you here."

His fingers tightened around her arm almost to the point of hurting, then released her as if her skin were poison. Calvin's expression was unreadable, almost frightening Abigail. Then he turned away.

Abby stared at his broad back, her heart pounding against her temples and her breathing unsteady, until he threw open the door to the house and disappeared inside. She winced when it slammed closed after him.

"So," Bernice, who had been standing at Abby's side for God knew how long, said with forced cheerfulness, "that was your new butler?"

Chapter 14

The worst part about admitting you were wrong, Abigail thought as she gazed silently at the closed door across from hers, was not doing it to yourself but to the one you had treated unfairly. Most especially when you were rather adamant in your self-assurance that it was you who were right. She sighed.

Abigail wasn't certain but had a sneaking suspicion a full hour had passed as she stood staring at Calvin's bedchamber door. She was trying to gather her resolve, but her heart only continued to pound heavily in her chest and her leg was starting to hurt.

She took a deep breath and lifted her closed hand to knock.

"He isn't there, lass."

Abigail released a startled gasp before turning to regard the woman who stood at the top of the stairs. She didn't try to pretend she didn't know what her cook was talking about. "Do you know where he is?"

Mrs. Poole shook her head, opening her own chamber door. "Haven't seen him since breakfast. His lunch plate is still in the kitchen. Margot said she saw him walking away from the house. Said he looked a bit perturbed."

Abigail winced. "Did she say if she saw he had all his belongings with him?"

Mrs. Poole looked back over her shoulder, her eyes reflecting sympathy as they met Abby's and she shook her head.

When the older woman had closed her door for her afternoon nap, Abigail did not move away from Calvin's bedchamber. Without qualm, without thinking about it so long she would lose her resolve, she reached for the doorknob. She made a valiant attempt at ignoring the rush of relief she felt when her gaze immediately fell across the opened valise in the middle of the floor. A small smile tickled the corner of her lips as she spotted a familiar coat thrown across one of the chairs. The expression in her gaze turned thoughtful as she let the door fall closed again.

"Thank you, Timothy," she said an hour later. She rested a gloved palm on the other's shoulder as he carefully set her on her feet. Abigail gave him a brief pat on the back when she caught him nervously eyeing the pedestrians moving up and down the earthen road that bisected North Rutherford. "I'll be quick. I promise."

Timothy nodded, not meeting her eye. He did not lean comfortably against the side of the carriage as Calvin had when he brought her to the village, but climbed back into the driver's perch. He kept his head down. Abigail glanced back over her shoulder before entering the dress shop and felt a pang of sympathy for Timothy. He clutched the reins to him as if waiting for her to come running back and ordering him to bolt.

A bell not unlike the one above the door of the bookshop announced Abigail's arrival inside the boutique. The small building smelled of perfume and clean linens. It was crowded, but not untidy. There were tables of folded materials, various dressmaker's dummies all clad in gowns that varied in price from those the lower middle class could afford to those in loftier ranges. There were only two other women in the shop, both familiar to the newcomer.

Marcella Rueben looked up from the length of silk she was scrutinizing, her ugly frown of concentration quickly disappearing in lieu of a pretty, artificial smile.

"Hello, Lady Wolcott." Her jovial voice, as with everything else about the coldly attractive woman, was fake.

Abigail offered the other only a brief nod, not even bothering to force a smile, before moving to the back of the shop. An ignorant observer might think her unpleasant and the wealthy merchant's daughter the opposite. Abigail didn't care. She was well aware of the sort of woman Marcella was; she smiled in your face and said nasty things behind your back. She had been one of the instigators in all the talk that had revolved for a short time around Sebastian Black, Bernice's husband. She had also, as Abigail heard it, made certain the entire village of North Rutherford knew when her engagement had ended because she was hideously disfigured.

Abby made herself push away the memory as well as the remembered disgust as she came to a halt at the worktable where the proprietress of the dress shop sat. Her head was bowed over the near-translucent bit of lace she was sewing, her brow furrowed in concentration. Without looking up from her work, she said, "Good afternoon, Lady Abby." Her tone indicated genuine welcome and warmth.

"Moira." Abigail smiled. "How are you?"

"Staying busy." Her dainty hands moved fluidly over her needle and string, even as she peered up from under her brows, making sure Marcella was out of earshot. She spoke softly, "I've been working on that pair of breeches you asked about. I think I should like to take a few more measurements, if you do not mind. Of"—she nodded downward—"your right leg. I think the breeches should have more give there."

"All right." Abigail nodded, noting the distinct difference in the ways Marcella and Moira had looked at her injured leg. The latter woman had been the first to make clothes for her after the accident; it had been her idea to lift the hem so that her skirts would not get caught in her brace. "By the bye, Moira, do you happen to have extra material of the heavy sort you showed me for my riding coat?"

"Yes." The seamstress put down her needlework to offer Abigail her full attention. "I ordered several yards of the wool in black and brown, besides the blue I'm using for your coat. Did you decide you wanted another made?"

"More or less." From the corner of her eye, Abigail saw a dummy clad in a rather beautiful nightrail. She spoke absently as she eyed the simple cut of the gown, the square neckline and gauzy folds of silk that draped from it. "The coat will not be for me, however."

"Oh?"

"It's for . . . a friend." Abigail suddenly realized she never thought she would say that about a man who was not her brother since her accident.

"A lady friend?"

"No."

"Oh." Moira's tone suddenly changed. She produced a writing tablet from under the various scraps of material on her table. "Do you have his measurements?"

Abigail's brows snapped together as she turned back to face the woman. "Well"—she propped her crutch against her leg and held her hands apart—"his shoulders are about this large. His arms from shoulder to wrist are as long as mine from shoulder to fingertips." She thought about it a moment, then said, "I believe he's about three times as big as I."

Moira stared at her.

Abigail blinked. "That doesn't help very much, does it?"

The seamstress scribbled something on her tablet. "It is a gift, hm? I shall do my best, and if it isn't right, you send him here to have it fitted properly."

"Thank you."

"And when do you need it?"

"I know it is a lot to ask but," Abigail tried, "this afternoon?"

Moira's brows lifted, but a moment later she shrugged. "Give me two hours."

Abigail smiled. The other woman was already

moving toward her workroom when she called after her, "Moira?"

"I'll have the nightgown ready also," she called back over her shoulder.

Abigail turned to leave the shop, certain that Timothy would not mind the wait if he could go down to the bookshop and sit with Emily, whom he had a small crush on. She caught sight of Marcella watching her from beneath her brows and had a feeling the woman had heard her less-than-adequate measurements for the gentleman's coat.

"There is something peculiar," Bernice said by way of greeting, "about her relationship with that man."

The two women standing on the other side of the opened door, soft golden light from the beeswax candles inside creating a warm glow behind them, did not appear taken aback with either Bernice's presence in London or her lack of greeting.

"You think so too?" Harriet lifted a brow.

"Come in, Bernice." Augusta moved out of the doorway.

"Definitely." Bernice slipped out of her ermine-lined cloak, handing it over into Augusta's waiting hands. "I saw as much today, when I called on Abigail."

"What happened?" Augusta's voice was muffled from the cloakroom.

"That awful Lord Raleigh and his hired thug made an attempt at frightening Abby again."

"Another message on her wall?" Harriet's stocking feet were silent on the wood floor as she led the way to the parlor. "Did Dobbs refer to her as a birch, perhaps?"

"Message?" Bernice blinked. "No, they shot at her."

"My God," Augusta gasped, pressing a hand to her throat. Her face appeared strange when it was lacking a smile. "Is Abby okay?"

Bernice propped herself on a high-backed chair that was worn in spots. "A little scratch on her ear. They didn't mean to hit her, I think, just frighten." She waved her hand dismissively. "You know Abby. It takes more than thinly veiled threats from rotten excuses for human beings to get her riled."

"Yes." Augusta's smile returned.

"It was not the shooting, in truth, that interested me."

Harriet peered at Augusta from the corner of her eye. "The woman is rescued from thieving villains, has a pistol pointed at her in the middle of a ball, marries an infamous earl, and thinks she's seen it all."

Augusta chuckled from where she sat beside Harriet on the settee. "Go on, Bernice. What was it that interested you about the whole scene?"

The other woman's eyes gleamed like the bronze of an ancient statue behind her spectacles. "At the time the viscount's *accidental* gunfire occurred, Abby's new butler arrived."

"Handsome, isn't he?" Harriet wiggled her eyebrows.

"Yes, and, I believe, not a man I should like to have angry with me." Bernice shook her head. "After what those men did to frighten Abby, I thought he was going to come to blows."

"With the viscount?" Augusta's expression registered some of the same wonder Bernice had felt hours before.

The other woman nodded. "He went after the two of them like he had no concern for Raleigh's station or the fact that together both men were larger than himself."

"I've never seen a servant actually argue with the nobility," Harriet said. "None has ever argued with me."

"You've never had a servant," Augusta pointed out.

"I'm not a member of the nobility either." Harriet shrugged, unconcerned.

"He and Abby argued as well." Bernice ignored the others' byplay, too ensconced in the matter that had taken up a lot of her thoughts since leaving the Wolcott estate. "She was upset at Mr. Garrett for interfering in her affairs and, I think, a little put out that he might believe she needed him to take care of her."

"What did Garrett have to say?" Harriet folded her legs beneath her, fully enthralled with the story.

Bernice glanced between her two friends and said softly, "He told her he would not leave her to harm. He promised to watch over her."

Augusta released all her breath in a quiet rush.

"That's not all," Harriet encouraged, "is it, Bernice?"

The other woman shook her head, remembering the entire scene. Recalling the strange but sudden certainty she had that Calvin Garrett was going to kiss Abigail in the middle of that field. To the women seated across from her, she asked, "Do you remember when that Collins fellow snuck into my home and I had to knock him over the head with my water pitcher?"

"I'd like to think it was a move you learned from me." Harriet grinned.

"Yes, well, when I screamed, I heard Sebastian break my door in. I went running down the stairs and to him as fast as I could. I must have looked a fright, but I remember thinking he looked even worse than I did. Upset."

Augusta said softly, "He was worried something had happened to you."

"Yes." Bernice felt her heart swell at the memory.

"But what does that have to do with Mr. Garrett?"

"The way Sebastian looked at me then was how Garrett looked at Abby."

"Bloody hell," Harriet whispered.

"He kissed her," Augusta said. She nodded when the other two gaped at her. "She told Isabel and me the other day at the shop. He kissed her, and she kissed him back."

"He's handsome," Harriet said again, her tone thoughtful, "but not in the same way that Patrick Valmonte was handsome. Just to hear Garrett speak . . ." She shook her head, struggling for words that were so easy for the two women who read love stories. "He is different."

Augusta shook her head, perhaps remembering sitting beside Abby's bed as the other woman pretended her broken leg didn't pain her. "After their engagement ended," she said sadly, "she stopped reading the books we love so much. It broke my heart."

"Bernice?" Harriet frowned worriedly. "Why are you grinning like that?"

* * *

The soft folds of fabric rested silently atop her head as Abigail froze. Her arms were still lifted above her head to slip on her new nightrail as she listened to the sound of heavy footfalls in the hall. There was a muted creak of the bedchamber door across from hers opening then falling closed again. From wherever Calvin had been all day, he had returned home.

A slight tug brought Abigail's gown over her head and a second made certain it was in its place. A heartbeat later she snatched up her crutch and was moving through her door and to the one across from it. Old habits as well as the urgency of her stride had her hand on the doorknob and it turning before she even bothered a warning.

Abigail immediately, upon entering Calvin's bedchamber, wished she had remembered to knock.

She dropped her gaze to her stocking feet. "Excuse me," she said quickly, breathlessly. "Tuttleton told me I never had to knock, and I suppose I forgot. . . ."

When Calvin remained silent, Abigail lifted her gaze to peer across the room through her lashes. Besides not having spoken a word since she barged inside his room, he hadn't moved a muscle. He still stood by the washstand, only a single taper illuminating him in the room that was dark and untouched by the light from the hall. His boots lay on their sides on the floor beside his feet; his shirt hung open with the sleeves folded back. Her gaze moving to his face—the tense muscle in his jaw, the line of his lips pressed together, and the dark expression in his eyes—Abigail thought he looked tired and angry.

She cleared her throat. "Perhaps I shouldn't have come," she said. "I just wanted to apologize. For earlier today, I mean." She peeked at Calvin again and, seeing him still in place, began to worry. "I'm afraid I was upset and a bit blunt when I spoke to you. I'm sorry if I—"

"Get out."

Abigail blinked. Her chin lifted and her heart stopped when she realized Calvin had finally moved and it was to come right at her. She struggled to come to grips with his escalating anger in the face of her apology. "Have I made it worse?"

"*Yes.*" The hiss of his tone and the tightening of the muscles across his face suggested Abigail and Calvin were not discussing the same thing.

Although he was closing in on her, his steady steps echoing heavily against the walls, Abby could not make herself move. She shook her head. "I don't understand."

"Do I look like your last butler, Lady Abigail?" His warm hands lifted and circled her bare upper arms.

"Tuttleton?" She shivered. "No."

"Have I ever struck you in any way as comparable to the man?"

Abigail looked up from the large hands that could have circled her arms twice. His hold wasn't painful, just tight and rather unnerving in its presence. Her heart pounded against her ribs. "Not really." The words came out shaking.

Calvin's face came close to hers so that she could see the white of his clenched teeth. The heat from his body stirred the air around them and made her throat dry.

"Do not"—he said the words evenly, without moving his jaw—"mistake me for an old man who has forgotten what to do with a woman." His eyes burned like blue flames against her flesh as they lowered between them, running along the exposed line of her neck and the gentle curves of her breasts pressed against the bodice of her nightgown. "Come into my room like this again, Abby, and I'll show you that I do know what to do with a beautiful woman."

Quickly, pointedly, but with a surprising amount of gentleness, he turned her away and gave her a small shove toward the door. She left the room on numb legs with her hands shaking and gasped when the door slammed closed after her. She did not blink, did not breathe, until she had crossed the hall and was safely in her own bedchamber. Once there, she released the pent-up breath she'd been holding and dropped her forehead against the cool wood of the door.

It came out of nowhere.

The urge curled around her spine and squeezed, a tingling sensation spreading out to her fingertips and toes. In the silence of her darkened bedchamber, where no one could see, least of all the man who had just thrown her from his room, Abigail gave into the inclination. She smiled.

Chapter 15

After the scene with Raleigh and his cohort, Calvin had to find an outlet for his rage at the two men who were trying so hard to frighten Abby, the woman who was trying so hard to pretend they didn't affect her at all. Her thinly veiled threat that his post was on tenuous ground had made Calvin want to throttle her. Not because she was so damned stubborn, but because of the ease with which she had given the warning. As if it would not be difficult for her to be rid of him. As if Abby felt nothing compared to the certainty Calvin had that he belonged there.

He had gone walking, ignoring the beat of the sun on his back and his increasing hunger as the day wore on. He found his way back to the pond where he had kissed Abigail and she had appeared to enjoy kissing him back. The spot only made him angrier, so he walked on. He had made it around the entire perimeter of her property and was back at the estate by nightfall. Not before having destroyed three animal traps he found at the edge of her land and two he could see on Raleigh's.

By the time he had eaten the cold beef and cheese Mrs. Poole had left out for him and gone up to his bedchamber to wash, his anger had diffused to a simmer and he had made a deal with himself.

He would not kiss Abigail, despite the fact he had been sorely tempted to do so on many occasions since their first shared embrace, ever again. He would make himself look upon her solely as her brother's sister and a woman whose only relationship to him would be employer and unknowing charge. If he had to stay up all night, he would have no more dreams about her from which he would wake up painfully aroused.

Then she had walked right into his bedchamber without even bothering to knock. The light from the hall illuminated her like a mocking thing, the flickering sconces laughing silently at this sudden taunt at his resolve. Abigail's chestnut hair was in loose upkeep, countless tendrils escaping from her barrettes down her nape and at her temples. Her skin had been flushed and her chest rising and falling quickly as if she had hurried from her room the moment she realized he was in his. The only article of clothing she wore was a simple nightgown with shell sleeves and a lace décolletage above which the uppermost curves of her breasts were exposed. The material cinched tightly beneath the swell of her breasts then dissolved into frothy layers of silk through which Calvin could clearly make out the curve of her hips and the tapered length of her legs.

The fates had sent her—Calvin would tell himself after he ordered her none too kindly from his room—to tempt him. To test the steely resolve he had set within himself. He only had to remember the startled look in her gaze when he wrapped his hands around her painfully soft skin and the moistness of her ragged breaths against his own lips to know with grim certainty he had thoroughly failed his test.

Despite the cold water he had used to bathe and the half-dozen glasses of brandy he gulped down before falling back onto the bed, he was painfully awake as the glow of the moon across the ceiling gave way to dawn's first light.

He had given up on sleep long before, but waited until the sun had begun its ascent to push himself up to a sitting position. His eyes felt grainy, his mouth dry, and his face itched where a night's worth of beard had taken root.

Even though the only sound she made was the light tapping on the door, he knew it was Abigail.

Despite his night without sleep and consequently sour mood, he was tempted to smile when he saw her through the opening door. All he could make out of Abigail was her face. She wore a pale violet bonnet that matched her gloves, and her darker coat was buttoned up to her neck. Another garment of black hung over her free arm.

"Good morning, Calvin," she offered carefully.

"Good morning, Abby." He was surprised she was talking to him after last night. Had been certain as his hours of wakefulness droned on that he would have to make apologies this day. After all, she had come to his room only to express regret for her treatment of him, and he had rudely thrown her out.

"I was just on my way out—"

"Let me put on my boots"—Calvin nodded— "and I'll be down."

"That won't be necessary." Abigail shook her head. "Some of my friends are coming to get me. We're going to the bookshop."

Calvin wondered what made the shop so popular that the woman frequented it more than once a week.

"Tomorrow evening, however, I shall need you to accompany me to London. Thomas is throwing another party for my sister."

"All right," he said, suddenly aware that they were speaking to each other with careful politeness. The way tentative strangers might. He couldn't say he appreciated their almost-too-civil tones.

"I have something for you," Abigail was saying, looking slightly embarrassed as she held up her arm.

He frowned, reaching for the length of dark cloth.

"I hope you do not mind," she added as if suddenly worried he might take the gift as an insult. "It's just that you always seemed uncomfortable in yours."

"A coat?" He held up the garment, noting the silk lining and sturdy wool that constructed it.

"A gift." Abigail lifted gloved fingers to toy with the lapels of her own coat. She looked from the jacket he held to his face then back again. Her brows crinkled, as if she read something adverse in his expression. "If you do not like it, you don't have to wear it, of course. It may be a little large for him, but I'm sure Timothy can use—"

"It's the nicest thing anyone's ever given me, Abby."

Abigail laughed. "You don't have to make me feel better. Of course you've received nicer things from a friend or relative."

"No." He didn't think his father's timely death counted as a present, just an obscure twist of fate. Calvin met Abby's gaze and, with just that contact, prevented her from turning away. "I have never received a gift from anyone. Ever. Thank you."

"Well." Abigail nodded, and he thought he saw a slight twitch at the corner of her mouth. "I had best get downstairs. Bernice will be here soon."

"Abby?"

"Yes?"

Though Calvin did not look up from the coat in his fists, he knew she had stopped in the doorway.

"You need not fear any unwanted attentions on my part." He slowly lifted his gaze to her gloved hands, then to her buttoned coat. "You should not feel you have to blanket yourself from head to toe to prevent my want of you."

She stared at him a long moment before realizing what she was doing. Her laugh was high and nervous. "That's silly, Calvin. I'm not afraid of your"—she swallowed—"attentions. I am dressed like this because, as I already mentioned, I am going out. One never knows when it will start to rain."

Calvin lifted a brow.

"Really." She smiled much too brightly.

He couldn't help it. There was something undeniably captivating about such nervousness from a woman who made a point to be self-assured. The fact Calvin could see her breasts rising rapidly beneath the material of her coat and gown didn't hurt either. As he moved nearer to the doorway in which she stood, he saw her eyes go wide in the shadow of her bonnet.

"I didn't alarm you at all last night?"

Her lashes fluttered; she felt his words as the caress he had intended them to be. "No, sir." She cleared her throat. "I should not have barged in here last night without gaining your permission, and it was most unseemly of me to do so in only my nightgown. Improper, I should think."

"I suppose one could blame it on your interruption and attire"—Calvin cut his nod off short—"except . . ."

"Except?" Abigail blinked up at him, and it was all he could do not to grab her by the shoulders and drag her into his bedchamber.

"Except"—he set his new coat neatly across his shoulder, then lifted a hand to either side of the doorjamb—"you were very discreet in knocking at my door this morning and are dressed very respectably—rather spinsterlike, in fact."

Despite the fact he was a large and looming form above her, she frowned at that. "And?"

His lips curved into a slow smile as his gaze moved to her full and perfect mouth. "And I want to do to you the same things I wanted to do to you last night."

"Oh." The word was barely audible, breathless. It left her lips parted.

Too much, he decided as he stepped toward her, for him to take. She didn't move as he reached out to capture her arms much the same way as he had the night before. The material of her coat was warm and soft, but nowhere near as much so as her skin had been. Abigail's chin lifted as she watched him close in on her, and as his head lowered, the very tip of her tongue peeked out to wet her lips.

Calvin groaned and brought his mouth to hers.

"Abby!" Margot's voice pierced the heavy silence between them. "Lady Abby?"

"Yes." It came out a whisper. Then Abigail blinked and looked toward the stairs. "Yes?" she called louder.

"I see Lady Black's carriage coming up the drive!"

"Be right down." Abigail turned back to Calvin, taking a deep breath. "I should go."

"Yes." He nodded, releasing her and stepping away. He watched as she turned and walked quickly from him and didn't miss, when she was halfway down the carpeted stairs, her look of utter bewilderment as she peeked back.

"This is all too much," Abigail breathed, staring—gaping, really—at the women seated in the carriage about her.

Augusta was on the cushioned seat beside her, Harriet and Bernice in the one directly before them. Each woman was an individual, yet all were friends despite their varied likes and dislikes and different stations in life. At that moment they made a powerful force intent upon one task.

It was not bad enough that they had questioned her thoroughly about her trembling hands when she had boarded the carriage, but they also had to bring up the topic at hand. A topic that horrified Abigail at the amount of thought it took up in the others' minds.

"Forgive us, Abby," Augusta said, "if you think us overly forward in concerning ourselves with your personal life in such a way."

Harriet folded her arms beneath her breasts, closely scrutinizing the face of the woman seated across from her. "You have actually never thought of it yourself?"

Abigail wondered why the other women did not notice the stifling heat in the carriage. She unbuttoned her coat and reached for the ribbons of her bonnet. "I have gone to great pains to keep from thinking about it, Harriet."

"So you admit, you've thought about it because you had to make yourself not." The other woman grinned.

"I saw the way he looks at you, Abby," Bernice said.

"And you did say you shared a kiss," Augusta added.

Abigail's brows drew together as she began to fan herself with her bonnet. She offered each of the women a reprimanding scowl. "Is this what you do to occupy yourselves when I am not about? Fret over my love life?"

Bernice's brows lifted above the rims of her spectacles as she returned, "And you did not discus my relationship with Sebastian before we were married?"

"That was different." Abigail couldn't quite hold the other woman's gaze, well aware Bernice's affair with Black had been all they spoke about until they were certain of the earl's intentions toward her.

"It's true we have moved on to other concerns." Harriet shrugged. "It is somewhat disheartening to one's own lack of a liaison when you are certain your best friend most likely shares intimate embraces with the man she loves every blasted night of the week."

"Sometimes twice." Bernice grinned.

When the others laughed, Abigail could not bring herself to refrain from joining in.

"It is unseemly," Abigail said when she had sobered enough to do so, "to even attempt such a thing."

The others fell quiet as well, save for Augusta. She smiled gently as she spoke. "I have never seen you fret over what others think of you. If anything, I've witnessed you relish in proving everyone wrong in all they imagine that you cannot accomplish, by doing so much with your life."

"Proving that I can care for myself without the aid of a husband or my good brother is one thing. Tempting ruination is another." Toying with the silken ribbons of her bonnet lying across her lap, she said, "He is a man under my employ, and I"— her lips curved in a half smile—"I am the town spinster."

"Opinions of those who believe you a spinster simply because you are an unmarried woman of nine and twenty should mean less than nothing to you." Bernice glowed in her pale yellow-and-pink-patterned dress. "They are exactly the kind of people who often miss out on the most wonderful friends."

"Whoever would find out, anyhow?" Harriet brought up what Abigail had never thought about. "You live in the middle of nowhere and have only a few servants. I have only met the man once, but from what you and Bernice have told us of Calvin, he does not seem to be the sort to share his personal affairs with others."

I hardly know anything about him myself, Abigail acknowledged inwardly.

"After everything that happened with Valmonte," she said aloud, "I never imagined I would even want to share the company of a man again, let alone . . ." She turned her gaze out the opened carriage window.

"We shouldn't have said anything." Bernice's hopeful expression crumpled. "I'm sorry, Abby."

Without even knowing she was going to until the confession parted her lips, Abigail said, "Last night, I ran into Calvin when I was wearing only my nightgown." She took a deep breath. "He told me, very crossly I might add, that I should never do so again because it made him . . . want to do things."

The women's mouths fell open in unison.

"This morning he said much the same thing to me again, even though"—she couldn't bring herself to look at the others anymore—"I was dressed as you see me now."

"What did you do?" Augusta asked.

"On both occasions, I must admit, I ran away." She let her eyes travel back to read her friends' expressions. "After both occasions, however, I felt sinfully pleased with myself."

Not a single look of judgment or disapproval

crossed the others' features. In fact, their lips curved in rather sweet and all-too-knowing smiles.

Bernice leaned forward, resting her hand atop Abigail's braced knee. "Though our attempt was rather lacking in polish, we wanted to let you know that if you did decide you enjoyed Calvin's company and wished to establish a relationship with him, we will not judge you."

"But we will insist you tell us all the details," Harriet clarified.

Chapter 16

Dinner that evening was a terrible affair. The tension around the table was a near-tangible thing; it hovered over the beef brisket Mrs. Poole had made like a thick fog and pressed down on Abigail with invisible weight. She was as certain that she wasn't the only one who felt it as that she was the one who had in all probability caused it. Actually, she decided as she downed most of her wine in one swallow, it was her friends' fault.

If they hadn't put to voice what she had been carefully not thinking about, Margot wouldn't be sharing dinner conversation mostly with herself, Mrs. Poole wouldn't be demanding to know why Abigail was pushing her food around her plate, and Timothy wouldn't be looking up from his own meal and blinking with puzzlement. Amidst all this, things were even worse for Abigail herself. She decided to blame that on Harriet, Bernice, and Augusta as well.

When Calvin had come to join them for dinner,

she had been unable to meet his eye—whether because of their last encounter that morning or the conversation in the Blacks' red and ebony carriage, she was uncertain. She could feel herself as the object of his attention, however, as he sat across from her. The clink of his silverware drew her gaze across the table, and she found herself watching the deft movements of his fingers around his fork and knife. Once, she tracked the journey of a sliver of potato to his lips, watched as his lips parted then closed over the tines of his fork, was mesmerized by the flexing of his jaw muscles as he chewed.

When he abruptly stopped, her eyes flashed upward and met his through the soft glow of the candelabra set between them. His face showed no emotion, his gaze unreadable, as they faced each other.

Abby had excused herself before dessert was served, though Mrs. Poole had made her favorite fruit salad. She pressed her back to the closed door of the parlor once she was safely inside and released the breath she felt like she had been holding since dinner began. Stabilizing the erratic beat of her heart only through her willpower, she moved to the closest place to sit—the pianoforte, near the opened window.

The bench was cushioned, and she fit to it with a sad sort of remembrance. Her fingers ran over the keys, playing a familiar tune at less than half its usual tempo. She closed her eyes and pressed her forehead to the cool wood, remembering. She saw herself in London, not at the home she had shared with her brother and sister after their parents' death but in the expansive parlor of the Valmonte family.

She laughed as her fingers pounded at the keys of the family's piano, and above the sound of both her laughter and the music she could hear Patrick's clapping. On a whim she shot to her feet, knocking the bench over with a bump of her thighs, grinning, as her fast-paced waltz became a country jig. When the song reached its end, she looked up, smiling with wisps of her hair falling from the barrettes her younger sister had carefully placed in it.

Patrick walked toward her, no longer clapping, but smiling. He held out one elegant palm, his beautiful green eyes shimmering. "Dance with me."

"There's no music," she said breathlessly.

"That never stopped us before." His lips curved in a perfect smile.

Abigail's eyes went from being loosely closed to tightly shut as she tried to hold back tears that had not threatened in a long time.

"What is the matter with me?"

"Besides being too stubborn for your own good," Calvin said, "I would say nothing at all."

At the sound of his voice, old feelings scattered, to be replaced by those that were a great deal more difficult to deal with. Abigail's head flew up, and she stared at the man who had appeared silently in the room, closing the door after.

He did not look apologetic for interrupting her solitude, but said, "Margot and Mrs. Poole have turned the topic to female undergarments. Timothy and I made a run for it." Without waiting for a response, he stepped farther into the room, his gaze shifting to Abigail's hands, limp on the piano keys. "Do you enjoy playing?"

"I used to." She drew her hands into her lap. "I'm afraid I'm not very skilled at it any longer."

"What you were playing when I came in sounded

nice." He reached out and pressed down one of the ivory keys. A low note rang out from the chords and shook the instrument.

Abigail noticed his hands were long, his fingers tapered and his palms calloused. When he had touched her bare arms the night before, it hadn't felt like the occasions when Patrick Valmonte had. She couldn't say the fact displeased her.

"I apologize, Lady Abigail"—Calvin's blunt words cut through her thoughts—"for what I said to you this morning and last night. Sometimes, I forget . . . "

Abigail blinked at the last, and then shook her head. "Think nothing of it, Calvin. I hardly remember anything at all," she lied.

"Then why were you so uncomfortable at dinner?"

She almost gave a physical jerk. She peered at him from the corner of her eye and said, "It would have been polite not to mention it." She shifted on the bench, wondering where she had left her crutch.

"I do make an effort, Lady Abby." Calvin knelt and straightened again, holding the length of wood. "But it is difficult for me to feign interest in things that bore me and pretend to be unaffected by that which I find intriguing."

"Mrs. Poole was right." Abigail did not look at him and made certain her fingers didn't touch his as she took her crutch. "You do have a peculiar way of talking."

"I paid someone," he said plainly, "to teach me how to speak correctly."

"Why?" She paused in rising.

"It made me more suitable, I thought, for my new station in life."

Abigail asked, "When you went to work for my brother?"

His gaze shifted, and when he spoke she thought she saw the muscle in his jaw work. "Yes."

"Your coat looks as if it fits well." Abigail eyed the garment briefly before moving across the room and farther away from Calvin. In fact, the jacket Moira had made fit him perfectly. The material clung to his broad shoulders but not to the point of near-bursting. The sleeves reached completely to his wrists, and the sides narrowed at his slim waist. The dark wool did nothing to make the man who wore it appear lighter. His skin was dusky from the sun and drawn taut over sinew.

"It does." She could feel him watch her move and felt as if her leg was dragging even more than usual under his scrutiny. "Abby?"

She had made her way to one of the tall windows in the back wall, where she pretended to look into the night beyond though all she could see was the reflection of herself and the room behind her. Calvin was gazing intently at her back. "Yes?"

"You are certain I did not frighten you?"

There was something touching and ever so slightly amusing in his earnestness. If he only knew how his words and touch had made her feel. . . .

"I am certain, Calvin." She managed a smile as she said, "In truth, it was something my friends spoke to me about today that has me out of sorts."

"And what was that?"

Abigail saw her eyes go round in the pane of glass before her. It was not Calvin's boldness at asking such personal questions—she had found she'd grown accustomed to his audacity some time ago. It was the fact she had set a trap for herself.

"Nothing, really." Her laugh sounded forced to her own ears. "Silly rubbish."

"Something," Calvin countered, "that upset you."

"Oh, I'm not upset. Just a little flustered." She winced at her much-too-bright tone.

"What did they say to you, Abby?" Her heart stopped when she saw him begin to move across the room behind her. "I must admit the idea that anything in this world can fluster you is interesting."

"I'm not all that unapproachable, Calvin." She rolled her eyes.

"No," he chuckled, "but you do try."

Abigail propped her free hand on her hip to scowl at his reflection.

"Did they say something about Raleigh?"

"No."

"Did it concern the bookshop you frequent?"

"No."

"About me?"

Abigail's hand tightened about her crutch. "That's absurd. What could they possibly have to say about you?"

"Lady Black did witness our quarrel yesterday morning." Calvin stopped not far behind her. His hands, she saw, had curled into fists. "Perhaps she told the others and they believe you should rid your home of my presence."

The shout of laughter that escaped her was genuine. "Quite the opposite, sir." She shook her head, seeking to rid herself of the demons haunting her by bringing them out into the open. "If you must know, they actually believe that I should consider having a love affair with you."

If anything, it was worth saying just to see the generally unruffled man stare at her in shock.

Abigail laughed at his expression. Her amusement died quickly, however, and her smile trembled when his eyes took on a distinctly thoughtful cast.

Abigail cleared her throat. "Isn't that preposterous?"

"Is that what you think?"

She frowned, not certain when she had lost hold of the conversation. "Yes."

"Because you are a woman of rank and I am nobody?"

"Because you are under my employ," Abby insisted. "I cannot imagine what people would say about it."

"Ah, you do not like me then?"

A passerby might have found their relaxed exchange about such a personal matter amusing.

"Calvin, if I did not like you, I would not have you in my home."

"You did not enjoy our kiss?"

Abigail gasped, spinning around only to realize he had moved in closer still. She was forced to look up into eyes like blue storm clouds.

"No," he said slowly, shaking his head as his gaze dropped to her parted lips, "I am positive you liked it."

His only touch was that of his lips on hers. He did not hold her arms, did not put his arms around her back and pull her toward him. Calvin was giving her the room she might need to run, but running was the last thing Abigail wanted to do. The warmth of his lips, the pressure of his mouth on hers, was even better than she remembered. She felt as if the kiss held her as her legs quivered and her hands began to shake. Abigail curled the fingers of her free hand into the lapels of Calvin's new coat. He groaned, as if that had been the sign he'd been waiting for, and lifted a hand to cup the back of her head. His mouth slanted across hers and his lips parted. She felt the moist tickle of his breath and then a violent shiver when his teeth closed gently over her bottom lip.

"I must admit"—his lips continued to brush hers as he spoke—"I am inclined to agree with your friends' scheme."

Abigail should have stepped away, made space between them, left the room if need be, but did not. She only shook her head. "It is madness."

"Why, Abby?" The hand that had been cupping the back of her skull slipped down to wrap about her nape. His thumb gently brushed the back of her ear. "We are adults; we can do what we want."

"If anyone found out, I'd be ruined." She let her head fall forward, her forehead resting in the clean hollow of his neck.

"I would not let that happen." Calvin's hand dropped lower; his palm moved down her spine and pressed her to him. She felt parts of her burn as her breasts came into contact with the hard wall of his chest. Through her gown and chemise, his jacket and shirt, she could still feel the heat of him. "I would make it good for you."

The intimate kisses they had shared had been incredible; the idea of something that went beyond those embraces brought back memories for Abigail. Realizing the implication of her words, she said, "Since the end of my engagement, it is one of the few things I do not miss about being in a relationship."

"You and Valmonte?" Calvin's hot breath stirred the hair at the top of her scalp. His intent was apparent.

Abigail took a step back, not meeting his eye as she nodded. She didn't want to explain her reasoning at the time or her belief that Valmonte would be the man she loved for the rest of her life. A week after she had shared herself with him, he had caused the accident that nearly killed her.

"If you do not miss it," Calvin said, "then he did not do it right."

Abigail's chin slowly lifted as he released her. Amazingly, his lips were curled upward as he took a step back.

"If you change your mind, Abby"—he inclined his head, his expression serious—"you can find me in the bedchamber across from yours. Feel free to barge in at any time of night without knocking." He turned away, walking toward the door. "I have been having trouble sleeping, anyway."

"Calvin?" She wasn't sure what it was—his complete lack of concern over the fact that she was a woman of a less-than-unsoiled reputation, the gentleness of his touch on her nape and back, or his words—but something caused an odd sensation inside her. It went well beyond the passion ignited at their kiss. Deep in her breast, her heart stopped pounding heavily and started to tremble, like the fluttering of butterfly wings.

He lifted a single brow, looking back over his shoulder.

"You can be infuriating at times, sir," she told him from where she still stood near the window.

"Arrogant beyond words and almost—no. You *are* obstinate." Abigail took a deep breath, and, when she felt her heart perform that strange quiver again, she smiled. "You most certainly, however, are not a nobody."

Chapter 17

"You made quite an impression"—the voice was familiar—"on my cousin, you know." Katrina Raleigh's silhouette blocked most of the afternoon sun where Calvin had left the rear stable door open. She waited until he put down the bale of hay he'd been carrying and was looking at her. Then she entered. Her hips swayed more than necessary as she stepped toward him. "You were all he could talk about after the incident with Lady Wolcott."

"Good." Calvin made no effort to hide his dislike for the other man. "Then he won't forget to stay away from her."

Katrina was garbed in a blood red riding gown with matching boots, gloves, and bonnet. Looking at her, Calvin couldn't help but recall what Abigail wore when she went riding. He smiled.

Katrina's lips curved in reply to a signal he had not sent. "You seem awfully protective of her, Calvin." Her eyes moved to where his neck was exposed between the opened top buttons of his shirt, then as far down as the waist of his breeches. She looked up at him from beneath her brows. "It's adorable, the way you take care of a woman all alone in the world."

"She's not alone." Calvin reached for the hay bale again, hefting it to Achilles' stall. "And she doesn't need my protection. She does well taking care of herself."

"You must admit"—Katrina followed him—"there are tasks that are insurmountable to a woman with her physical limitations. Things she cannot do that other women can."

Calvin's brows snapped together, but he remained silent. He eyed Achilles while setting the hay within the animal's stall and thought the horse met his gaze with a shared amount of disgust.

What a foul amount of irony it was that the woman he hardly liked was laying herself out on a platter and the one he wanted more with each passing day held him at arm's length.

When he turned, Katrina blocked the opening in the stall. She ran her gloved fingertips below her neck, where a great deal of skin was exposed in her low-cut bodice.

"It's stifling in here."

"Then you should go."

Katrina's lips pursed in a pout for only a moment. "Did I upset you with what I said about Abigail? I didn't mean to. It's just"—the woman's smile had returned as her chin lowered—"there are paths a woman can choose to take, very exciting journeys, when she is physically capable."

Calvin did not disguise his actions as he started at the toes of Katrina's boots and let his gaze travel the length of her. By the time he reached her torso, her breasts were heaving. He stepped closer to her, and she lifted her face.

"Some paths have been used more than others," he said. "Now, if you'll excuse me, I have to get a lot of work done before I take my lady to London this evening." He brushed against her as he passed through the stall, but there was nothing lingering in the encounter. Calvin ignored the sound of her boots stomping away as he moved in the opposite direction.

He didn't realize the other woman was standing there, in the shadows of the corner near the building's entrance, until he was almost on top of her.

"Abby?" He came up short.

"Funny," she said. "Lady Raleigh never came to visit Tuttleton." She held out a covered plate. "I thought you might want to eat before we go. I had Mrs. Poole put together an early dinner."

Calvin took the plate, not knowing why he should feel so guilty. Abigail's eyes flickered in the gloom before she turned away and pressed all her weight into the half-opened stable door. "Abby, I wasn't—"

"I have to get ready, Calvin." She did not look back as she walked away from him. "Perhaps we can talk later."

He did not try to speak to her again, just stood there with the warm plate she had brought to him. An action, he was certain, most ladies did not perform for their servants.

He watched Abigail as she moved quickly back to the house, the wind sending waves through her skirts and exposing the slightly uneven sway of her hips. Calvin's jaw tightened to the point he thought his teeth would crack when he saw Abby's head lower and the woman lift a hand to the lower half of her face.

"Don't be petulant, Katrina." Edmund Raleigh took his cousin's chin in his hand and turned her away from the mirror. "Tell me what happened."

"Nothing, Edmund." Katrina rolled her eyes. "We spoke for barely five minutes. Then he was off to do her bidding."

"You found out nothing about him?" Raleigh let his hand drop.

"No more than what I already knew." Katrina turned back to her full-length mirror. Except . . ." She paused in laying her dark hair over her shoulders.

Raleigh lifted his brows at her reflection, waiting. They made a perfect pair in the oval of reflecting glass: elegantly dressed, handsome, and wealthy. Nothing at all like Lady Abigail in her unfashionably cut gowns and the butler who bore the self-importance of a man who served no one.

"I think there is something unusual going on between Garrett and Lady Wolcott, or at least he would like there to be." Katrina made a face. "There is something about his tone when he talks about her. It makes one ill."

Edmund's lips curled into a smile, his plump cheeks rounding. "So that is what has gotten you out of sorts."

Katrina snorted, her delicate nostrils flaring unbecomingly. "I've seen men fawn over women before."

"Yes," her cousin acknowledged, "but usually they do so over you and not an aging spinster with a misshapen leg. You made an offer no man can refuse, and Garrett did." Edmund's eyes gleamed. "That must have been quite a blow to your ego."

"Don't be an idiot. What do I care of what a servant thinks of me?"

"Especially when you know you are beautiful," Edmund said deep in his throat, his hand lifting again to run along the curve of her breast. He watched her face in the mirror as Katrina's eyes slid closed. "That was as far as your conversation went?"

"He left," she said absently, concentrating on the feel of Edmund's hand as it covered her breast and squeezed. How dare Garrett turn down her veiled offer? She was exquisite. "Said he had a lot to do before he took his *lady*"—her lips curled around the word like an insult—"to London."

Edmund kissed the pale and cool skin of her neck, her jaw, then flicked his tongue across her ear. Into it he spoke. "They are going to London, you say?"

It was unnerving—if the word was accurate— having him wait for her at the end of the stairs. Abigail began down the carpeted steps quickly, not realizing he was there until his gaze lifted and hers dropped. In the light of the downstairs tapers and the sconces mounted on the wall behind her, she saw Calvin focus on her kidskin slippers and move his survey upward over her raspberry-colored gown. Her steady gait only faltered a little under his close scrutiny before she lifted a gloved hand to the rail and continued down the stairs.

Her cheeks felt warm where the spiral curls

Margot had carefully shaped brushed against her skin. Abigail couldn't walk away from the last step, as Calvin didn't budge where he stood before her. She stared at his neck for a full minute, waiting, then finally let her gaze lift though her chin did not.

It was what he had been waiting for.

"You are beautiful, Abby."

In the silence that followed his guttural words, Abigail could hear her own breathing shudder in her chest. It had been so long since she had received such niceties from a man, she forgot how to respond. She considered answering in kind, as she was certain Calvin—clean shaven, the hair brushed back from his forehead still damp and smelling of soap—looked better than any man she would see at the soiree later that night.

"I had Margot get your cloak," Calvin said before she could manage a reply. He turned to lead the way toward the foyer. "It looks like rain."

"Oh?" Suddenly the fissures of sensation that had been trickling down her spine became cold nips of an invisible needle. She opened the front door, blinking nervously as she glanced between the clouds moving across the night sky and the carriage waiting in the drive.

Abigail jumped when Calvin set her black cloak across her shoulders. Her worry must have been evident in her expression as she glanced back at him, because he did not remove his hands, but gave her shoulders a gentle squeeze through the soft velvet.

"Would you rather not go out?"

The controlled gentleness of his tone irritated her for reasons she knew were irrational.

"I'll be fine." She ignored the forceful winds that tugged at the ends of her cloak and made the material billow in waves around her as she walked to the carriage. Abigail only got the cab door opened before Calvin slipped an arm beneath her legs.

She peered up at him as, in lieu of putting her arms around his neck, she folded them beneath her breasts. "There really is a better way of doing this."

He did not look at her as he moved up the carriage steps. "I prefer holding you." His tone hinted at an intimacy beyond helping her to her seat.

Abigail's hands gripped the edge of the cushioned bench as soon as Calvin set her atop it. She was silent as he carefully laid her crutch on the floor at her feet. He looked up at her as he straightened, and she was grateful for the shadows that shielded her from his intent stare before he dropped out of the cab and shut the door after.

She fell back against the cushions and released a heavy sigh as she listened to the sound of him taking his place behind the reins. She did not, however, hear him signal the horses into motion or the first thuds of hooves in the loose soil of the drive—the rumble of thunder above was much too loud.

Her hands shook, less than fifteen minutes later, as she tried to light one of the lamps swaying from a hook in the wall. On her third try—as Abigail struggled to ignore the foreboding sounds that suggested they were riding directly into the storm—the wick within the lantern began to glow. She sighed, fell back into her seat, and then scowled when the light quickly died. Her heart stopped when a brilliant flash of lightning succeeded where the lantern had failed and brought the inside of the carriage to light. Her concern grew, but not for herself.

Abigail lifted her open palm to bang on the wall that separated the cab from the driver's perch. Before she had a chance to ask Calvin if he wanted to turn back, she heard the sharp crack: not thunder but splintering wood.

Her heart leapt up to her throat as she heard the horses cry out in alarm then felt the carriage lurch. Abigail slammed into the wall, her teeth snapping together sharply as her skull made contact with the wood. She bounced up off her seat in a whisper of skirts, looking down at the hard floor below with sickened awareness.

"No . . ." It came as a whimper as she reached out for anything that might stabilize her. She caught the lantern, but it snapped off its hook a heartbeat later, and, despite trying to catch herself on her good leg, Abigail went down on her knees. As her right leg twisted beneath her, her brace allowing no give, deep-rooted pain returned to each nerve that ran through her leg. Blackness curled at the edge of her vision, and in it followed the cold tones of countless physicians, the pitying whispers of strangers, and her own agonized scream.

Chapter 18

Calvin threw himself from behind the reins before the carriage came to a complete stop, his heart slamming against his ribs as his feet hit the packed earth and he ran back to the cab door. He opened the door on a flash of lightning, and a violent wind caught the thin wood and slammed it back against the wall of the carriage.

Abigail was a pool of raspberry silk and black velvet on the cab floor. Her arms, gloved to above the elbow, stretched out across one of the seats. Her fingers dug into the cushions with enough force to nearly tear the fabric. Her face was hidden behind disheveled curls, her forehead pressed to the edge of the seat.

"Abby?" He took the stairs in one great step.

"Are you all right, Calvin?"

Her voice, uncharacteristically weak and trembling, cut into his heart.

"I'm fine. Lady Abby—"

"Good." She shifted only slightly and he saw her back jerk with pain. "Please, leave me alone."

Calvin had to bend, hunching his shoulders and bowing his head as he moved nearer to her. Through the thunder rumbling overhead, he thought he could hear the ragged sound of her breathing.

"Leave me be!"

Her enraged voice almost stopped him. Almost. "Like hell I will." He reached for her.

"*Don't*," Abigail hissed, her muscles so taut they quivered as he wrapped his fingers around her arms.

He knew she was hurt—it was evident in her huddled frame and voice. Yet he could no more leave her to suffer on the floor of the carriage than he could go back in time and fill in the rut that had put her there. Finding his way through the material of her cloak, he put an arm just beneath her breasts and squatted with his knees on either side of her.

"Hold on, Abby." His lips touched her ear as he spoke the words.

Her hands lifted to the arm wrapped around her, but only to try to pull it away.

Calvin ignored her silent attempts to dissuade him and straightened his legs, lifting her with him. He did not carry Abigail out of the carriage, but eased himself backward into the seat opposite the one she had been holding to for dear life. She came easily into his lap, the base of her leg brace thudding distinctly against the floor. He heard her take a sharp breath, felt her hands squeeze painfully into his arm. Then her body shuddered and she was turning, giving him a brief glimpse of her face.

Gone were the rosy cheeks of less than an hour

before and the beautiful glimmer of her eyes when she was coming down the stairs to him. The flesh beneath her cheeks was sunken in as if the pain had physically drawn her. Abigail's skin was pale, her bottom lip bright red where she had clasped it between her teeth, and her eyes shone with tears. Calvin saw all this in the heartbeat before she buried herself against him.

For the first time since he had met her, he was stunned into immobility by Abigail's behavior. Calvin sat stiff for perhaps a full minute, feeling nothing but her uneven breaths against his neck and the softness of her curls tickling his jaw. Her fingers had come up to his shoulders and twisted the wool of his coat in a fierce grip. It felt not unlike the hold she had on his heart as she fit so perfectly to him.

The stiffness swam out of him quickly. His head lowered until his lips were against the part in her hair, and his arms came up to wrap tightly around her back.

"It's all right, Abby," he said soothingly above her ragged breaths. "I have you."

"I apologize, Calvin," she said through her tears. "I shouldn't—"

"Don't." His jaw muscles worked fiercely.

"It hurts," she breathed.

"I know." Calvin lowered one hand to her injured leg, pressed it lightly to her thigh through the material of her skirt. He instantly wished he hadn't. The touch surprised her, made her leg jerk abruptly, and she released a pain-filled whimper.

"Sorry." Calvin immediately returned his hand to her back. "Sorry."

"I was frightened." She trembled. "More than I should have been, perhaps."

"Because of your accident?"

The top of her head bumped his chin as she nodded. Her erratic breathing had begun to steady itself, and she was no longer as stiff in his arms. Her forehead dropped to his shoulder, and though it was impossible, Calvin could have sworn he felt the heat of her tears through his coat and shirt.

"Would you like to talk about it?"

It took her nearly a full minute to decide. "No." She shifted against him again until her cheek lay against his chest. He could feel her gaze lift to his face. "What happened?"

"A hole in the road, almost as deep as the carriage is wide. I didn't see it in time. One of the wheels broke, I think."

"You are sure you're unhurt?"

He looked into her upturned face, cheeks wet with tears and brow furrowed in concern for him. Calvin used his fingertips to brush away the last of the dampness. Abigail's skin turned a becoming shade of pink.

"How are you?"

She sniffed delicately. "Embarrassed."

"Don't be. Your leg?"

"Sore." She scowled down at her bent leg as if to scold it. "I landed on my knee, where I had my break." Her gaze slowly moved upward, and she gave a start as if only now realizing she was atop Calvin's lap.

He didn't hold her back as she shifted off of him, though he was sorely tempted to do so. Since her silent tears had evaporated, the warmth of her bottom pressing so snugly against him had become appealing.

She braced herself with a fierce grip on the door-jamb and rested all of her weight on her good leg.

"May I ask you something personal, Abby?" He retrieved her crutch from where it had been lodged between the seat and the wall at the jostling of the carriage.

Abigail had been peering wearily up at the clouds swarming above them through the opened door of the carriage. "Yes?" She glanced back over her shoulder at him, her chestnut curls bouncing in the wind.

"Where was your fiancé when you were in the accident?"

He found himself staring at the elegant line of her nape when she turned away. "I did not notice where he landed."

Calvin's brows lifted at that, and his head bent as he moved closer behind her. "He was in the phaeton with you?"

There was a sharp crack of thunder before Abby said softly, "He was driving."

Calvin's strong dislike for the man Abby was going to marry three years before had commenced shortly after he'd met her. The pure, unadulterated jealousy had intensified his disliking for Patrick Valmonte when he found he had been the first to touch Abigail—to feel her wrapped tightly around him.

Hearing that the man had been driving the phaeton and might very well have caused the accident that injured her, he thought that perhaps along with his father . . . No. There had never been another man he did not know whom he hated as much as Patrick Valmonte.

* * *

"Yes," Abigail said, staring at the splintered remains and jagged chunks of wood littering the
ground, "I'd say it is broken." She tried to keep her
tone light, not looking at the man standing so
close beside her as she struggled to overcome her
embarrassment.

The pain had been awful, but she was certain
she could have maintained a modicum of dignity
had Calvin not put his arms around her. The
agony of her abused leg had been all too reminis-
cent of the pain of the accident. The fact someone
had come to her immediately and took her into a
comforting embrace had shattered something inside her. Something that had been born as she lay
alone in the icy waters of a river with a carriage
crushing her leg.

Her knee throbbed steadily as she glanced both
ways of the narrow road they had been traveling.
The wind whistled through the trees that bordered
the pathway, as steady as the ominous clouds that
had collected overhead.

"You should get back in the carriage," Calvin
said, still gazing at the hole in the earth as if he
knew something she did not. "It's beginning to
rain."

Abigail made a face. "Should we try to make it
back to North Rutherford?"

"It's about ten miles back." Calvin put his hands
on his lean hips, the wind tossing his dark-as-
midnight hair and the edges of his coat. His eyes
squinted a little as he surveyed Abigail from head
to toe, thoughtfully. "I could carry you that far."

"Absolutely not!" she gasped. "I can walk with
you."

Calvin scowled. A drop of rain caught in his thick lashes, and for a moment Abby was transfixed by the shimmering dot against his dark eyes. "You cannot walk that far, not after your knee was bruised. I will not tolerate it."

Abigail ignored the possession in his tone. The raindrop now clung to the end of a single lash. She was absently aware of similar beads of water sinking through her hair to her scalp and alighting on the skin of her nape. "I could wait in the carriage for you to return," she offered, not particularly caring for the idea herself.

"No," Calvin said quickly, leaving no room for argument. He blinked, and Abigail watched that little droplet of rain tremble then plummet toward the ground.

For some absurd reason, she thought it must have been nice to be that raindrop. She then frowned when Calvin folded his arms across the expansive breadth of his chest and approached her. He did not stop before her, however, but moved around Abigail, looking her up and down.

"What are you about, sir?"

"I could throw you over my shoulder. . . ."

Abigail gasped. "I would be unconscious within the first mile. All the blood would go to my head."

"You could climb on my back."

"What an interesting picture that makes." She glowered at him over her shoulder. She wasn't positive, but thought his survey paused overlong on the swell of her bottom. Abigail turned to face him. "Honestly, Calvin. I can walk."

He watched her lashes flutter as the rain increased, dampening her hair in earnest. Calvin reached for the hood of her cloak and drew it over her head. Then, without warning, he lifted her in his arms as he did when putting her into the carriage.

"Calvin!" She dropped her crutch and grabbed his shoulders.

"Yes, Lady Abigail?" He lifted a brow and turned in the direction of the village they had left behind. Calvin knelt briefly, and Abigail's stomach plummeted at the drop as he recovered her crutch.

"What about the horses?" She was grasping at straws and she knew it. It wasn't that she was uncomfortable in Calvin's arms—and that fact surprised her. It was that she was certain her weight was too much for him to bear for ten miles, not to mention the rain.

"No saddles."

"I can ride bareback," she insisted, looking over his shoulder and watching the carriage begin to shrink in size.

"For ten miles? I think not." Calvin shifted his arms, and she fell into his chest. She was very conscious of his arm's proximity to her bottom when he said, "Your backside would take a beating and be sore for days."

Abigail's brows wrinkled. She had been forced to put an arm around Calvin's neck; her free hand clutched a lapel of his coat. "It's a risk I'm willing to take."

"I"—there was something rather unsavory about his grin as he continued to gaze straight ahead— "find the thought less than agreeable."

"You are the most stubborn man I have ever met!" Abigail had to shout above a groan of thunder.

Velvet blue eyes locked with bay a moment before Calvin's damp lashes lowered in a wink. "I learned from the best." He chuckled at her baffled expression. "Do not fret, Abby," he said gently and pressed his lips to the space between her brows. "You were bound to meet your equal in obstinacy sooner or later."

It took great effort for her to refrain from lifting her fingertips to the place Calvin had so lightly kissed. She wanted to be certain it was not her imagination that made the spot so warm. She couldn't find the words to speak, and, as Calvin faced forward again, she noted the increasing dampness of the skin drawn taut over his sharp facial bones.

She released the lapel of his jacket and lifted her gloved hand to his cheeks and forehead, carefully brushing away the rainwater. His skin was warm through the material of her glove, and his muscles tightened as she touched them. Before his gaze could meet hers, she dropped her hand into her lap and looked straight ahead.

Chapter 19

"Leonard." Prudence Redman clutched at her husband's arm, her tone awestruck. "Do you think that carriage belonged to these folks?"

The old man's brows came together, two fat gray caterpillars kissing. His eyes weren't as good as they used to be, and he could barely make out the blur to the right of the road not far ahead. "I can't imagine why anyone else would be walking in the rain, Prue."

"She's not walking," Prudence clarified, where her husband's poor eyesight had left him oblivious. "He's carrying her. Heaven's, Leonard," she breathed, "he must have carried her four miles so far. What vigor!"

He elbowed his wife in her plump side. "I remember when you used to say the same about me."

"Hush," she hissed, but her wrinkled cheeks turned pink. Her bright blue eyes remained focused on the pair in the street. The man had stopped and turned himself and his charge to face them. He was tall and well muscled, with dark hair that lay damp against his skull. The woman he carried wore a lovely gown and cloak, most of her face hidden in the hood of the latter. It was peculiar, but Prudence could have sworn there was a distinctly horrified gleam to her eyes. "Stop the horses, Leonard."

The phaeton, Abigail told herself, was nothing like the one Lord and Lady Valmonte had given their son for his twenty-fourth birthday. It was not as fancy; its sides were caked with mud, and the horses that pulled it looked older than Abby. The man behind the reins guided the vehicle carefully near, and there was no devil-may-care gleam to his dark eyes. No drunken grin curling his lips.

"Hello, there!" The round woman seated beside him, a blanket thrown over her head, waved at the two in the road as if she had been waiting forever to see them.

"Good evening," Calvin called back. He began to lower Abigail to her feet, keeping an arm around her waist once she was grounded.

"That be your nice carriage with the broken wheel?" The old man spoke, exposing several spots where teeth should have been. It added, Abigail decided, a rather engaging quality to his smile.

She smiled back. "I'm afraid so. We hit a rather nasty hole in the road."

"That'll do it." He nodded.

"I said to Leonard you must be the folks from that carriage when we first caught sight of you walking." The woman dropped her blanket and, with a grunt, lowered herself from the phaeton. "I am an excellent judge of people."

"Are you?" Calvin was forced to look down at her as the top of her head of frothy white hair barely reached the middle of his chest.

"Absolutely." The woman glanced between Abigail and Calvin and pursed her lips for a moment. "For instance, I know that you both are in love."

Abigail felt her heart plummet to her stomach; she was very aware of Calvin's fingers flexing against her hip.

"I imagine you two must have been married for six years," the woman went on, completely unaware of the silence of the two with whom she was speaking. "Just like my Leonard and I when we were your age, I suspect."

Abigail blinked and had to clear her throat twice to speak. "Actually—"

"We haven't been married that long." Calvin made to hold out the hand not tightly gripping Abigail's side and produced her crutch.

"Oh!" The old woman stared at it, puzzled.

"Excuse me." Calvin gave the crutch to Abigail, meeting her gaze and—she thought—pointedly ignoring her stunned expression. He took the old woman's hand and bowed over it. "I'm Calvin Garrett," he said, "and this is my Abby."

She made herself ignore the way her heart fluttered its way back to its rightful place and forced herself to again smile at the woman.

"I'm Prudence Redman." She nodded toward the man still seated at the reins of the phaeton. "That's my husband, Leonard."

Leonard lifted his floppy hat to expose a bald and shiny scalp. "A pleasure."

"We have a farm just up around the bend."

"We're trying to make it back to North Rutherford," Calvin explained, "before the weather gets worse."

"I'd say you're out of luck, son." Leonard scowled up at the sky above, as if he could read the clouds. "It's only going to get worse. The on-and-off rain is bad enough, but there's a storm brewing. I'm certain of it."

"My Leonard knows the weather like I know people." Prudence beamed.

"Now, don't you go bragging, Prue. Just help that nice boy and his lady in here. We'll take them back to the farm for the night and then into the village in the morning."

Abigail almost laughed at the old man's decision to call Calvin *boy*. "We wouldn't want to burden you like that, Mr. Redman," she said. "I should hate to put you out when you aren't expecting guests."

"No bother."

"We have four children." Prudence was bragging again. "All with their own homes now, but there's still plenty of room at ours. Come along. Let's get you both warm and dry." She turned to lead the way, her great hips swaying side to side under her skirt.

Abigail felt Calvin's fingers lock around her elbow.

"Why did you let her believe we were married?" She barely moved her lips as she whispered. They were far enough behind the woman that she wouldn't notice.

"I couldn't," Calvin whispered back. "Not after what she said about knowing people." She felt him look down at the top of her head. "Will you be all right?"

"I think not," Abigail snapped. "I loathe lying."

Calvin's grip on her elbow tightened. "I mean in the phaeton."

Abigail frowned. She had almost forgotten about the phaeton upon suddenly finding out she was a married woman. For three years, she hated looking at the blasted vehicles. The one time she had tried to board her brother's, she had gotten physically ill, and he had felt obliged to sell the phaeton. She told herself it was the kindness that hovered around the couple that owned this vehicle like an aura that had stifled her fear. Not—she almost groaned when she bumped against him—Calvin's presence beside her.

"I think I will manage."

"Everything will be fine, Abby." Calvin's voice dropped even further as they neared the Redmans. "Just play along."

She turned to face him, ignoring the tremor that went through her when his broad hands wrapped about her waist to lift her into the phaeton. Abigail rested a palm on his shoulder, ignoring his much-too-engaging smile to scowl at Calvin. "I cannot imagine," she mouthed, "it can get any worse."

"I was wrong."

"I beg your pardon?"

Abigail winced as Calvin kicked the door closed behind them. Her eyes opened back to the bedchamber that had once belonged to the Redmans' only daughter. There was a dressing screen, washstand, a bed Abby barely glanced at, and a dressing mirror on the opposite side of the room from the door. Gazing at the reflection they made in the glass, she in Calvin's arms with her own wrapped loosely about his neck, Abigail was reminded of wedding-day traditions and not the necessity of having to be carried, as her throbbing leg would not allow her to climb the stairs. To anyone who didn't know better, Calvin might appear a groom carrying his bride over the threshold to the bed in which they would consummate their marriage.

"Put me down, please."

She saw Calvin's brow lift in the mirror before he was setting her gently on her feet.

"What is wrong?"

Abigail wondered if he was deliberately being obtuse and was almost certain of the fact as he moved past her to sit on the edge of the bed.

"Your falsehood is what is wrong." Her crutch thumped against the wooden floorboards as she moved around the bed and to the washbasin Leonard had filled for them. "You have gotten us into quite a mess, Calvin. Now we have to share this room for the night or look like charlatans to two of the kindest people that have probably ever walked the earth."

"I like the room."

Abigail paused in splashing water against her heated face to gape at Calvin's reflection in the mirror above the ceramic basin.

"The bed is small." He fell back onto the quilt Prudence Redman had stitched when her daughter was a babe. Calvin slid the palm of one hand under his cheek and smiled a wholly wicked grin. "But if we both lie on our sides—me snuggling up behind you, of course—I think we'll fit nicely."

Abigail's mouth dropped open, fat drops of

lukewarm water dripping off her chin and back into the basin.

"You could curl up behind me, if you'd prefer." He appeared to consider it before nodding. "Yes, I think I would like to feel you pressed up against my back. You'd have to remove that damned thing bracketing your leg, though. I'd hate to imagine what would happen if you accidentally kicked me in your sleep."

Abigail applied her full weight to where her brace wrapped around her slipper and spun to face Calvin. She fisted her hands on her hips and glared at him. "I'm glad you find this so blasted funny."

His expression went serious as Calvin sighed, then rolled up and out of the bed. He reached for one of the towels beside the washstand, and Abigail found herself unable to move when he began to dry her damp cheeks and forehead. "I know you are uncomfortable with tonight's sleeping arrangements, Abby," he said. His gaze was focused not on her eyes, but her mouth. "It might shock you to know that I am uncomfortable also, but for reasons you cannot imagine. I joke to get my mind off of it."

"What reasons?" She frowned up at him, slightly irritated by his tone.

"Gentlemanly obligations"—his eyes finally lifted to meet hers, and the tapers spaced about the room flickered his gaze like fire—"and an overwhelming desire to disregard them." Calvin turned away, pressing the now-damp cloth to the back of his neck.

Abigail watched him move around the room to a chair near the door. "I hate to tell you this, sir," she said, letting the corners of her mouth curl a little, "but as a humorist, you leave a lot to be desired."

"Opinion noted." Calvin shrugged out of his still-damp coat and threw it across the chair. He sat down to remove his boots.

Abigail quickly moved her gaze to the room's only window, watching rain pound against the glass. The water shone like diamonds every time lightning flashed. "Leonard was right," she said absently.

Calvin chuckled. "Apparently his knowledge of weather surpasses his wife's knowledge of people."

"I wonder why Prudence thought that we were married." Abigail's eyes went wide when she realized she had spoken the thought aloud.

"Because I was carrying you, perhaps," Calvin said quickly, as if he had been giving the matter some thought during the cabbage dinner the old woman had prepared. "I doubt many ladies allow their servants such liberties."

Abigail frowned, not caring for the separation his tone implied. Before she could speak, she was surprised by his touch on her bare arm—her gloves had seemed a little much as she assisted the farming couple in setting their battered dinner table. She was even more surprised when her head turned to the naked wall of Calvin's chest.

"You can have my shirt," he said, holding out the garment, "to sleep in."

"I can stay in my gown." She dropped her gaze quickly to her feet; she couldn't, however, manage to draw it away in its journey down. She did not miss the dark, curling hair that tapered into a thin line before disappearing into his breeches.

"It's wet," Calvin said to the top of her head. "Soaked through to your shift, I imagine."

The undergarment did, in fact, cling wetly to her legs.

"Take it, Abby. I won't have you fall ill."

She ignored the shaking of her fingers as she reached for Calvin's shirt. Fortunately, so did he. Abigail found shelter behind the dressing screen, and as she was tossing her gown over the top—spreading the material out to dry—the room got dimmer. Calvin was putting out the tapers.

"Do you mind if I take the blanket from the end of the bed? I'll need something to put on the floor."

She shielded her naked breasts with her arms for a moment before the idiocy of the move hit her. Calvin's voice was from across the room.

"Certainly." Abigail reached quickly for his shirt and almost sighed at the warmth that remained a part of the garment like Calvin's ghost. It smelled faintly of rain and sweat and an odor she identified only as Calvin himself. She frowned, looking up from the buttons.

"I should take the floor," she said.

"No."

"But you walked a long way carrying me, and that cannot be good for your back. The hard floor will make it worse."

"I said no, Abby."

She held most of her weight on her good leg as she stared for a moment at the blank wall of the dressing screen. Her thoughts went back to what he had said only minutes before.

"I think," she said, loud enough for her roommate to hear, "you may be right about why Prudence thought what she did."

"Yes?" She had an idea Calvin was watching the dressing screen.

"Perhaps"—Abigail laced her cool fingers together—"she sensed that I did not think of you as my servant, Calvin. I like to think you are my friend."

There was something unexplainable in his tone as he said, "Come to bed, Abby."

She almost did exactly as he ordered until her leg brace made contact with the floorboards. The shirt she wore came to her knees, and she was struck by how large the man who wore it was, most especially since the garment was too small for him. Abigail's thoughts drifted in that direction for a moment only before she—for the first time in a long time—was struck by the crudity of her right leg. Besides where her skin was red from her brace and her knee was swollen from the fall she had taken earlier, a vicious scar ran across her shin, nearly an inch wide and four times as long.

"Is your back turned, sir?" She tried futilely to tug the shirt down further.

His chuckle was dry. "Not to shock your ladylike sensibilities, but I have seen women in less than what you are now wearing. I imagine the nightgown you wore two nights past showed more flesh."

She struggled to find the words to explain it was not the fact of being seen in his shirt that bothered her, but the idea that he would see the ravages of the accident on her leg. A purely feminine, if not downright vain, part of her recalled him saying she was beautiful as she came down the stairs of her home hours before. She had an idea that if she saw Calvin look at her with the disgust that was quite unavoidable given the circumstances, something inside her would fall apart.

"I'm already lying down, Abby. You are safe."

* * *

After moments of waiting, imagining she was peeking out from behind the dressing screen, he heard her pad quietly to the bed. There was a squeak of long-unused springs as she sat, then the sound of brass hitting wood. Lying with his neatly folded coat as his head's only protection against the floor, Calvin realized she was removing her leg brace.

He rolled to his other side and saw, from under the bed, the assembly of wood and metal brackets and leather bindings with their brass buckles being set on the floor. As he watched, Abigail's delicate ankles, so small he might have fit a single hand around both, disappeared upward.

Calvin's lower body tightened at that infinitesimal glimpse of bare skin, and he was suddenly glad he had not seen Abby in only his shirt.

He was on the brink. He had known it since she had stood before him with her damp ball gown clinging to the curves of her breasts and the swell of her hips . . . perhaps even before. He had been teetering on the verge of a fall ever since she had informed him of her friends' idea of an affair between them both. It would take little to send him over the edge.

Thomas Wolcott and the conspiracy for her protection be damned.

As faint as the fluttering wings of a baby bird, Abigail whimpered.

He frowned, his ears hurting with concentration.

The bedsprings squeaked once and then again. Abigail sighed. It was the resolute sound of someone aware of a long night of pain ahead of them.

Calvin eased onto his bare back, stared at the ceiling as he asked, "Would you like me to rub it?"

"I beg your pardon?"

He almost laughed at the shock in her voice. "Your leg."

"Oh." He thought he detected a hint of disappointment in her tone. It made him wonder what she thought he meant. "No, thank you."

"I might be good at it."

"Shall I ask Katrina Raleigh to be certain?"

Her words chilled him to the bone. "Abigail, it wasn't what you thought."

"No?" A strange noise came from the bed, a stifled sound.

"Believe it or not, she was attempting to seduce me." For some unknown reason, he wanted it clear to her that the woman meant nothing to him.

There was that peculiar sound again, and Calvin wasn't certain, but it sounded like Abigail snorted.

Calvin sat up, sincerely praying that she had covered herself up beneath the bed quilt. "I had to ward off her advances."

"How dreadful for you, Calvin." She was beneath the blankets. Abigail had a hand over her mouth, and a tear trickled from her eye as she slowly turned her head in his direction. "It must have been quite frightening being accosted by a woman less than half your size. However did you make it through unscathed?"

Through Abigail's tears, Calvin saw, her eyes were alight with humor. His eyelashes drew together warningly. "Are you laughing at me?"

Abigail couldn't hold back her giggles any longer. She let her hand drop to her side to expose her curved lips. She laughed aloud. "Not at you, Calvin.

I'm just remembering Lady Katrina's face. She appeared very perturbed that you did not take her up on her not-so-veiled offer."

"I'm glad you found a traumatic episode in my life so amusing." He tried to keep his tone stern, but his grin betrayed him.

Abigail roared at that.

He couldn't help it; her amusement was infectious. Her neck arched as she buried her head into the pillows. Calvin began to laugh with her.

"You saw the whole thing?"

Abigail nodded, unable to speak.

He realized when she had left the stables so quickly, it was because she was as struck by the hilarity of the situation.

"Forgive me, Calvin." Abigail shook her head against the pillows, trying to calm herself with a deep breath. "I don't mean to tease you."

"I think you do," he countered.

She looked at him, lips still curved. "Perhaps." Abigail's gaze became thoughtful, barely visible in the light of the single taper he'd left burning. Her laughter faded. "Why?"

He lifted a brow in question.

Abigail propped herself on one elbow. "I didn't think men disregarded the attentions of women like Katrina Raleigh. She's beautiful."

Calvin thought about telling Abigail that the woman was nothing in comparison to her. Even now, with her hair disheveled and his steward's overly large shirt engulfing her frame, she was a sight to behold.

"I have dealt with women like her before, Abby," he said instead, deciding that in giving up every little bit of honesty he could, he might be saving himself. "To put it politely, they seek the excitement they think cannot be found with men of their rank. They thrive on being with someone with an interesting past. Dirty hands, so to speak."

"How many women have approached you in such a way, Calvin?" Her fine brows came together.

"That is unimportant," he dismissed quickly. "I only fell for the ploy once and learned my lesson well."

It had been shortly after he moved into the estate that had belonged to his father, when associates of the man he had never met before heard about the events of Calvin's life. The daughter of the marquis' best friend had offered her friendship to Calvin, introducing him to all the best parties and London's elite, then proved herself unable to keep her hands off of him on the carriage ride back to their homes. It had been almost three months before Calvin realized he was being used—not introduced to Jessica's friends, but shown off.

"Some men do not mind." His jaw clenched. "But I refuse to be any lonely rich woman's entertainment."

Abigail was no longer looking at him, and Calvin began to wonder if he had said too much, but he instantly understood her saddened expression when she spoke.

"Is that what you think of me, Calvin?" Her voice was so low, it was near inaudible. "Why I brought up the idea of an affair?"

"I have never once thought that about you, Abigail." He shook his head, his words earnest. "You like to rescue people, not use them. Besides"— he made himself smile, hoping it would break through her somberness—"you do everything you can not to like me."

"I like you, Calvin," she said with an honesty that touched his heart. The way she looked up at him from beneath her lashes touched other parts of him.

"I wish you wouldn't speak to me like that." His tone was gruff, low.

"Why?" Her head tilted, and his fingers began to itch to sink into the soft hair that slipped across her shoulder.

"It brings thoughts of your ruin to my mind."

Abigail blinked, her eyes staying shut longer than necessary. When she focused on him again, the tilt of her chin and the steadiness of her gaze hinted at a decision made. "At my age, ruin is beginning to sound exciting."

"Was your"—he searched for the right word—"relationship with your fiancé not exciting?"

She considered his question for so long, he began to think that he had offended her. Then her lips curved in a half smile. "I used to read these awful books, love stories. They were quite atrocious, really. Fantasy tales geared toward women. Reading these made me expect more of my fiancé. I was disappointed in Patrick Valmonte." She tried to chuckle, at her own logic mayhap, but her dry laughter died off quickly as she saw Calvin's expression.

"I would not disappoint you, Abigail."

He heard her breath stop, felt his own quicken, when she sat up. Her hair parted into two thick curtains that hid most of her face from view. Abigail watched him closely as he rose up on his knees.

He reached out, fully expecting her to shy away. She did not move, however, as he slid his hand beneath the blanket of her hair to cup her cheek. Calvin held his breath as one of her hands lifted; it was cool and shaking as she used it to cover his. The softness of her skin, the warmth of her touch, unmanned him.

His jaw clenched before he made himself speak again. "No one need ever know." Calvin didn't give a damn if everyone in England knew she had given herself to him. Only the idea of others discovering she belonged to him, and thus putting her reputation at risk, stilled him. "I wouldn't let anything happen to you because of this."

Her fingers weren't long enough to wrap around his hand, but she needed only to tug slightly to bring his palm to her lips. Her eyes crinkled at their corners as she said into his hand, "I'm not sure. . . . After the accident, I never . . ."

"We'll make it like you walk, Abby." He finally gave in to the urge to touch the soft locks of her hair, the fingers of his free hand sifting through the silky stuff, brushing it back from her lovely face. "Slow and steady."

Her lashes dropped, but he felt Abigail's lips curl against his palm.

Chapter 20

Abigail was very conscious of the oxygen that had accumulated in her lungs and there remained as Calvin's hand lowered until the pad of his thumb encountered the seam between her lips. She had never known there was such a concentration of nerve endings in her bottom lip until he slowly dragged his thumb back and forth across it. From that light touch, she felt heat spread out to her limbs and goose bumps stretch across her arms. Her eyes were just about to slip closed to allow her full attention to the sensation that was being evoked when his touch disappeared.

Abigail's lashes lifted, and, as she met Calvin's eyes, her pent-up breath left her in a silent rush. His gaze was that of blue flames. The heat of it stretched across the space between them and scared her heart.

"You are certain, Abigail?" The words came out rough and dry, as if Calvin had been holding his own breath.

Her attention drifted from his eyes to his cheek-bones standing out stark against the planes of his face. It slipped across his nose and noted a slight bump that suggested it may once have been broken. Abby looked at the line of his mouth and ticking muscle in his jaw, and, as her gaze lifted back to his, it hit her. She was very certain she wanted to be with Calvin. It was rather astounding how the lines of his face, the breadth of his shoulders, and everything he was had become so dear to her in so short a space of time.

"Yes, Calvin." Her words, even in the small room, were barely audible to her own ears. "I am certain."

Calvin heard. He was off the floor in a fluid move that made Abigail's eyes go wide. Her eyes went wider still when, barely a heartbeat later, she found herself lying back against the mattress. Calvin's knees were on either side of her hips, his bare arms holding him steady above her.

He had given her only one chance to change her mind, which was just as well. When his mouth lowered to cover hers—with a gentleness that rivaled his rushed climb onto the bed—Abigail's mind went blank and all the reasons why she shouldn't be doing this disappeared. Her hands opened then closed reflexively in the quilt beneath them, and the moment she felt Calvin's lips part against hers, Abby let hers do the same.

A certain amount of female delight rushed through her as she heard Calvin sigh. The sound dissolved into a groan when her tongue boldly met his searching one. She pulled back quickly then, nipping at him with her teeth.

He broke the contact, tearing away as if it took

great effort, and then released a very low chuckle. From the corners of her eyes, she noted the muscles defined in his stretched arms were quaking slightly.

"Has anyone ever told you"—his breath fanned her face as he spoke, smelling faintly of the gin he and Leonard Redman had shared after dinner— "that your kisses make a man forget himself?"

"No." She shook her head against the embroidered pillowcase and smiled a little. "But I haven't kissed all that many men."

She could feel the heat of his naked chest through the material of the shirt she wore as he lowered himself to his elbows, but he put none of his weight on her.

Calvin lowered his mouth to hers once more, but only briefly. As she clung to his full bottom lip almost greedily, he shook his head. "No more of that. You'll make me humiliate myself."

On the first and only occasion Abigail had been intimate with Patrick Valmonte, there had been few words. Those spoken had come from her, to ask him if he would kindly move the arm that was pulling her hair and politely informing him that she could hardly breathe when he pressed his shoulder across her nose. He had never complimented her on the way she kissed, never told her she made him want to lose himself. He had certainly never traced the underside of her jaw, as Calvin was doing now, with the wet, hot tip of his tongue.

Abigail shivered as his kisses moved to the hollow behind her ear, then gasped when his teeth bit down softly on her lobe. From far off, she was aware of the night air caressing skin that had been covered by her shirt only moments before and the faint sound the shirt made when Calvin used one hand to lay it open across the bed. Abigail had been so lost in his kisses that she hadn't even noticed he had gone to work on the buttons of her shirt. Then she gasped, heard Calvin's breath come out as a hiss against her ear, as his large palm cupped one of her bare breasts.

"You're so soft, Abby." His lips brushed her ear as he spoke, and she wasn't sure if it was that or the things his hand was doing that made her shiver. Much like the astonishing sensations that had erupted from his touch on her lips, her breasts swelled and nipples hardened at his caress. His thumb moved in a circle, just barely brushing the peak of her breast and making her legs shift impatiently between his. "Perfect." This he said against her throat.

Abigail held her breath as Calvin's mouth made a damp track down from the hollow of her throat. Her teeth clenched together when his ragged breathing tickled her oversensitized flesh. Then she released a grateful sigh when his mouth closed over her breast. Her eyes closed and her hands released their fierce hold on the bedclothes to sink into his thick hair. He growled down in his throat, shifting his weight to his other arm as he began to stroke the breast his mouth wasn't worshiping.

Clenching her teeth together, Abigail let her fingernails brush lightly across Calvin's scalp. He shook, and she was tempted to smile, but the urge was taken over by one to scowl. She had thought the extra attention Calvin was offering would end some of the need that was nagging at her insides. Instead, it was making her desire worse. Her body felt drawn to a breaking point she had never known before. Something strange was happening to her. All at once she was restless; part of her wanted Calvin to cease with his expert ministrations and part of her knew she would scream if he did. And there was a place, down low in her belly—perhaps not in her belly at all—that was beginning to throb in time with the beat of her heart.

Then Calvin's teeth, in a move she was sure sought revenge against the occasions she had nipped at his tongue and lips, closed almost delicately upon her nipple. Abigail did scream, but Calvin moved quickly. His mouth, open over hers, captured most of her cry.

"The room beside this one is occupied," he reminded her breathlessly.

She barely heard his words, but was arching her back. In Calvin's movement to silence her, the heated skin of his chest had brushed across her overly sensitized flesh. The coarse, dark hairs continued to tease her breasts to the point of being painful. Abigail took handfuls of Calvin's soft hair and tugged.

"Calvin . . ." The whimper sounded not of her own calm and collected voice.

"Are you alright, Abby?" He frowned down at her, searching her face as he made to again lift most of his weight from her quivering body. "Did I hurt your leg?"

She groaned, holding back an unladylike curse. "I need . . ."

"What, sweetheart?" He brushed her sweat-dampened hair back from her face, his expression concerned.

"*Calvin.*" How could she possibly tell him when

she wasn't sure herself? How could a man who was normally so intelligent be so agonizingly obtuse?

Abigail's legs shifted again, doing nothing to still the throbbing between her legs that had only gotten worse. A new thought occurred to her then, and before she could think twice, she lifted her legs. Bringing most of her lower back off the mattress, she locked her thighs about Calvin's lean hips and pressed herself against him. Her hands moved from his hair to the damp skin low on his back and pressed him downward.

Calvin cursed, a foul word that might have shocked Abigail were she not releasing a much-relieved sigh. Calvin's weight was a wonderful thing atop her. His skin, save for where he still wore his breeches, covered hers completely, and, at the most intimate place, where her body cupped his, he throbbed in time with her.

She was smiling this time when it struck her: even this was not enough. "Bloody hell," she said into the space between his neck and shoulder.

"Abby." Calvin pushed himself up out of her hold, looking as if her reluctance to release him caused physical pain. "Give me a moment, sweetheart. It will be all right."

Now, she realized, *he understands. Thank God.*

He sat back, dislodging her legs, his hands immediately moving to the buttons of his breeches. Abigail watched his movements with greedy, hungry eyes, relishing the play of muscles in his arms and the way his stomach rose and fell rapidly in time with his breath. His fingers slipped on his last button, and her gaze lifted to his face. Abby realized, without any kind of timidity, Calvin was looking at her much the same way. He devoured her with his eyes.

She wrapped her arms around his shoulders when he fell forward again, returned his kiss with everything burning inside her. Her knees lifted, his hips moved forward, and then he was inside her.

This, she understood, was what she had needed.

"No!" Her fingernails dug into the skin of Calvin's back as he pulled away.

"Shhh . . . " He kissed the spot between her furrowed brows, the end of her nose, and then eased forward again.

Abigail's lower body tensed. Her skin felt as if a slow fire were burning across it. "What . . . ?"

Calvin's hips flexed, then again. Again.

Her eyes opened wide. "Calvin?"

"It's all right, love." It was difficult for him to form the words. His gaze held hers as he smiled.

Calvin moved his hips again, and this time Abigail's lower body moved of its own volition, meeting his halfway. Her mouth fell open as she sucked in a great gasp of air and the world shattered around her. Behind the roaring in her ears and through the waves of unequivocal ecstasy rolling through her, she was aware of Calvin clutching her to his chest. His whole body went extraordinarily rigid before a great tremor shook him and he gasped into Abby's hair.

"Perfect."

He couldn't possibly . . . not now.

Calvin let the decision settle upon him, much

like a heavy weight around his heart that threatened to smother those that had burned to life inside him since the night before. Since perhaps even before Abigail had wrapped herself around him, offering a precious gift in herself.

He almost smiled as he remembered the sudden surprise that passed across her face—the way her heavy-lidded eyes suddenly went wide and her mouth slipped open in wonder. Abigail had been a sight to behold as she was lifted to her peak for the first time. Later, when Calvin folded her in his arms, breathing none too steadily himself into her disheveled hair, the sound of her happily bewildered laughter was like music to his ears. It also led him to believe that Patrick Valmonte had, in fact, been a very disappointing lover.

"Son?"

Calvin's attention moved only momentarily from the packed earth of the road beside the still carriage to the old man standing at his phaeton. "Yes?"

"I said, I think that wheel will do nicely, at least until you and the missus can acquire a new one." Leonard Redman removed his hat to wipe the sweat from his bald head.

Calvin's back, beneath the material of his shirt and jacket, was damp with sweat as well. Though it had been fairly early in the morning as they began to remove the fragments of the old wheel to the carriage and replace it with one Leonard had found amidst the junk in his back field, the temperature had been warm and the air humid from the rain. Calvin was aware of the odor of his own efforts gradually overpowering the sweet scent of Abby that had been in his shirt when he donned it.

"Thank you again." Calvin nodded to the old man. "This will get us back into North Rutherford, if not to Abigail's home."

If Leonard noticed the slip of the younger man's tongue, he did not show it. As he hefted himself into the phaeton, Calvin let his gaze move back to where it had been fixed for a long time, even as they worked on the carriage.

Abigail had told him she found lying loathsome; only recently was he realizing he did not particularly care for the act himself. If not to the Redmans, to Abby herself. As he watched her sleeping that morning, unable to take his eyes off the soft curve of her cheek and the pale slope of one exposed shoulder, Calvin had decided he was going to tell her the truth. He would face what was sure to be her understandable rage and begin the process of making amends. Making, if he could, a permanent place for himself in Abigail's life.

Calvin felt a muscle in his jaw begin to flex steadily as he stared at the indentation in the road that caused their accident. Despite the pouring rain that had lasted until the break of dawn, little of the dirt had been packed down. The hole was still present: large, with flat sides. The hole, in fact, was shaped almost exactly like a square.

If Calvin told Abigail the truth, she would send him away until he could find a way to earn her forgiveness for his lies—he could hardly imagine her understanding her brother's logic. While Calvin was gone, she would be alone at her estate. For all accounts and purposes, left at the mercy of the wolf who lived on the property that bordered hers. She was too damned stubborn to realize she needed him with her.

His gaze burned into the section of missing earth as if his stare alone could make it disappear.

"If you're thinking what I'm thinking, Calvin," Leonard called from his phaeton, "I can understand why you look so angry."

"What are you thinking?"

"Someone dug that hole." Leonard held the reins in one hand and fisted the other on his hip. "Stupid youngsters playing a prank, I imagine."

No, Calvin thought, *neither Raleigh nor Dobbs was young*.

"They probably never meant for your lady to get hurt."

They meant to hurt her, alright.

Leonard's next words finally permeated the grim cloud around Calvin. His tone was jovial and perceptive to the point of drawing the other man's gaze back to him.

"You can't tell that to a gentleman who believes his woman is in danger, though." Leonard grinned. "She may not be your wife, but it's pretty clear Abigail is yours."

Calvin met the other's gaze evenly. "Yes."

To keep it that way, he would continue with his lie.

Chapter 21

"By the bye, how did you and Calvin meet?"

Abigail restrained the urge to groan aloud and sent a silent curse to the man who had disappeared before she had even awakened that morning. She scooped up another spoonful of the porridge Prudence had made for breakfast and took her time swallowing as she searched for a plausible response. Not only did she not like to lie, she wasn't very good at it.

"My brother"—she was pleased it wasn't a complete falsehood—"introduced us."

"How nice." Prudence took Abby's empty bowl before the younger woman could even think about getting up herself. "Leonard and I met at church. He used to pull my hair and step on my skirts. I hated him." She grinned over her round shoulder. "We were, of course, only ten at the time."

Abigail smiled back, pushing up from the table. "Let me help you clean, Prudence."

"Nonsense, dear. You're a guest." The older

woman had the bowl and spoon cleaned and put away before she even finished the sentence.

"I can't tell you how much we appreciate your kindness, most especially helping us with the carriage."

"Oh, Leonard had no use for that wheel anyway." Prudence wiped her hands on her apron. "And to tell you the truth, I like the company. My Leonard's a sweetheart, but I get tired of hearing about horse teeth and crops all day. It's nice to have a woman to talk to."

Abigail nodded, leaning heavily on her crutch when her knee gave a slight twinge to remind her of the circumstances that brought them to the farm. "I didn't have many friends," she said, "until after my accident. While I was recuperating, some ladies I had encountered only briefly once began to visit regularly. I think, had I never had my accident, we may never have met again."

"I believe everything happens for a reason, Abby," Prudence said thoughtfully. "Maybe you had your accident so you could have these friends."

It was true. Had she not been in the awful wreck, she may have never gotten to truly know the women who were now her best friends. She would have married Valmonte and perhaps never known the kind of man he really was. She wouldn't have moved into the solace of the country, never met Calvin. It was frightening, really, what she may have lost had she not nearly died.

"I think I hear them coming." Prudence had tilted her head to the side to listen before speaking. She linked her arm through Abigail's as they stepped outside to watch the two vehicles approach. "You shall have to come see us again, Abby."

"Absolutely." She nodded, her eyes on the man behind the reins of the carriage. Something inside her was instantly aware of Calvin's grim expression, the tight set of his jaw and tenseness in his shoulders.

"Abigail was just telling me how you both met, Calvin," Prudence said as he dropped from the carriage.

His brows only snapped together briefly, a movement Abigail was certain only she had seen. "Yes," Calvin said without looking at the short and round woman next to her, "at a party."

Abigail winced.

"A party?" Prudence blinked.

"Yes," Abby said quickly. "That's where my brother introduced us."

"I see." Prudence smiled with understanding.

There was something controlled about the way Leonard cleared his throat before addressing his wife. "The hole that caught their carriage was not an accident."

Abigail's eyes went wide, darting to the man who had come to stand before her. He remained silent.

"No?" Prudence said.

"I was telling Calvin it was probably young pranksters not knowing someone could actually get hurt," Leonard explained.

"Indeed." Prudence appeared as horrified as Abigail felt. "Abby or Calvin could have broken their necks."

Abigail's breath froze in her lungs as an awful picture formed in her mind. She saw Calvin being slung from behind the reins and crashing to the ground to lie unmoving. She went cold all over as she focused again on the man who could have died driving her carriage. It would have been, she was uncomfortably certain, her fault.

"We should go." Calvin reached for her elbow, his tone devoid of any emotion. "I'll have to get a new wheel made, and you need to send word to your brother as to why you didn't make the soiree last night."

"Yes," she said. She paused to address the old couple standing before their home, arms linked loosely around each other. "Thank you." She managed a smile. "For everything."

"Remember what I said, dear." Prudence waved.

Abigail was stiff in Calvin's arms as he lifted her into the carriage. There were things, perhaps, that should have been said after what transpired between them the night before. But her mind was on other matters entirely.

"There will be a road," she said after she was seated, "before we get into the village. It goes to the right; you will see a sign for another farm like this one. Please take us there instead of home."

Calvin straightened from where he had set her crutch on the floor of the cab. His brows drew together.

"Please, Calvin. It is important." She did not look up as she spoke, afraid that he would be able to see her guilt before she could explain.

"All right, Abby." He waited a long time, perhaps to see if she would lift her head, and then closed the cab door.

Abigail was dimly aware of the carriage beginning to move, slightly lopsided now with Leonard's wheel. She was concentrating on what she would say to Calvin, how she would explain to the man who had been so kind as to defend her from Raleigh that it was, in fact, all her fault that the viscount was so intent in his hatred for her.

The sign before the road read only HUTCHINSON and bore an engraving of a trio of horses. Calvin brought the carriage up to the large stone house that sat in the center of the clearing. There was a stable—as big as five of Abigail's—set off from the house, and the land was divided into at least a half-dozen fenced sections. Within a few of the pens, horses of varied breeds basked in the sun.

"This is where I purchased Achilles," Abigail said as he lifted her from the cab. She was noticeably stiff in his arms and wouldn't meet his eye. Not for the first time, Calvin wondered if her reticence was due to embarrassment from the night before.

Regret.

A woman had appeared at the door of the house as Abigail was lowered to her feet. She was petite, with silver hair and intelligent brown eyes. The front of her apron was dusted with flour and butter. "Good morning, Lady Abby!"

"Maggie." Abigail smiled and lifted a hand.

"Do you need to speak with Luther, or are you just visiting?"

"Visiting," Abby returned. She slipped her arm into her crutch and began to move toward the fence nearest the stables. She did not look back to make sure Calvin followed, only said, "Luther Hutchinson, Maggie's husband, is one of the best horse handlers in North Rutherford. In all of England, I should think. He led a regiment in the cavalry during the war."

As if on cue, two men departed one of the stable's many openings. One had hair the same hue as his wife and a face that bore the results of a life of hard work and happiness. The man beside him, leading an irritated stallion by the reins, was almost identical save for his black hair and unlined face. Father and son nodded their greeting before turning their full attention to the horse.

"Hutchinson takes excellent care of his animals," Abigail was saying as she stopped before one of the larger fenced areas. There were five horses in the pen, four lingering beneath a shade tree and an aged mare that was sauntering to where the two humans stood.

Abigail propped her crutch against the wooden fence, resting her weight on a corner post as she reached out to the mare.

Calvin watched Abby gently stroke the animal's white muzzle, understanding hitting him the moment she finally turned to look at him.

"When I was in the phaeton accident, both horses pulling the vehicle went over the bridge with me. The first died immediately. The second, the one that landed in the water not far from where I lay, lived until my rescuers came. She had to have been in awful pain; I was told she had broken two legs and the remnants of the reins were cutting into her throat." Her voice was soft, her gaze haunted with the past. "I could hear her breathe in the storm. She did not die, though, until right after I was taken from the river." Abigail looked back to the old mare. "I know it sounds ridiculous, but I would have been more afraid, more willing to die, had I not heard that horse. Had I believed I was all alone."

She took a deep breath, squeezed her eyes closed, regained her composure. "When I heard Raleigh take the whip to this mare, I couldn't bear it. She had been unable to keep up with his hunting team, I think. I could not imagine he would miss her were she gone."

"You did take the horse," Calvin said.

"Yes." Her gaze met his again. "Tuttleton and I brought her here. Mr. Hutchinson saw the whip burns on her and accepted the mare at his farm with no questions asked." Her smile was bittersweet. "I like to believe my actions justified, but it still remains that I am a thief."

"Is this when all the trouble started with Raleigh?" Calvin's eyes drifted to the horse and then her haunches, where the scars of her torture remained. He scowled.

"We lived in communal dislike before his horse went missing, because of the parties and traps. The viscount thought it was Timothy and his father who had taken the animal. One of his servants reported seeing a large man and a smaller one leaving the property with it."

"The small man was you."

Abigail nodded. "Tuttleton refused to defend himself; in an effort to protect me, I believe. When I stood up for him and Timothy against the magistrate, insisted I knew their whereabouts all evening long, my stables caught fire."

A lazy breeze laid a tendril of her hair across the bridge of her freckled nose. "I am sorry I did not tell you this sooner, Calvin. I truly thought I could manage the battle on my own. The idea that what I did could have cost you your life yesterday"—she took a deep, shuddering breath—"is quite unbearable. I shall, of course, write you an excellent reference when we return to the estate. So you may leave as soon as you wish."

His attention moved from the horse to the woman gazing so intently up at him. "And if I do not wish to go?"

She blinked. "Certainly you do not want to keep under the employ of a thief who has put your life in danger?"

"I know of no such person." Calvin slowly shook his head, reaching out with one hand to tuck the wispy tendril of her hair behind an ear. "You did not steal the viscount's horse, as I see it. You saved her."

Abigail released a long, slow breath. She looked down at the ground by his booted feet. "He must have had Dobbs dig that hole in the road. I took a fall, but you could just as easily have been injured. Had you broken your neck, as Prudence said, it would have been because of my actions."

Calvin captured her delicate chin, gently lifted her head. "Listen to me carefully, Abby." He waited until her bay eyes met his before speaking again. "You will stop this at once. What is done is done, and if you could change the past, I highly doubt you would not have rescued this horse from whatever Raleigh had in store for her."

She shook her head.

"I do not blame you for what happened yesterday," Calvin went on. "Raleigh would never have known to set the trap had I not told his cousin we were planning to take the road."

"But Calvin—"

"No." He covered her lips with his thumb and almost forgot what he was going to say. Almost gave himself up to the texture of her mouth, as he had the night before. "You brought me out here believing I would think you a thief and God knows what else. I am telling you that I do not. Nothing you have done in the past, certainly nothing you did because you believed it was right and would save another creature's life, will ever change the fact that you are my Abby."

He expected her to scowl at the intent of his words, the possession they implied. Instead, her expression reminded him a lot of the wonder she had shown the night before as she clutched to him as if for dear life.

"Now"—he dropped his hand before he was tempted to kiss her in the sight of anyone passing by—"let us get back home. I don't want you on your leg any longer than necessary until you are feeling better."

They turned together toward the carriage and had made it halfway in shared silence before he felt her touch. Her free hand brushed against the material of his coat, as if unsure, then settled neatly in the crook of his arm. He looked down at her as she carefully kept her own gaze focused on the carriage, then let his hand come up to cover hers.

Chapter 22

"You are certain you don't wish me to send for Dr. McKinney?"

"I'm fine, Margot, really." Abigail met the other woman's gaze evenly when she paused in dumping the last pail of steaming water into the bathtub. She wished Calvin hadn't shared their mishap with the two women who had clogged the front door in their efforts to meet the carriage's arrival.

"Calvin had to carry you up the stairs."

She wished he hadn't done that either.

Abigail had already removed her gown and was in the process of reaching for the ties of her slip when she spotted the pink abrasions across her skin; burns from Calvin's morning beard brushing her breasts. She reached for her stockings instead. "My knee pains me still, but it is nothing to fret over. Calvin didn't even give me the chance to tell him I could manage on my own."

"At least," Margot huffed as she set a chair near

the bathtub, "let Mrs. Poole make you one of her poultice wraps."

Abigail's nose wrinkled, recalling the foul odor of the last wrap the cook had concocted for her. When she looked up from her last stocking, however, Margot's expression was vaguely warning. "All right." She added quickly as she slowly made her way across the room to the tub, "But I will not wear it all day. Strange insects began to hover about me when I wore the last too long."

"Good enough." Margot finally smiled. "Do you need anything else, Abby?"

"No. Thank you for preparing the water for me."

She was already slipping her bare feet into the hot tub when her maid closed the bedchamber door. Abigail tugged her slip overhead and tossed it onto the chair beside her crutch and sank gratefully into the water. The steam rising off its surface smelled faintly of roses, and Abigail smiled at Margot's thoughtfulness.

Harry gave her a dirty look when she lifted the washcloth from the side of the tub, the end of which the rabbit had been happily chewing. Abigail applied the rag gently to the tender abrasions just below her collarbones; the fading red marks seemed to be her only proof of what had happened with Calvin the night before. She had been worried, when the sun rose and she registered what had actually taken place, things would be different between them. Though Calvin had made no mention of the change in their relationship that morning, she was certain Mrs. Poole and Margot would notice something out of sorts.

As it was, everything appeared the same even to

Abigail. Calvin had kept himself an arm's width apart from her as they moved from the carriage to the house. He hadn't spoken save to tell the others of the accident, and as he carried Abby up the stairs, his hold was less intimate than it had been before they spent the evening together.

Abby frowned as she dipped her washcloth into the water then held the dripping cloth above where her bent knee broke the surface. It was red, slightly swollen still, and the hot water stung at first. Carefully, she laid the washcloth across her knee and sighed when there was a slight break in the pain.

Only when she closed her eyes did the dark thoughts begin to register. Perhaps Calvin wished the events of the night before hadn't taken place. That was impossible, though, for he hardly seemed ill at ease at the time. That, of course, had been before he knew the woman he was making love to was a charlatan and a thief.

Abigail's lashes lifted. Uneven tendrils of her hair had slipped from the loose knot she had put them in; their tips were dampened in the water as she bowed her head. It was a difficult task, allowing herself regret at having something that had been so blissful end so quickly.

She did not hear the bedchamber door open, only the dull thud of the wood settling back into the jamb. She frowned at her reflection in the water, lifted her chin, then gasped.

"Calvin!" She yanked the washcloth from her knee to hold open at her breasts.

His dark gaze moved slowly from her barely covered skin to her flushed features. He lifted a brow. "I need to speak with you."

Abigail's disbelief rose as he continued into the room, pausing to scratch the spot above Harry's nose on the way to the bathtub. "Can it not wait?"

"Are you shy, Abby?" Calvin's lips suddenly curled. "Not the sophisticated air of a woman partaking of an illicit affair." He straddled her chair backward, breeches going tight across muscled thighs she had been much too eager to wrap her legs about less than twelve hours before. His gaze held hers, all too amused. "Shall I point out it is nothing I have not seen—or touched—before?"

But it was. Abigail's gaze moved quickly, darting between the man seated near the bathtub to where her bare knee broke through the water's surface. The room had been all shadows last night, and Calvin's intent gaze—as far as she recalled—had spent most of the time reading her expressions as if they were food and he a starving man. His large hands, calloused from working on her estate, had cupped her breasts, run across the skin of her arms, and gone so far as to tightly grip her bottom, but they had never strayed so far as her legs. He had not felt the ragged scars that marred the one or seen the red and puckered flesh so unlike the pale skin around it.

Meeting his eyes again, she shifted slightly, trying to pull her leg down further.

Calvin's brows drew together, his smile slipping away. "You want me to leave?"

It was much the same tone he had used before, when she had been sprawled on her back and breathing heavily, her skin damp with his and her own sweat.

"How is your leg?"

She had grinned at the dark ceiling, something

reassuring in the weight of his arm thrown across her naked waist and his ragged breathing fanning her ear. *"What leg?"*

"What was it you needed to speak to me about?" Feeling painfully self-conscious with only the thin washcloth covering her torso from view, she casually crossed her arms across her chest and wrapped her fingers about her shoulders. She pressed her cheek to the back of one hand, hoping, as she peered up at Calvin, she looked demure and not like an insane woman.

"I'm leaving for London tomorrow."

"Oh," she breathed, feeling her heart sink. He had, apparently, been lying when they were at the Hutchinson horse farm. "Oh."

"I will be back, Abby." He scowled as if he could read her mind and was rather annoyed by her lack of faith. "I have some personal errands I must run."

"Might I be of help in any way?" She could have sworn that the force with which her heart again lifted reverberated through her ribs and against the arms crossed at her chest.

"No. There are a few loose ends I must attend to."

Abigail's lashes lowered thoughtfully. There was something almost cryptic about his tone.

"If there is anything you need before I go in the morning, let me know." He gently nudged Harry away with his boot when the rabbit started sniffing his laces as one might a fine wine. "I know I still have to get the damned wheel for the carriage, Timothy needs my help with the horses, and I don't like you having to go up and down the stairs alone."

"We'll be fine without you, Calvin." Abigail chuckled, but instantly wished she had chosen different words when Calvin's features went grim and his gaze cold. It was surely impossible, but it almost appeared as if she had hurt his feelings.

"Yes," he cleared his throat, rising from the chair, "well—"

"I will miss you, though," Abigail said quickly, lifting her chin.

He stopped in turning toward the door, glancing back at her over one broad shoulder. "It will only be one day."

Although her independent nature sorely tempted her to do so, Abigail would not relent. "Still," she said and smiled.

Calvin turned completely round, an impressive figure in the light of the sun from a nearby window. His dark hair shone like the wings of a raven and his eyes like the ocean. His expression was serious to the point of being grim as he moved back to the bathtub and squatted on his haunches beside where only a little of her legs were under the water.

She shifted.

"Abby, about last night . . ."

"Are you referring to our accident?" She sincerely hoped he was as she lowered one arm, slipping it beneath the water as she reached for her unsightly knee.

"No." He rested his forearms along the side of the bathtub. "After."

"Calvin, you don't have to—"

"I don't want to make you uncomfortable, Abby." He spoke over her nervous words. "I just wanted to assure you again that I would do nothing to dishonor you, and, though there might be a time when you doubt my intentions, I assure you I would never do anything to hurt you."

She blinked at that, quietly covering her knee with her open palm. "Why ever would I doubt you?"

His attention had been diverted by the sound of splashing water. His gaze took its time in traveling the length of her wet form, then halted above where she was spreading her fingers as far as they would go about her knee. "Does your leg hurt?"

"No," she said quickly. Her knuckles went white as she gripped her knee.

"What are you about?" He reached for her wrist, his long fingers circling it as if she were as dainty as a child.

"Calvin, don't." Abigail wasn't sure why she even bothered to fight his grip; he lifted her hand from her leg as if she hadn't done a thing to restrain him. His dark brows crumpled; his mouth became a blunt line as he gazed at her knee. "I wish you hadn't done that," she whispered, looking away.

"Abby . . ." The hair at her nape rose on end as he ran his fingertips, so lightly she might have imagined it, across the thin line of one scar. "It must have been horrible for you."

"Others"—she thought of Bernice's husband, whose scars could not be hidden as easily as hers—"have had it worse." Her eyes slowly drifted back to the man who was almost stroking the second scar beneath her kneecap. "It looks worse than it really was."

Calvin smiled. "Liar."

Abigail's lips pursed. "If you are quite finished

investigating my disfigurement, sir, I should like to finish with my bath."

He broke eye contact, watching his hand as it slipped above her knee and deeper into the water. His fingers glided smoothly across her inner thigh.

Abby sucked in her breath.

"I'm not quite finished, Lady Abigail." Calvin looked at her through his thick lashes.

"Calvin!" She brought her legs together, trapping his hand farther from her knees than the apex of her thighs.

"Yes?"

Abigail struggled with the calmness of his tone. "You're getting your shirt wet."

He appeared totally unconcerned that his sleeve was soaked up to the elbow. "It will dry." He lifted his free hand, brushed his knuckles across her heated cheek before pushing aside her hair to whisper against her ear, "Open." His fingers trapped under the water, tickling the underside of her legs, left no doubt as to what he was talking about.

"I don't think—"

She felt his hot breath against her cheek only a moment before Calvin covered her mouth with his. The remembered sensations of the night before came to life as if they had been dormant for moments instead of hours. A not-unfamiliar warmth spread throughout Abigail's body as Calvin parted her lips with his and sank his fingers into her hair.

It was he who broke away first, rough breathing fanning Abigail's face as her lashes lifted and her gaze met his. She realized that his kiss had stunned her, made her body dissolve almost lazily, and had given Calvin the leeway he needed to move his hand under the water to the core of her.

His gaze held hers, refusing her any respite against the heat of his stare as his fingers ever so slowly began to stroke. Abigail released a ragged gasp, one hand trembling to grip the side of the bathtub and the other reaching for the wet material of his shirt. As his fingers parted her beneath the water, hers gripped the material of his shirt so tightly the fabric nearly tore.

"Calvin?" It parted her lips as a whimper.

"Do not worry, love." He kissed her once, lingeringly, before letting his forehead rest against hers. "Let me touch you." And then his fingers found a very sensitive place between her legs.

Abigail's breathing stopped; her eyes squeezed closed. Tension radiated through her body from the place Calvin was now slowly circling with a single fingertip. Suddenly the water was much too hot, his touch more than she could bear. Even still, when she released his shirtsleeve to dig her fingertips into the sinew of his arm, it was not to push him away. She rocked her hips upward at the same time she pushed Calvin's hand against her.

He laughed in her hair, but it was not a sound of amusement at her expense. The sound was coarse, an odd mix of pleasure and pain.

"Lady Abby?"

She froze at the soft tap on her bedchamber door, felt Calvin do the same. Abigail's eyes flared wide, meeting his of smoky blue before they moved to the door.

"Abby?"

"Yes." She had to clear her throat when the word came out hoarse. "Margot?"

"I've your poultice wrap," the other woman called through the door.

"My what?"

"The wrap Mrs. Poole made." Margot's tone became perplexed. "For your leg."

"Oh."

"Shall I bring it in for you?"

"No!" Abigail winced at the escalated pitch of her voice. "Thank you, Margot, but I will come downstairs to read in a few moments. I'll put it on in the parlor."

"All right, then."

Abby sighed, avoiding Calvin's gaze.

"Are you feeling well, Abby?"

She gasped, certain the other woman had vacated the area before her door until she spoke again.

"You sound a bit shaky."

Abigail pressed her open palm against her forehead and took a deep breath. "I'm fine, Margot. I'll be down in a moment."

"All right," Margot said again, and this time Abby could hear her footsteps retreating from the door.

The sound of his hand in the water was loud as Calvin wrapped his fingers around her thigh. He gave her leg a gentle squeeze.

"You should go," she whispered.

He nodded and rose to his feet. Instead of moving toward the door, however, he reached for the towel that had been lying across the chair. Calvin held out a hand to Abigail.

Her nerves were much too frazzled for her to argue. She laced her fingers through his much larger ones and came to her feet. Painfully conscious of her nakedness in comparison to his fully clothed state, she avoided eye contact until she had wrapped the towel under her arms and across her breasts. Calvin's hands rested lightly around her hips as he waited until she finally lifted her lashes.

His gaze was fixed on her mouth, still swollen from his kiss of moments before. When he bowed his head, however, he did not brush her lips with his, but her still damp shoulder.

Abigail stood for a long moment beside the bathtub after Calvin had gone. Her skin slowly dried, and Harry curled up between her feet, and she continued to gaze in horror at the door the man had closed after him.

It had not been part of her plan. She had never imagined that an emotion beyond desire was what had backed her longing to be with Calvin. She had certainly never considered she might love the man.

Chapter 23

"Ah," Thomas Wolcott said with mock sorrow, "I had thought you possessed more staying power."

"I'm in London for the day." Calvin seated himself across the table from the other man. "I return to North Rutherford in the morning."

It was early in the afternoon, yet nearly every table at Justin's was occupied. Calvin wrapped his fingers around the dark tea the server had brought, eyeing the tables about theirs to make certain no one was close enough to overhear.

"I'm glad to know Abby has yet to frighten you away." Thomas was adding heaping spoonfuls of honey to his own tea as he spoke. "My sister puts on a great show of being strong, but she is just as delicate as any female."

Calvin gazed into the depths of his cup, the brew inside a shade of brown not unlike Abigail's eyes. "You underestimate her."

"You believe she is not delicate?"

Calvin made himself ignore the mental picture

of Abigail in her bath, tendrils of damp hair clinging to her cheeks, holding his gaze in silent wonder as he gently stroked her. "I did not say that." He cleared his throat. "She took Raleigh's horse."

Thomas sputtered, almost choked on his tea. *"What?"*

"The man is a bastard. He was abusing the animal, and Abby could not stand it. She and the deceased Mr. Tuttleton secreted the mare away to a safe place."

"Bloody hell," Thomas breathed. His face had turned a shade of red at odds with his freckles and hair.

Calvin's jaw clenched. "Raleigh and a reprobate by the name of Dobbs—in the short time I've shared her company—have threatened Abby, caused her carriage to be in an accident"—his fingers went tight around his cup until his knuckles turned white—"and fired a bullet that grazed her ear."

"Jesus." Thomas put his cup atop the table with a loud bang. "I have to get her out of there at once."

"She won't go."

"She can stay with Jeanette and me."

"She won't go, Thomas. That is her home." Calvin shook his head. "If she will not retreat due to threats made on her person by men who care not if they do her real harm, what makes you think she will listen to you?"

"I am her brother. She is stubborn—"

"You have no idea."

"—but she will listen to reason, I'm sure."

"She is an intelligent female, and she listens to her heart. Her heart belongs to her home in the country, her friends and servants." His brows drew together at the last. Did Abby have any intention of opening her heart to a man that was part of her staff, her lover, and a liar?

"Then I will go to her," Thomas said. "Make certain she is safe."

"How will you explain the way you obtained your knowledge on the matter?"

"I shall have to tell her the truth."

"No!" Calvin said it with a roughness that startled the other man. He took a deep breath, not meeting his best friend's gaze. "You'll like as not upset her more than she deserves right now. I'll protect her. I'll take care of this."

"How?" Thomas signaled for a server, ordered a brandy.

"First, I shall have to get rid of the village magistrate. He's in Raleigh's pocket."

"How do you propose to do that, may I ask?"

"I have a plan. I'm meeting with my man of affairs later this evening to put it into play." Calvin scowled. "Men like Kingsly leave a bad taste in my mouth. They're easily bought and sold like cattle and do the biddings of those who pay them like sheep."

"Abby!"

"In here, Margot." She had already set aside her account book when she heard the front door down the hall being thrown open. She was on her feet, moving across the room, when the other woman burst into the study.

"You should come quick, my lady." Margot was breathless, her hair frazzled as if it were an extension of her emotional state. "They're outside."

"Who?" Abby felt a heavy weight in her stomach.

"It's that awful Mr. Kingsly. He won't leave poor Timothy alone."

They stood just outside the stables, Timothy with his head bowed, his features unreadable, and Mr. Kingsly pointing at his chest. Abigail could hear the older man's raised voice from the moment she left the house.

"I think you're lying to me. I think you *do* know where it is!"

"What's going on?" Abigail's tone was strong, never hinting at the discomfort she felt. Her anger rose when Timothy lifted his chin, his dark eyes taking her in with undisguised relief. Abigail was rigid as she maneuvered herself between the two men, ignoring the ache in her knee at the abrupt movements.

"I hate to be the bearer of bad news, Lady Wolcott"—Kingsly folded his arms across his chest—"but your stableman here is a thief."

Margot gasped from where she had moved to wrap her meaty arms about one of Timothy's.

"No, Abby," Timothy said in a shaking tone that was heartbreaking.

"That is the most ridiculous thing I have ever heard in my life." Abigail lifted her chin, meeting Kingsly's mean little eyes.

"I have a witness who says he dropped his hunting rifle right outside your property, Lady Wolcott, and then he saw your man here going off with it later that day."

Her brows slowly drew together, awareness dawning. "Dobbs did not drop the weapon, Mr. Kingsly. It was taken from him when he nearly shot my ear off."

Margot gasped again.

"So you admit"—Kingsly smiled as if he had won—"a member of your staff did steal one of Lord Raleigh's best guns."

"Did you not hear her say she was almost injured?" Margot said in a horrified tone.

"He heard me, Margot," Abby said grimly.

Kingsly's grin wavered. "Now, insofar as the man who originally took the gun has left North Rutherford, I am obliged to take matters up with the other seen with the weapon."

"How do you know Mr. Garrett is not here?" An icy shiver stole down Abigail's spine. Her head turned, her gaze focusing on the stretch of property that bordered hers. In the distance she saw the figures of three individuals, two on horseback.

Margot said something coarse and sinful under her breath.

"I feel I should take your stableman with me," Kingsly was saying. The wax he used to set his mustache gleamed in the sunlight.

Abby heard Timothy release a grunt of worry before she faced the magistrate again. "I think not."

"He was seen with the gun, Lady Wolcott." The man's voice bordered on whiny.

"Prove it, Mr. Kingsly. Show me this gun Timothy has. Let's go to his room in the stables now, shall we?"

"He was there already," Timothy said, glancing at the magistrate for only a second before looking down at the tips of his worn boots, "when I got in from taking Achilles out. My room's a mess."

Abigail's teeth clenched together, well aware Timothy kept his room so neat and tidy it was unbelievable. "Did you find the gun?" she asked Kingsly.

"No, but—"

"Then you have no proof, do you, sir? No reason to take Timothy away or bother us any longer."

Kingsly blinked, his mouth opening and closing like that of a fish out of water.

"Now, I'll ask you only once to take your leave," Abigail snapped. "Good day, sir."

"You cannot speak like this to a man who protects the community," Kingsly croaked, red rising from his neck to his cheeks.

"I am not speaking to a man who protects my community." Abby linked her arm through Timothy's, and she and Margot began to guide him toward the safety of the house. "I am speaking to you."

Chapter 24

He walked from his own home, his gait steady and even as the bustle of Town gave way to the less populated neighborhoods of great stone mansions and manicured lawns. He was a man with a purpose; it was evident in the grim angles of his face and his rigid stride, so no one stopped him as he stepped through the iron gates of the Valmonte estate and through the front door. The doorman had been pressing a buxom maid against the entry wall, running his fingertips across the lace of her décolletage, and fairly jumped out of his buckled shoes when Calvin entered.

He met the other man's gaze steadily, ignoring the gaping woman behind him. "Take me to Lord Valmonte," Calvin ordered.

The doorman eyed the breadth of Calvin's shoulders beneath his somber black greatcoat, the size of his hands curled into fists. The younger man's hands were almost delicate, and his shoulders, where his shimmering pink jacket fit tightly to them, slight. "Yes," he said. "This way, sir."

Only the fireplace illuminated the parlor. Most of the room was in shadows save where Patrick Valmonte sat in a high-backed leather chair directly before the hearth. Calvin could see little of the man—as his chair back was to the door—save his stocking feet stretched out on the carpet, the length of one arm, and the empty snifter he held loosely in elegant fingers.

"A visitor, my lord," the doorman announced quickly and disappeared.

Calvin's brows drew together as he glanced at the closed door. He could never imagine Mrs. Poole or Margot permitting a stranger into Abby's company without making certain their employer would be all right. When he faced forward again, Calvin saw Valmonte had risen.

He blinked slowly, drunkenly, at the man who had invaded his privacy. "Do we know each other, sir?"

Just looking at the man whom Abigail was going to wed made dark jealousy curl down Calvin's spine. The fact Valmonte, even in his drunken state, appeared elegantly collected didn't help either. His brown hair was swept neatly back from his forehead and tied at his nape. His face—high cheekbones, dimpled chin—and soft gray eyes were clear evidence that he was unmarred with childhood traumas and hunger. The man, in his expensive attire and perfectly tied cravat, had never had a day of suffering in his life. He had not hesitated to abandon Abigail when her life had become difficult.

"No." Calvin stepped farther into the room, onto

the thick Persian rug circled by the firelight. "But we both know Lady Abigail Wolcott."

Valmonte flinched as if he had been hit. "Abby?"

The familiarity cut into Calvin's heart. "Don't call her that. Only her friends call her that."

"You are Ab—Abigail's friend?" The other man had not moved from where he stood at the chair.

Calvin felt his lips curl. "You could say that."

"Forgive me for being so bold as to ask"— Valmonte's voice was soft, almost musical—"but why are you here?"

Calvin himself hadn't known why until that moment. "To call you out."

"Call me out?" The duke's face went slack. "You cannot be serious."

"Mr. Emanuel Fitzherbert and Abby's own brother will serve as my seconds. I'll leave you a night to appoint yours."

The brandy snifter hit the carpet, but did not break. Valmonte's hands hung limp at his sides. "Good God, man! What is this about? I've done nothing to warrant such extremes."

"You're a thief," Calvin said, then shook his head. "No, you are even worse than that. There has to be a more suitable name for a man who preys on the kindness of a woman whom he should protect. Monster, perhaps?"

"I don't understand." Calvin was tempted to believe the other man as he frantically shook his head. "Is this about the accident?" Valmonte lifted his palms up in supplication. "I was drunk and stupid. I admit I was pushing the horses much too hard. I did not know what I was doing afterward. I took quite a blow to the head, I swear it."

"I don't want to hear your excuses, Valmonte."

Calvin's hands shook, his fists were drawn so tight. A picture was being formed in his mind as the other spoke: Abigail in a carriage bent on destruction.

"I saw her in the river." Valmonte's hands trembled, his eyes watery for a reason that went beyond drunkenness. "She was staring at the sky, not blinking. I thought she was dead. What else could I have done?"

Then it hit Calvin, a silent rush of awareness. It explained why Abigail was so hell-bent on depending on no one. The one man in the world she should have been able to rely upon in her ordeal had failed her.

His control snapped like a twig. One moment Calvin was near the door, the next he was across the room. He gripped Valmonte by the lapels of his coat and slammed him against the stones that surrounded the fireplace. A rush of satisfaction coursed through his blood when he heard the other man's teeth crack together.

"You left her there." Calvin's voice was deadly soft as he spoke through clenched teeth. "You drove the phaeton over the bridge, saw Abby fall. Then you left her there to die."

Valmonte could not argue. His shirt was drawn tight across his neck, his face turning a brilliant shade of red.

Calvin didn't care. "You son of a bitch!" He slammed him against the hearth again.

"Patrick?" It came from the opened doorway, a near-shriek. *"Patrick!"*

Calvin glanced back over his shoulder, saw the pale figure in the frothy white robe. The woman—

ONE NIGHT TO BE SINFUL 249

a girl, really—looked no more than seventeen. Her blond hair hung in tangled disarray about her shoulders. Her blue eyes were wide and went swiftly from being frightened to angry.

"Who is this man, Patrick?" she demanded, fisting her hands on hips thin enough to be a boy's. "Have you been gambling again?"

Calvin released Valmonte, who crumpled, coughing, ungracefully to the floor.

"Answer me, Patrick!" The woman bounded into the room toward her husband, completely ignoring the man who had almost killed him. She tapped her foot impatiently on the floor. "I thought I told you I did not want you visiting those gaming hells. I cannot believe you told me I could not purchase that diamond brooch from the jeweler, then went out and wasted money away on your bloody hobby."

"Elizabeth . . . ," Valmonte croaked, crawling up to his knees.

"I do not want to hear it!" She kicked him sharply in his side, sending the man back to the floor. "I will not stand for this. I'm telling Papa, and he'll be none too pleased with you, sir." Elizabeth promptly burst into hysterics. She was a great deal less attractive with spittle flying from her lips and mucous bubbles erupting from her nostrils. "I hate you, Patrick Valmonte. You have ruined my life!" She ran from the room screaming.

Calvin lifted a brow, waiting until Valmonte groaned and sat up. He propped his back against the wall, offered the standing man only a brief glare before tentatively touching his side. He winced in pain.

"Never mind finding seconds, Valmonte," Calvin

said. "Death would be an all-too-pleasant release. I think the prison you have locked yourself into now satisfies me."

"Go to hell"—Valmonte's voice was no longer musical, just coarse and breathless—"whatever your name is."

"You will no longer take stipends from Abigail."

Valmonte peered up at Calvin from beneath lowered brows. "I do not take stipends from Abigail."

"Your initials are in her account book."

"Not mine." Valmonte shook his head and groaned when his eyes rolled. He rested his head against the wall to stave off dizziness. "Why would I need Wolcott money? I have plenty of my own. Plenty from my lovely wife."

The man was not lying. Calvin scowled at the observation. *Then who the hell was P.V.?*

He stepped over the other man's sprawled legs, running his fingers through his hair as he moved to leave the parlor.

When Valmonte spoke, he had to clear his throat twice before the words would come out. "How is she?"

Calvin stopped and slowly turned back into the room. Gazing at Valmonte's features, he rethought his earlier idea that the other man had never experienced suffering. Then he relished in his own smile as he said, "She's wonderful."

"Where, pray tell, have you been?" Emanuel Fitzherbert said by way of greeting. He had made himself comfortable in one of the settees of Calvin's study. He held a fine ceramic saucer and a nearly full cup on his lap.

"I had to pay a call across town." Calvin shrugged out of his jacket and tossed it onto a chair on his way to the drink table.

"Not tonight, Garrett. You're hardly five minutes late." Fitzherbert glanced between the clock in the corner to the man who was removing the crystal stopper from a decanter. "For the past fortnight, you have been missing. Your staff told me you left town."

Calvin leaned back against the drink table and took a long swallow of gin. "I was assisting a friend in a matter of import."

"You have friends?" The accountant was slight, a foot shorter than his employer and about half as wide. His hair was pale, as were his eyes, set behind a pair of wire-rimmed bifocals. He had always been unconcerned with Calvin's larger size, just as he had been with the other's rough appearance when he'd been hired.

"If you are finished"—Calvin downed the last of his drink and moved toward his desk—"I should like to get to the matter at hand."

Fitzherbert immediately set his coffee aside, opening the leather case he had propped against his legs.

"It is a bit, I think, out of the realm of a normal man of affairs." Calvin regarded Fitzherbert from across the top of his desk.

The other man glanced up over the rims of his specs. "I am not your normal man of affairs."

Calvin nodded. He and the other shared a bond; they had both spent most of their childhoods on the streets. Whereas Calvin had used his fists to get by, Fitzherbert had used his uncanny knack with numbers. "Have you heard of North Rutherford?"

"I've visited before." Fitzherbert opened a note-book on his lap, produced a quill out of nowhere. "It's not far from London."

"Not even a full day's journey," Calvin nodded. "I'd like you to go there tomorrow. Use my car-riage. Locate the magistrate, Kingsly, and deliver to him a sum of five hundred pounds."

Fitzherbert paused in writing. "Five hundred, you say?"

"Yes. Inform Mr. Kingsly that the money will as-sist him in his move from North Rutherford to wherever else in England he desires to go."

"The magistrate has plans to leave?"

"He will after you speak to him," Calvin said. "You tell Mr. Kingsly that a benefactor who sur-passes a certain viscount in integrity does not be-lieve his services are required in the country any longer. Tell him that either he takes the five hun-dred pounds and leaves, or said benefactor will pay him a visit. Assure him that after the visit, he will wish he had made the move."

"Excuse me for interfering"—Fitzherbert wet his lips—"but making such threats borders on ille-gal practices."

"Rest assured, Fitzherbert," Calvin countered grimly, "Mr. Kingsly has proven himself unworthy of any type of consideration. He has put my friend, a woman, in harm's way."

"Might I know this woman?"

"I doubt it." Calvin's lips curved a little. "She's a bit reclusive, my Lady Wolcott."

"Not Abby?" Fitzherbert's brows lifted.

Calvin frowned at the other man. "How do you know her?"

"I assisted her and some lady friends in a financial matter not long ago."

"What matter?"

Fitzherbert met Calvin's gaze. "I'm afraid I'm not at liberty to discuss their personal affairs. They were all very nice to me, though I could hardly take credit for helping them as much as the Earl of North Rutherford did." He smiled. "Lady Abby sent me a basket of fruit and pastries on my birthday."

"What would I have to do," Calvin inquired, "to convince you to tell me what you worked on for Abby?"

"Do me physical harm, perhaps. Yet even then I might not talk." Fitzherbert chuckled. "It's of no use to you, however. I am certain Lady Abby would not make friends with the type of man who assaults others."

Recalling the near-unconscious Valmonte he had left behind, Calvin lifted a brow.

Chapter 25

The sun had almost completed its descent upon the horizon. Abigail gazed at the orange crescent disappearing into the earth, her cheek resting against the wooden handle of the pitchfork, and had to concentrate to keep her mind blank. As a breeze lifted the tendrils of hair that had fallen across her brow as she worked, she told herself it would be of no use to replay her last conversation with Calvin. Recalling that he said he would be back before nightfall the day after he departed the estate was of no help. It hadn't been, at least, the last ten or so odd times Abby had done it before.

As the afternoon sky turned from blue to shades of purple and pink, Abigail turned back into the stables and began to focus on not worrying.

The tines of the pitchfork skidded across the stall floor, sending hay into the air and across the horse that had been patiently awaiting his afternoon meal. Achilles looked up from his feed and glared at Abby through a mane laced with straw.

"Don't look at me like that." She reached out to pluck the strands of hay from the gray's thick mane, using the pitchfork as a make-do crutch. "I know I don't do it like Timothy. We're just going to have to make do," she told both the horse and herself, "until he comes back."

"Where did he go?"

The familiar voice sent Abigail's heart slamming against her rib cage.

He was nothing more than a large shadow until he took the steps that brought him away from the light of the setting sun and into the building. He wore breeches she had never seen before—they fit him correctly—his wide-brimmed hat, and a familiar black coat. His jaw was clean-shaven, his eyes crisp and alert, and Abigail wondered if he was even more handsome than she remembered.

No, she decided, his features were just unbelievably welcome.

"Abby?" He frowned when she did not speak. "Where is Timothy? Why are you feeding the horses?"

When he came closer still, eyeing her from head to toe, she was absurdly self-conscious of the way she looked. She wore an old brown walking dress and a coat she had stained long ago with wine. Her hair was damp with sweat at her brow and nape; more of it had fallen out of her braid than not. Abigail pressed the sore and red palm of one hand to her heated cheek.

"He went to Lady Black's estate for a few days." She considered telling Calvin the entire story about the magistrate's visit and her decision to send Timothy somewhere safe. The idea that he had been gone but one day and a problem had occurred was somewhat disconcerting. "He's helping her staff at their stables."

"Then you should have Margot doing this." Calvin reached for the pitchfork, leaving Abigail no choice but to grab hold of one of the stall doors.

"Margot is in the village." Abby took a deep breath as the wind pressed the remembered scent of him to her nose. "She took the mare to run a few errands and pick up something for me at the bookshop."

He leaned the pitchfork against the wall, lightly patting Achilles on the muzzle when the horse sniffed at his coat sleeve. "Mrs. Poole?"

Abigail laughed aloud at that. "You cannot be serious."

The silence bordered on uncomfortable when Calvin only lifted a brow at her.

"Well, then"—she tried to forget the awkwardness that hung in the air about them—"did you tend to everything you needed in London?"

"I believe so." Calvin nodded and offered no further explanation as to what exactly he had been attending to.

Later she would tell herself it was the unnerving silence that made her talk and, as she had nothing else to say, blurt that which had been hanging at the back of her mind like a dark cloud. "I was beginning to worry you had found yourself another position." Her smile felt crooked as she said, "I thought you had left me behind."

His expression had been curious and concerned when he entered to find Abigail working in the stables. Now, however, his features underwent a drastic change. His jaw went taut; the skin beneath his high cheekbones sunk inward as if he was struggling with an emotion Abby could not identify. The look in his eye, the glimpse of blue fire, reminded her of the occasion he'd gone after Dobbs and his gun.

Abigail was so absorbed in the play of emotions across Calvin's face that she did not realize his intent until he moved. A startled gasp escaped her when his fingers closed around her upper arms. She stumbled on her weak knee only a moment before her legs hung weightless beneath her and her feet lifted off the hay-strewn floor. Calvin lifted Abigail until she had no choice but be eye to eye with him.

His voice shook with intensity, and Abby felt her own body quiver in response when he said, "I would never leave you behind, Abby. Never."

Perhaps she knew all along, since the night of the carriage accident or even before. It fully hit her then, however, when Calvin pressed her into the wall of his chest and kissed her, that this was and had always been more than an uncomplicated affair. She would have never shared her personal feelings, her entire self, with a man she could not love.

Telling Calvin was not a possibility. The man had never expressed anything to her that suggested he might feel the same, and there were other reasons she refused even to think about. Yet he had proven himself a faithful companion in the short time they had known each other, a gentle lover who had shown her how wrong she was in believing there was nothing extraordinary in a man's touch. It was improper for her to tell Calvin he was one of her best friends, and she certainly couldn't convey her thoughts that she might be falling in love with him.

But she could show him.

His groan reverberated against her breasts as she sank her fingers into his hair, sending his hat to the ground. She wrapped her free arm about his nape and let her eyes slip closed as she opened herself to his kiss. His lips did not simply meet and hold hers, however, but were everywhere at once. The curve of her cheek, the soft skin of her temple; he lifted her high against him to gain access to the hollow beneath her jaw. Heat coursed through Abigail's body as his large hands pressed flat against her back and lower until her bottom filled his palms.

Abigail jerked nervously, grabbing at Calvin's shoulders as her back encountered the stable wall. His hands had moved down the backs of her thighs and pressed up at her knees.

"Calvin?" Alarm tinged her tone as she felt her skirts lifting and the man holding her bring her legs up around his waist. His hand was moving dangerously close to her leg brace, her very unattractive leg brace that would—she was certain—devastate the moment.

She was pushing at his shoulders, gasping against his mouth. "Stop, Calvin! You mustn't—"

Then his hand was running down beneath her knee, across the bulky brace as if it were nothing. Nothing.

Calvin's fingers wrapped easily about her booted ankles, bringing them around his back. He winced when their bodies made contact, and Abigail was certain it was just as she feared, her brace was disturbing him, but she must have been mistaken.

Calvin steadied her against him when she tried to shift away, brought one arm around her back and his other hand to her nape.

"No, Abby, hold on to me." The words came from low in his throat, his lips barely moving to utter them. "Hold on."

He used his thumb against her jaw to keep her head lifted as he pressed his brow to hers. His skin burned like fire where they touched, and Abigail could feel the heat coming off of him where they did not.

When Calvin again covered her mouth with his, she was ready. Her thoughts were effectively shifted from her worries over that ridiculous brace to the feel of his tongue moving across hers and his hand slipping between their bodies. It disappeared under the hem of her gown, above where the smoothness of her stockings gave way to bare flesh. Then, at the same moment he slipped inside her, he pressed his thumb to that tiny bit of sensitivity he had first tested while she was bathing two nights before.

Abigail's eyes went wide, her mouth falling agape on a breath that stretched her lungs to near bursting. Calvin met her gaze evenly, his mouth a grim line, and his nostrils flared as he waited for her to accustom herself to his intimate touch, the feel of him inside her. Very slowly, he began to move his thumb in the small circles that had nearly driven her mad beneath the water of her bath.

Her fingernails dug into the material of the coat stretched across his broad shoulders. She heard Calvin take a ragged breath that dissolved into a groan as she rolled her hips against his fingers, wanting him to move his hand faster against her, wanting more. He bent his legs, and Abigail gasped at the slight drop. Her eyes slid closed on a moan as Calvin brought his hips up again.

He started slow, just as he had with those all-too-delicate circles, rocking his hips up and down. Abigail's feet, crossed at the ankles, bounced against him, and her back brushed the wall. Her eyes slowly opened; heavy eyelids at half-mast as she heard the harsh sound of her own erratic breathing interspersed with whimpers she hadn't even realized she was making. Calvin's brow was furrowed as if in concentration, his teeth bared in a grimace. Whereas his whole body was taut and hard, hers grew softer and her limbs so heavy she could hardly hold her arms up.

She felt that same vexing ache throughout her body, but where she had been certain on their first occasion together it would only get worse, Abby knew there was an impending release in the torment of Calvin's touch. She reached for it, rocking her hips faster still against his until she realized she couldn't do it on her own.

"Calvin," she cried, dropping her forehead against his chest, "please . . ."

Then his fingers shifted, from the circles that only seemed to make the wanting worse, to a long and deliberate stroke. His fingertips moved from that hidden bud of pleasure to right above where their bodies were joined.

Abigail's back arched, her head lifted, and she cried out her release at the rafters.

She heard the slam of the hand that had been touching her intimately against the stable wall beside her head. Calvin sank into her one last time, head buried in the curve of her neck, so her own sweat-dampened skin caught the sound of his hoarse shout.

His legs gave out, and suddenly Abby was falling. Calvin's strong arms wrapped securely around her back as he dropped to his knees on the stable floor, she still wrapped around him and he still trembling inside her.

"Abby . . ."

His breathing was hot and damp against the top of her head, but she could not bring herself to look at him. Not yet. Not when the tears were still in her eyes and she was on the verge of baring her heart. She buried her face against his chest, wrapped her arms tightly about his waist, and held on as if the sheer force of her grip would keep them together like this forever. After a moment, she was aware that Calvin's own arms did the same about her.

He made a joke, something about how if she had been more accurate with a pitchfork, they would be on the hard ground and not a soft pile of hay. It was enough to make her giggle softly into his shirt. Whatever heaviness had been weighing down on Abigail after she had tightened her thighs fiercely about him and screamed, passed. Her forehead lifted from his chest, and he brushed her hair off her face with an open palm.

"Where is your crutch?"

"At the front of the stables." She pointed to where the opened doors gave way to the mounting shadows of night.

Not without regret, not without more than a little longing to remain at the core of her forever, Calvin disengaged himself from Abigail and carried her with him as he rose to his feet.

She fit so perfectly to him—her arm around his waist and his about her shoulders—that when he lifted the wooden crutch from where it had been leaning against the wall, he did not relinquish it to its owner. She was obliged to hold him to maintain an even gait back toward the house.

Calvin had wanted her in his comforting embrace since he had spoken to Valmonte and inadvertently discovered the man had left her alone and certainly terrified in the icy waters of a river. The moment he found her in the stables, a well-worn gown clinging familiarly to her curves, it was all he could do not to take her then and there. His reserve had been completely shattered when she said she thought he had left her.

Recalling the languid gleam in her lovely eyes as he pressed her into the stable wall, the way she clung to him as if she would never let him go, his body trembled.

"Are you cold, Calvin?" Her tone was polite, her expression concerned as she gazed up at him.

He shook his head and, unable to resist the urge to take her into his arms again, stopped halfway to the house. He cupped her shoulders with a gentleness he feared he had not used with her moments before and pressed a kiss between her brows. She stood there a long moment afterward, her eyes closed and her swollen lips curved.

"Hello, there!"

Calvin felt Abigail tense. Their gazes met then turned toward the woman who approached on horseback. Margot waved happily.

Calvin noted, as he pushed Abby's crutch into her hand and took a step to separate himself from her all-too-intoxicating touch, the other woman appeared totally unconcerned—decidedly nonchalant, in fact—with the embrace she found her employer and fellow servant sharing. She slid easily down from the sidesaddle of the mare and reached for the satchel that hung on the horn.

"I was worried," Margot said as she marched toward them, "I'd not make it back before nightfall."

"You hardly did." Abigail took another step away from Calvin, and he heard her draw a deep breath. She brushed ineffectually at her hair, as if only now realizing it had spilled down her shoulders in lovemaking.

"I have an excellent excuse for my tardiness, though." Margot propped a hand on her hip, including both Calvin and Abby in her delighted gaze. "Prior to taking my leave of the bookshop, Miss Harriet told me some very interesting news." She opened her satchel and produced a flat object wrapped in protective cloth. "Oh! Here is the sign she wanted you to consider."

Calvin did not miss the way Abigail's hand shook as she took the wrapped parcel.

"What is this interesting news, Margot?" he asked.

Her eyes gleamed as they met Abigail's. "Mr. Kingsly has disappeared."

Calvin felt his lips curl in the darkness.

"I beg your pardon?" Abigail sounded surprised and rather elated.

"Not disappeared, exactly," Margot clarified. "Moira said she saw him pack up his belongings in a carriage and depart the village. He mentioned something to the gentleman with whom he boards about going to be with his family in Sheffield."

"Goodness," Abigail breathed.

"Goodness, indeed, Lady Abby." Margot grinned. "It appears you gave him quite the fright in your encounter yesterday."

Calvin could sense the woman beside him tensing as grim awareness curled down his spine. "Yesterday?" He looked down at her, certain she was deliberately not meeting his eye.

"Well, let me get this old girl into the stables." Margot reached for the reins of the mare. She glanced over her shoulder as she began to guide the animal away. "Perhaps tomorrow we can send for Timothy to come back home?"

"Yes, of course." Abigail smiled and nodded. She offered Calvin a brief peek before wincing and turning back toward the house.

"Abigail . . . ," he spoke warningly.

"Yes, Calvin?" She pushed open the front door and stepped inside with a sigh. Setting the package Margot had given her on the hall table, she began to shrug out of her coat.

"Are you going to tell me what happened yesterday?" He rested his hands on his hips, watching her as Abby reached again for her wrapped parcel.

She clutched it against her chest as she looked up at him. "It was nothing, really."

"You sent Timothy away," Calvin reasoned aloud, "because you believed he was in danger from Kingsly."

"If you must know, Calvin," Abigail sighed, "Mr. Kingsly accused him of stealing a hunting rifle that belonged to Lord Raleigh."

"The one I took from Dobbs?" Calvin's brows snapped together when Abby nodded. "Son of a—"

"Yes," she interrupted quickly, moving out of the foyer and toward the staircase, "we were all very upset. Most of all Timothy, who wouldn't steal a loaf of bread was he starving."

"I dropped that damned gun in the dirt where Raleigh and Dobbs stood."

"Kingsly had this ridiculous story that someone had seen Timothy with the gun. He acted as if he were going to take Timothy away with him." Abigail paused at the foot of the stairs, shook her head. "I would not allow it. I sent Kingsly away and Timothy to my friend's home just to be safe."

Calvin had followed close behind Abby, but she hadn't realized it until he covered her hand with his on the railing. "Why didn't you tell me?" He was aware of the proprietary tone of his voice even as he spoke. He was certain the woman looking up at him, the one he had held quivering in his arms less than an hour before, would become indignant with his high-handed protectiveness.

Instead, she smiled reassuringly. "There was no need, Calvin. I know you like to believe you know what is best, but I have taken care of myself for twenty-nine years. As you can see by what Margot told us, I actually do manage well on my own."

His lips parted to tell her that what she said wasn't exactly true. He had been the one to go after Raleigh and Dobbs when they nearly shot her, he who had carried her after the accident they had caused, he—in fact—who had induced Kingsly's departure.

Gazing down into Abigail's features, still flushed from his lovemaking, Calvin caught himself. Her bay eyes shimmered in the candlelight, and her nose wrinkled a bit as she smiled. His mouth snapped closed as he lifted his free hand and traced the curve of one cheek with his knuckles.

"You are right, of course," he said then and wasn't sure he was imagining the swelling of her breast.

"Calvin." Abby's lashes lowered, crescent-shaped shadows appearing at the top of her cheeks. "I'm glad your home."

"I'm glad to be home." For the first time in his life, Calvin realized he actually felt at home.

His head bowed, Abigail's chin lifted, and Mrs. Poole cleared her throat. Calvin and the woman he'd been about to kiss jerked away from each other as if they were young lovers caught by a condemning parent.

The old woman hardly glanced at them, however, but moved directly toward the staircase. She halted before she passed Abigail and turned back down the stairs, moving with obvious intent toward Calvin.

He frowned when she began to brush her hand vigorously across the back of his breeches. She gave him three good swipes with her open palm and then returned to the stairs.

"Good night then," she grunted as she disappeared up the staircase.

Calvin looked up from the small pile of hay Mrs. Poole had dislodged from the back of his breeches.

"Good night, Mrs. Poole," he said. He met Abigail's gaze, shimmering with amusement. "Sleep well, Lady Abby."

She surprised him, rising up on her toes to press a quick kiss to his cheek, and was gone.

Chapter 26

The box was sitting atop her desk when she arrived in her study the next morning. It was a plain white thing, approximately a foot wide and just as tall. Abigail's brows drew together as she glanced between it and the empty doorway.

She leaned her crutch against the desk and reached for the box. It was light and made a faint, unidentifiable sound when she shook it. Lips pursed, she slipped off the lid.

A small sound of wonder escaped her as she reached inside and removed the hat. It was simple in form, a flat top and a wide brim of chocolate brown. The lining was silk and soft to the touch. The folded sheet of foolscap at the bottom of the box caught her eye.

A sturdy hat for a gentleman who enjoys late night rides.
Or a woman pretending to be one.
-C

Abigail moved to the nearest window, where she could make out a slight glimmer of her reflection in the glass pane. The hat fit neatly atop her skull, and she found that all her hair could be hidden within its satin hollow.

Patrick Valmonte, during his courtship of her, had given Abby expensive items—the usual frippery expected of a doting and wealthy admirer. At the end of their engagement, she had given the diamond earrings, gold pendant molded in the shape of a heart, and delicate pearl bracelet to the Church.

She removed the hat and held it to her breast, where her heart was pounding out a steady cadence, when there was a soft rap on the doorjamb.

"Mrs. Poole," Emily said apologetically, "told me to come right in."

Abigail turned to face her closest friend, silently reprimanding herself for wishing she had been another, like Bernice or Augusta. Someone she could speak to about the matter pressing down on her heart. The ton referred to Emily Paxton as the Queen of Ice, but Abby believed they went too far. Circumstances beyond what anyone would ever know had made Emily into the composed woman she was today. The last in the world, perhaps, that would wish to be bothered with matters of love and longing.

"Good morning, Emily." Her smile was genuine as she moved away from the window. "What brings you by today?"

"I was in the area, visiting the bookshop." She entered the room, removing her dark maroon bonnet. Her eyes drifted to Abigail's hands. "Nice hat."

"Thank you." Abigail dropped the hat back into its gift box, smiling to herself.

"Is everything all right, Abby?" Emily asked in her usual direct way.

"Yes," the other woman replied much too quickly. Her own dry laugh made her wince before she inquired, "Why do you ask?"

"You appear anxious." Emily went to work on the buttons of her dark coat as she sat at the edge of a high-backed chair. "The only time I've ever seen you unsettled was the night Bernice was accosted by those two ruffians." Her dark brows lifted. "It was she who told me about Mr. Dobbs taking a shot at you."

"I'm fine." Abigail lifted a hand to where only the faintest scratch remained from the bullet grazing her ear. "Had he intended me any real harm, he would have done it."

Emily nodded. She folded her hands in her lap. "Bernice also told me about Mr. Garrett."

"Oh?" Abigail dropped back in her chair. She couldn't quite meet her friend's eye.

"That he confronted the viscount about what had happened."

"Oh." Abigail sighed with relief.

"That he appeared to have feelings for you that went beyond the call of a servant's duty to his mistress," Emily continued matter-of-factly. "And you him."

Abigail's heart stopped as her lashes lifted. She and Emily's eyes met across the desk: rustic brown locked with somber blue.

"Tea!" Margot barged happily into the silence that filled the room. She set her tray, laden with cups, a silver pot, and a plate of scones, on the edge of Abby's desk. "Good morning, Emily. Three spoons of sugar, no?"

Emily nodded politely at the other woman. "Thank you."

"Let me have that coat and bonnet as well." The maid reached for the articles of clothing with one hand as she held out Emily's tea with the other.

The moment Margot was gone, Abigail could feel Emily's gaze upon her again. "You know, despite the fact I am quite a novice when it comes to matters of romance," she said, "I do have other qualities that suit. I listen very well, I should think."

"I'm afraid"—Abby blew lightly at the steam rising up from her own cup—"you'll think me ridiculous. I am certainly of an age beyond such impractical ideas."

"I would never think any such thing about you, Abby." Emily's friendship, stark in its devotion, hinted that there were things residing in the woman's character that went well beyond her strict self-control.

"I think . . ." Abigail shook her head, smiled at her own reluctance to admit her feelings even to herself. "I love him, Emily."

"I see." The other woman's features betrayed no sign of emotion.

"He is quite possibly the most wonderful man I have ever known. He is intelligent, and strong, and"—she faltered only slightly—"he makes me feel things that I never felt with Patrick Valmonte."

"That's fortunate, considering what an ass Valmonte turned out to be."

Abigail's laughter surprised herself. She did not miss the slight twinkle in her friend's eye. "The reason I am unsettled, as you so politely put it, is that I am uncertain of Calvin's feelings toward me."

Emily's lashes drew slightly together. "I suppose it's out of the question to simply ask him?"

"I couldn't possibly." Abigail shook her head vehemently.

"Things are never as easy as I believe they should be," Emily said, not without a little self-derision.

"Be honest, Emily." Abigail set her cup and saucer neatly atop the desk. "What do you think?"

She expected her friend to bring up the discrepancies in their rank. To point out the dangers of laying one's heart on the line, leaving one open to the abuse of someone who might not feel the same. Instead, however, Emily said something that gave Abigail pause to wonder if perhaps she knew more about the true nature of love than she liked others to believe.

"I think"—her tone was gentler than the other woman had ever heard it before—"it is human nature to love and want to be loved in return. If so many individuals across the world feel it, it cannot be so wrong."

Abigail took a deep, shuddering breath. "Then what should I do?"

"I have no earthly idea," Emily said evenly and smiled.

Gazing at her friend's smile—the slight imperfection of it, Abigail believed, restraining her more than her strictness—she could not help but grin back.

She was about to compliment Emily's talent for listening, but suggest her advice left something to be desired, when Margot screamed.

"Good Lord!" Emily surged to her feet at the same moment Abigail was reaching for her crutch. They moved through the study door together as the sound of the scuffle down the hall increased.

"Get out at once," Margot huffed as they entered the foyer. Her face beet red, arms shaking at the force she was applying to them, the woman finally lost her battle with the front door. She stumbled backward, not falling onto her rear only because Emily ran forward to catch her beneath the arms.

The door slammed back on its hinges and the man who had been battling Margot for God knew how long stepped inside, triumphant. The odor of liquor permeated the air around him, filling the space of the foyer so that Abigail wondered if the man had not bathed in it. A cold chill settled around her heart as he blinked blurrily until he was able to focus on her.

"You are not welcome here, Mr. Dobbs," Abigail said calmly, her knuckles going white around the handle of her crutch.

Margot steadied herself quickly with Emily's assistance then ran around the man at the door to get outside. She offered neither Abigail nor Dobbs a passing glance.

"I don't care what ye did to that scrawny magistrate to make him leave the village"—Dobbs pointed at Emily, frowned in bewilderment, then aimed his encrusted fingernail at Abigail—"but I can't be ran off so easily."

"All right." Abigail nodded in understanding. "Good day."

Dobbs scowled at her amiable dismissal and stumbled farther into the foyer. His hip hit the edge of the table against the wall, toppling the vase atop it. Flowers scattered across the tabletop and water poured down its side. Emily had to step aside or the man would have brushed her with his stained coat.

"Ye had best take your high and mighty arse out of Rutherford"—Dobbs belched, and Abigail winced as a pungent cloud of his breath wafted toward her—"if ye know what's good for ye."

Oddly enough, not more than six feet away from the man, Abigail was not afraid of Dobbs. She wasn't certain if it was his pitiful drunken state or the fact she was no longer alone with him in the darkened woods, but Raleigh's cohort was less than intimidating. All that really worried Abby, in fact, was that she might not get him out of her home before he vomited on her clean floor.

"Do you have a broom, Abby?" Emily inquired rather politely considering the circumstances.

Abigail read the intent in the other woman's gaze. If they were lucky, they could shoo the cretin out like a rat. "In the kitchen."

Emily turned to leave the room, but came to an abrupt halt when Dobbs lifted the vase he had just knocked over and hurled it against the wall a hand's width from Abigail's head.

The other woman slowly moved to Abigail's side, her jaw set.

"Stop this at once, Mr. Dobbs," Abby ordered, as if speaking to a child.

His thin lips curled into a sickening grin. "I warn ye, lady, something real bad might happen if ye don't take Lord Raleigh's offer."

"What offer?" Her brows snapped together.

Dobbs reached into his coat pocket and extricated an empty bottle. He shook it just to be sure before letting it slip from his fingers. He reached into his opposite pocket.

"I told ye before," he was saying, "the viscount is going to buy yer property."

"And I told you that I would not have it," Abigail snapped, her patience waning. "Get out of my house." Even as Dobbs took another step toward her, parting his lips to speak, she caught the shadow appear in the opened doorway behind him.

"An' what if I don't?"

"Then I shall put you out," Calvin said. He stepped out of the glare of the sun and into the house, shoulders tense and features ruthless. His eyes gleamed as they inspected Abigail from head to toe. "You are all right?"

She nodded, but before she could speak Dobbs began to cackle.

"I knew yer man was back." He shifted sideways to peer at Calvin. "I saw ye last night. I had come to pay a call on Lady Wolcott an' heard ye both in the stables."

Abigail gasped. A muscle began to click in Calvin's jaw as his gaze slowly shifted from her to the man in the middle of the foyer.

"Saw ye," Dobbs went on, heedless of the dangerous ground on which he walked, "hiking up her skirts, going at her like she was a common whore."

"That's enough," Emily said coldly. She reached out to hold Abigail's shaking hand.

"Tell me, man"—Dobbs's voice dropped to a loud whisper as he offered Calvin a man-to-man wink—"didn't it hurt to have that crippled leg digging into yer ribs?"

It was over fast; Abigail thanked heaven for that

much. One minute Dobbs was laughing merci-
lessly and then he was lying flat on his back. Calvin
stood over the unconscious man, hand still clenched
in a fist and teeth pressed together.

In the quiet that followed, Abigail was lost on a
sea of embarrassment. The fact that the vile man
lying in a drunken heap on the floor had watched
them the night before threatened to make what
she and Calvin had shared of themselves a dirty
thing. It also exposed her to one of her dearest
friends as not unlike "a common whore."

Emily stepped away from Abigail's side and
walked on silent feet to where Dobbs lay. She
glanced up at Calvin from the corner of her eye
and said, "Excellent."

"Thank you," he returned.

Chapter 27

As the village appeared over the horizon, Calvin thought he heard Abigail release a sigh of relief. She had chosen to sit not inside the carriage, but on the hard wooden driver's perch beside him. It had been wishful thinking on his part that she did so just to be close to him. He had counted over a dozen times since they left the estate for the business district of North Rutherford that his companion watched the road before them—searching for any hint of danger.

She was mostly quiet, sitting beside him with the rising sun casting her face into shadows beneath the brim of her straw bonnet. The most she spoke to him had been her request that he take her to the bookshop. It was, in fact, the most she had spoken to him since the night before and long after the episode with that blackguard, Dobbs.

Calvin had made an attempt at conversing with Abigail when the moon rose high in the sky and she was alone in the parlor. She was a solitary fig-

ure before the hearth as she crumpled the deed
Raleigh had sent Dobbs to deliver. As if the com-
pressed document vexed her still, she tossed the
ball into the fire.

As she watched the flames greedily devour the
paper, her eyes reflected the glow and her chin
lifted in a not-unfamiliar gesture of tenacity. Her
voice was soft, however, barely audible when she
sighed, "I grow tired of it all."

Calvin had gone to his bed leaving his door partially ajar. He did not close his eyes until he saw the
light beneath the door across from his fade to
black.

When he realized Abigail was still in no mood
for shared banter on the way into the village, he
began to preoccupy himself with attempting to
come up with a way to be done with Lord Raleigh
and his lot once and for all.

"Calvin?"

He hadn't even realized she was speaking to
him. He glanced at Abigail from the corner of his
eye before guiding the carriage in the direction of
the seemingly abandoned bookshop. He was more
than a little surprised that her lips had curved into
a sudden smile without him even realizing it.
"Yes?"

"I asked if I thanked you, sir," Abigail repeated
herself patiently, "for my hat."

"It fits then?" The hat had been a last-minute
idea, after he had exchanged his tailor-made attire
for clothing he had borrowed from one of his servants and was departing London in a much-used
hackney.

Abby was nodding. "Very well, with enough
room to hold all my hair."

He had told the clerk at the shop the hat was a gift for his son. The clerk had eyed Calvin's clothing suspiciously before allowing him to even touch the hat—understandable considering the hat probably cost as much as the entire suit Calvin wore.

"You shouldn't have spent your money on me, Calvin. There was no need."

"I wanted to," he returned evenly. In truth, he wanted to give her something better, but expensive jewelry or another silken nightgown of the likes he had seen her in before would have caused suspicion. "Besides," he said, "what with you providing my salary, giving me a place to rest my head, three meals a day, and a coat better than any I've ever owned—I was starting to feel like a kept man."

He grinned, but his brows drew together abruptly when she looked away. Her smile faded.

Without even thinking about it, he reached out and covered her skirt-blanketed knee with one palm. Waited until she again looked at him before speaking. "I did not mean that with any disrespect, Abby."

He had brought them to a halt before the bookshop with its blocked windows, unaware of the two women who had slipped from its depths until the smaller one cleared her throat.

Calvin had encountered the tall woman in Abigail's study. The other, who was staring with some horror at the hand draped across Abby's knee, he had never before met. He dropped off the side of the carriage, ignoring the latter's still-dismayed expression, as he moved to help Abby down.

"Good morning, Harriet." Abigail smiled at the

two, though she wouldn't meet the spectacled woman's gaze. "Isabel."

"Abby." Harriet grinned back, lifting an open palm to shield her eyes. "Mr. Garrett."

He returned her bright greeting with a nod. Uncertain of how to deal with the entirely too wide eyes of the smaller woman in the high-necked gown, he decided to ignore her.

"What did you think of the sign?" Harriet asked, appearing unaware of the discomfort wafting off the woman beside her.

"It was quite excellent." Abigail held up the wrapped parcel she had held on her lap for the journey into the village. "You did a wonderful job developing the new design."

The other woman shrugged, embarrassed. "I just drew up an idea. A craftsman in London did all the work."

"Do not downplay yourself, Harriet. We must hang this right away. I'm sure it will catch the eye of everyone passing through North Rutherford."

Harriet was turning red. "Go on."

"Shall we bring out a chair to stand upon?"

"I said, go on." Harriet fisted her hands on her hips, her face shifting into an amusingly threatening mask.

Abigail chuckled.

"I'll go get the chair," Isabel offered, as if she was searching for an escape.

"I could hang it." Calvin's gaze moved between the wrapped sign to the hooks dangling from the awning at the front of the shop. "I don't need a chair."

"Thank you, Calvin." Abigail smiled despite

Isabel's groan and went to work on peeling the protective wrap from the sign.

Calvin hardly looked at it until it was lifted above his head. What he first noticed was that the design was quite fantastic. At its bottom was an open book and running up the sides of the wood was a delicate line of ivy speckled with plump flowers. The inscription in the fine wood appeared to be done of pen rather than the chisel of a craftsman. PRECIOUS VOLUMES BOOKSHOP.

Calvin froze before he had managed to slip the sign onto the hooks.

Precious Volumes.

P.V.

He looked down his shoulder at Abigail. She was gazing, puzzled, at the curve of his lips.

"What is it, Mr. Garrett?" Harriet asked.

His eyes remained fixed on Abigail, the woman he had been so certain would never give money to an ex-lover. The woman who had, in fact, not.

"You own the bookshop, Abby?"

It was Isabel who cleared her throat, her stare glacial over the rims of her spectacles. "We are all investors in the shop, sir."

He turned his grin on her, and she blinked. The sign slipped easily into place, and Calvin let his arms drop to his sides.

"How did you know?" Abigail inquired quietly.

Hell. He frantically searched his mind for a response, any that had nothing to do with him snooping in her personal accounts only a day after they met. Luckily, everything in his thoughts was falling into place.

"I've never seen a woman frequent a shop as

often as you did this one," he said, "especially when it is not open. I am embarrassed I did not think of it sooner." That much was true. He was astounded that his own jealousy of a man who had once been a part of Abigail's life had blinded him to everything that had been right before his very nose.

"Oh." Something about the way her lashes drew slightly together gave Calvin a sinking feeling in his stomach. It was almost as if she was uncertain whether to believe him or not.

"We like to keep our ownership of the store private," Isabel said pointedly.

"Some," Harriet added, "have distinct notions as to a woman's place in the world. Married, bearing children, caring for the home. Not owning a business that sells books many believe would give those with weak constitutions a fit of the vapors."

"I have recently developed an appreciation for females of an independent nature," Calvin said to Abigail.

Harriet's attention drifted between him and the flushed woman before she grinned.

Isabel disappeared inside the shop.

He should have known, he would tell himself later when he woke tied to the chair with his skull pounding. He felt nothing when he saw the woman's silhouette at the south opening of the stables. The hair did not rise at his nape, his lower body did not tighten, and his heart did not begin to beat with enough force against his ribs to make him shake. He felt nothing like he usually did when Abigail was near.

Still, Calvin expected no one else.

"Abby?" His eyes squinted in the gloom, the brilliant afternoon sunlight beyond the stable walls seeming to make the building itself as dark as dusk.

"No." Katrina Raleigh's tone had a mocking quality. "Not Lady Abigail. Sorry to disappoint."

She moved farther into the stable, and Calvin wondered at his stupidity for even imagining her shape—much too large for his taste up top and unbelievably lean everywhere else—was that of Abigail. Her features were drawn into a mask of composure, though the curve of her red lips and the gleam in her eyes were icy.

"What do you want?" It was hard to pretend to be of the lower class, hard to keep up the guise of servitude when dealing with an individual he baldly disliked at best.

"To make you a proposition."

Calvin stepped out of Achilles' stall. "I thought I made it clear that I don't want anything you have to offer."

"I think you should reconsider what you are saying, Mr. Garrett. Dealing with my cousin and I might prove very profitable."

At the thought of Raleigh, remembering Dobbs's presence in Abigail's home the day prior, he scowled. "I don't think so."

"No?" Lady Raleigh's delicate brows lifted. "Lady Wolcott must pay you very well if you would so easily turn away a hundred pounds."

"A hundred pounds?" His brows lifted with an interest he knew the woman would misunderstand.

"Yes." The word came out like the hiss of a

snake. "A hundred pounds free and clear if only you do one small task for us."

A cold fist gripped his heart. "What is that?"

"Get her to sell Edmund the land. Convince her it would be a sound idea to return herself to London with her strange friends and brother." Katrina eyed Calvin from his boots to his shoulders. "Things our associate, Mr. Dobbs, has reported make us believe she will listen to you."

"Nothing," Calvin said through his teeth, "your spy discovered would make Abby leave her home. No amount of money would ever make me betray her trust."

"Oh." Katrina batted her lashes, pantomiming regret. "We were afraid you would say that."

He heard the whistle of air, felt the slight breeze in the hair at the back of his skull. From the corner of his eye he caught another figure materialize from the shadows. He had only begun to turn his head when something heavy and hard slammed into the space above his ear. He fell forward fast, unable to control his limbs, and collapsed in the hay he had just scattered across the floor. Before the blackness closed in on him, as the shadows formed around the edges of his line of vision, he saw expensive boots step into view.

"Now we do it my way," Lord Raleigh said.

Chapter 28

Calvin returned to consciousness with a stealth that was at odds with the dull throbbing at the base of his skull. He did not jerk with alarm when awareness hit him, but remained exactly as he'd been while unconscious. Head bowed forward with chin to chest, hands tied to the chair behind his back, he let his eyelids drift upward only enough to look out from beneath his lashes.

It was a ballroom, that much was evident in the overwhelming floor space and the crystal chandelier that dangled from the ceiling. They had put him in the middle of the room—they being the three individuals conversing casually in the corner.

Lord Raleigh wore a bland smile as he watched Dobbs place a table atop the marble floor. Katrina Raleigh waited until Dobbs was finished, then arranged a quill and ink bottle, a sheet of foolscap, and a small vase on the table.

"There!" She smiled as if she were a child who had just finished setting her first table.

"Everything is ready then." Raleigh rested a hand on Katrina's hip, and Calvin felt something in his stomach churn at the odd affection that existed between the two cousins. "Now we just have to wait until our guest arrives."

"Do you really believe she'll come, Edmund?" Katrina's frigidly pretty gaze moved briefly to the man tied to a chair in the center of the room. "You don't think Mr. Dobbs was mistaken in believing there was affection between the two?"

"I wasn't mistaken." Dobbs's tone was slightly irritated. He stood with his large shoulders hunched and his neck sunk deep into the collar of his coat, glaring at his surroundings as if the upper-class frippery offended him. "I saw them going at it, I did."

Calvin's jaw clenched, his hands curling into fists. His tongue itched to say something to the bastard who had been a silent intruder to their lovemaking. Then, hands fisted and arms tense, he pressed against the rope that bound him in place. Everything in him snapped to alertness as the binding gave a little.

"We'll see," Raleigh was saying, "if you were right about what you said you saw, Dobbs."

"I was," the other man grunted.

With some effort, Calvin unclenched his hands and used his fingers to find the knot holding the rope together. The corner of his mouth twitched as he gave a brief tug and the knot loosened.

"Then she will certainly come," Raleigh continued, "and we can be finished with this business once and for all."

"Finished with her," Katrina snorted.

Calvin kept both hands behind himself, holding the rope about his wrists now. He wondered briefly what Raleigh had planned for the night. His gaze moved from the trio on the other side of the room to the ballroom's only exit, an opening not far from his kidnappers.

"There's someone coming," Dobbs said.

Calvin's attention jerked back to the man peering out one of the tall windows.

"It's her!" Katrina clapped giddily.

"No." Dobbs shook his melon-sized head.

"What do you mean, no?" Raleigh pushed the man aside to look into the night-shrouded land beyond the estate.

"It's a man."

Calvin frowned.

"Who is it, Edmund?" Katrina pressed up behind her cousin, standing on her toes to look over his shoulder.

"How the hell should I know?" Raleigh hissed, clearly disliking this change in his plans. "It's dark out there."

"I couldn't see his face," Dobbs said. "He has a hat on."

Calvin's heart stopped.

"Well"—Raleigh glared at his toady—"go find out who it is. Get rid of him, damn it."

Calvin's head slowly lifted, and he watched with sinking dread as the bulky man, nearly four times the size of the "man" in the hat, left the ballroom.

"Ah, you are awake," Katrina said.

Calvin bent his knees, preparing to rise. He could not have taken on both Raleigh and Dobbs, but the viscount alone was easily handled.

When the other man turned to face him, he folded his hands behind his back. His coat parted to reveal the pistol he had slipped into the waist of his breeches.

"What the hell are you doing?" Calvin demanded, staying in place.

The viscount sniffed. "I don't have to explain myself to some insignificant servant."

Calvin grinned darkly. "There's a lot you don't know about me."

Raleigh blinked, his own smile fading.

Lady Wolcott—
If you ever want to see your man alive again, kindly pay your neighbors a call upon sunset.

Abigail tore the note from the nail that had kept it on the stable wall; she had read the evidence that Calvin had been kidnapped half a dozen times in ever-increasing horror. It may have seemed unbelievable to anyone who did not know Lord Raleigh, but the woman who had seen the torn flesh of the mount that had failed him in the hunt and dealt with the pain of the carriage accident he instigated was unsurprised. Her hands trembled as she folded the note, her heart in her throat as she prayed Calvin had come to no harm.

She reached into her jacket pocket as she drew Achilles to a halt, fingering the folded sheet of foolscap that served as her only link to the man and those who had taken him. For a heartbeat, standing alone in the dark and gazing at the lights of the enormous house, she wished she had listened to Margot when she insisted Abigail should not go alone. Sensibility followed her doubt, however, as it had when she began to remove her gown for more comfortable riding clothes.

Timothy had not yet returned from the Black estate, so his assistance was not an option. Abby told Margot she wanted the older woman to stay behind with Mrs. Poole, just in case she didn't come back. At such a time, they were to go to the home of Sebastian and Bernice Black and get help.

A shuddering sigh escaped her, the last of her fear as she would have it, and Abigail lifted her chin. She did not tie Achilles' reins, simply patted him on his muscled flank briefly before turning toward the house.

She almost screamed when she slammed into the man.

"I forgot, I did," Dobbs said, wrapping his fingers about one of her jacket lapels. "Ye like to play dress up."

She held her tongue against a retort. Dobbs could perhaps learn a thing or two from her example. He wore breeches that were torn at one knee and a shirt bearing large stains beneath his shoulders. Abigail met his eye evenly, shifting her shoulder until her coat slipped from his grasp.

"I am here to meet with your employer." Her voice hinted at none of her fear or the worry that had consumed her since finding Calvin gone.

"He's inside."

When the man did not move, Abigail's brows lifted.

Dobbs's lips parted in a grin that exposed all his teeth and the places where several were missing. "I thought ye'd be all shriveled up underneath yer skirts, but when Garret had ye against that wall yer skin looked as nice as any naked lady I've seen."

Abigail's features betrayed her distaste.

Her heart began to pound in her ears as she was led through the maze of the Raleigh home. Not for the first time since receiving her note from the viscount, she wondered if this was some elaborate trick. The house was twice as large as hers—she'd give them that much—but she was certain they had passed the statuette of a bucking horse already. She parted her lips to insist Dobbs cease whatever game he was playing when they stopped before a closed door. Even as her guide—silent save for his grunting breaths—reached for the door handle, she heard Raleigh's voice and his cousin's high-pitched giggle.

Abby took a deep breath before entering the ballroom. She frowned over the unusual setting for the meeting between her and her nemesis, but quickly realized what the viscount had done, he had done for shock value.

The room was enormous, as big as her study and parlor combined. The floors were marble, the walls covered with a mural of plump cherubs dancing across the sky. A crystal chandelier hung from the center of the ceiling, directly above Calvin. Abigail came to a sudden halt when she caught sight of the blood on the collar of his shirt and then released a startled gasp when she saw where it had come from. His hair was matted down at one side, and brilliant red stains had dried around his ear and temple.

Her gaze shifted quickly to meet Calvin's, and something within her, the beating of her heart, steadied. He had been placed in the center of the elaborate room in an effort to make him look frail and bruised, inconsequential in his well-worn breeches and work shirt. Instead, he bore a negligence that hinted he could belong in a rich man's ballroom and anywhere else he wished.

Her fingers tightened around the grip of her crutch, her free hand clenched into a fist against her chest. She could not bring herself to speak, but asked him with her eyes—darting to the blood on his face then back to his—if he was all right.

He nodded briefly. His own gaze, such a dark shade of blue it was nearly black, tried to communicate something to Abigail as well, but the viscount's words diverted her attention.

"I'm glad to see you joined us, Lady Wolcott."

"I had no choice." Abigail faced him, unable to forget the blood on Calvin's face, the way he had been tied to the chair and put on display like a trophy. "Did I?"

"No." Raleigh smiled.

"What on earth is she wearing?" Katrina spoke to the man next to her, but her gaze remained fixed on the newcomer. "I don't understand it."

Abigail chose to mimic the same expression she had seen on Calvin's face as she watched him look the woman up and down in the stables. She surveyed Katrina's silken gown, low-cut bodice, and the lime green feather she wore in her hair with deliberate intent. "No, I don't suppose you do."

The other woman's lips became a thin line.

"Let's get down to the matter at hand, shall we?" Raleigh stepped to the side, allowing Abigail a better view of the table and single chair that had been behind him. "Would you care to have a seat, Lady Wolcott?" His gaze drifted to her braced leg, his smile too bright. "We wouldn't want you to take a fall."

"I am not here to play games, Lord Raleigh." Abigail let her fisted hand drop to her side. "You will release Mr. Garrett at once."

"Or else what?" Katrina pointed out, "There is no one to help you. Your lover is tied to that chair. Who will be of assistance, your friends? The Queen of Ice or the little nobody who married that monstrous earl?"

"You know nothing about my friends, Katrina Raleigh." Abigail's temper was holding on by a frayed string. She glared at the other woman. "You know nothing about friends in general, I suspect."

The other woman gasped. "Why, you bloody cripple—"

"Enough!" Raleigh held up a manicured hand, ignoring his cousin's indignation to focus on Abigail. "I will release your servant after we've hashed out the rudimentaries of our arrangement."

"I refuse to listen to anything," Abigail countered, "until you release Mr. Garrett."

"A word or two, Lady Wolcott. Surely you cannot be so stubborn as to refuse that?"

Calvin's low chuckle surprised everyone in the room. When Abigail turned her wide-eyed gaze upon him, ripples of awareness skidding down her spine, he had the decency to look chagrined. His eyes continued to gleam.

"I am tired of your bullying, Lord Raleigh." Abigail began to walk toward Calvin, ignoring the expression he suddenly bore, the slight shake of his head. "I will not allow you to harm my . . . servant."

"You will listen, Wolcott"—the click of the pistol being cocked punctuated her name—"or I will kill him."

Abigail froze, dragging her gaze from Calvin's to slowly turn back to the madman. He appeared unflappable in his expensive attire, his face composed, as he held the pistol aimed at the man in the center of the room.

As if from far away, Abigail registered Dobbs's pleased chuckle.

"You cannot just kill a man," Abigail said once she found the breath enough to do so. "You will not get away with it."

"Yes, he will," Katrina countered with relish. "We have concocted a plan. If it comes down to it, Raleigh will not kill your man Garrett. You will."

Abigail glanced between the cousins, not comprehending their twisted logic.

"Dobbs here has informed us of your, shall we say, passionate relationship with your servant. When he is found dead in the pond on your property, the whole village will know." Raleigh shook his head. "We will share what we heard of the fight you two had before the man disappeared."

"How we heard Garrett tell you he was leaving you for another"—Katrina's teeth shone like a shark's when she smiled—"more appealing woman."

"It shan't be long, I would imagine"—Raleigh shrugged—"before you are run out of North Rutherford, if not taken away in chains."

"That's the most ridiculous thing I have ever heard." Abigail's voice was a near-whisper as she read the intent in the duo's eyes. It was quite obvious, however illogical, the cousins meant what they said. Heart pounding frantically, she grasped at straws. "I don't know why, but Mr. Dobbs has lied to you. I would never have a relationship of the sort you imply with a man under my employ."

"I am not lying!" Dobbs blustered. "I saw them both in the stables."

"Stables?" Abigail let her eyebrows shoot upward. She shook her head, hoping her lips would not tremble as she curled them. "Not only am I having an affair with my servant, but I cannot even manage it upon my own clean sheets?" She would not look at Calvin as she took a deep breath. "I am crippled, sir, but not desperate."

"She is lying!" Dobbs hissed as he stepped forward. He pointed at Abigail as he defended himself to the viscount. "I know what I saw."

"So it would not pain you"—Raleigh ignored the other man, moving to where Calvin remained as a silent observer at the center of the room—"Lady Wolcott, to have Garrett's blood on your hands?"

"I'd rather you did not shoot him," she said thoughtfully, still unable to look at Calvin—fearing she had hurt him with her words. "It is very hard to find good help."

"Very well." Raleigh's smile grew as he let the hand with which he was holding the pistol drop. "You shall have your servant back unharmed. All you must do is sign the agreement my cousin has been so kind as to put out for us."

Abigail's attention moved back to the table at which Katrina stood, now dipping a quill into ink. Abby did not ask what the agreement was. She already knew.

"Do not, Abby." Calvin spoke for the first time since she'd entered the room.

Her gaze skittered to him in time to see Raleigh slam the broad side of his gun against Calvin's cheek.

"Stop!" Abigail's voice betrayed her, she knew, revealing her fear and, perhaps, her love. She took a step forward, and Dobbs closed his meaty hand around her arm.

Calvin's cheek had turned a brilliant shade of red, yet his face registered no pain. His gaze remained focused on the man who had hit him, his expression full of hatred that frightened even the woman who loved him.

Raleigh cleared his throat, turning away from the other. "I've been generous, I think, in my offer. Your house is not all that impressive, certainly not so nice as this one. Your land is excellent, however, ripe with animals suitable for the hunt."

"You shall even have until the end of the month to pack your belongings."

Abigail's empty hand shook as she let her gaze drift back to the document set in the center of the writing table. What in God's name was she to do?

Calvin moved almost imperceptibly behind the man who was using him as a pawn in his greed and hatred for her. He met her gaze, moved his head once to the right and then the left.

Her chin dropped and she moved to the table. The taper atop it flickered, illuminating the same words that had been penned on the document Dobbs had brought into her home the day before. The title she had burned.

Katrina held the quill toward her.

She looked to Calvin again—he did not shake his head, as Raleigh had turned to keep him in his line of sight. His eyes held hers, brooking no refusal.

Abigail pressed the tip of the quill to the document and began to write in her most elegant script.

She was very conscious of the woman looking over her shoulder as she penned *Go to he—*

"*Shoot him, Edmund!*" Katrina shrieked. "*She's not signing it.*"

Raleigh blinked with surprise, the pistol already taking aim at Calvin—Calvin, who had risen to his feet.

Abigail gasped.

The viscount released an almost comical sound before the other man wrapped his fingers around his wrist and twisted. The gun fell to the floor as Raleigh's body contorted backward then heaved forward when Calvin brought his knee up into his stomach.

Katrina screamed, glaring at Dobbs, who had been stunned into immobility. "Do something, you bloody fool!"

The blocky man moved surprisingly fast, but Abigail's mind worked faster. She closed both hands around her crutch, gritted her teeth as she threw back her chair. The base of the crutch, though she had swung it without bothering to aim, caught Dobbs at the base of his throat. He came to an abrupt halt, clutching both hands to his throat as his mouth opened and closed like a fish out of water.

Raleigh had fallen, but not without taking Calvin with him. He slammed the other's head into the floor, leaving him dazed as he frantically searched his surroundings. Raleigh began to crawl toward the pistol that had stopped against the wall.

Reading his intent, Abigail moved toward the pistol herself. She had taken only one step before something slammed into her back, knocking her facedown onto the floor. Katrina landed on top of her, releasing a string of curses. Abigail floundered, gasping for the breath that had been knocked out of her, but felt a rush of relief when Calvin propelled himself forward to catch Raleigh's stocking ankle. He began to drag the viscount—who was attempting to dig his nails into the marble floor—back to him.

Abigail's lips parted on an agonized groan when Katrina's knee dug into her back. The woman paused only to kick Abby's crutch out of reach before running toward the pistol.

"Calvin!" Abigail screamed, then screamed again when strong fingers wrapped into her hair and dragged her off the floor.

Calvin held Raleigh by the collar of his shirt, the man's face turning an odd shade of violet-red, as he stumbled to his feet. His gaze darted between Katrina and Abigail, who was kicking out wildly and digging her nails into Dobbs's hand in an effort to dislodge his painful grip.

"Stop her!" Abigail managed to offer the one shout before Dobbs slammed her forward into the table at which she had just sat. She hit the wood with enough force to send the table over, its contents scattering across the floor. Through the tears of pain that filled her eyes, she saw the taper almost douse, then the flame catch the paper she had neatly penned her curse upon.

Her wide eyes moved from the foolscap that was disintegrating into flames to Calvin, who had frozen halfway to Katrina, and then Katrina herself. Though her hand was none too steady, she smiled as she took aim at him.

Chapter 29

He turned away at the explosion, turned so his last vision before dying would be of Abigail. He only hoped that, despite her own battle with Dobbs, she would be looking at him, offering him one last gift of her peaceful gaze before Katrina's bullet found him.

Abigail was not, however, looking at Calvin. Her mouth hung slightly agape, her eyes wide, as she focused not on Katrina but a point just beyond the woman's shoulder. Calvin watched her wince, saw one of her hands lift up to shield her face and her eyes squeeze closed a moment before shards of sparkling diamonds scattered across her and Dobbs like rain. Not rain, Calvin realized. Not diamonds. Broken glass.

Katrina screamed, dropping the gun as she clutched her bleeding wrist to her breast. Calvin did not try to hash out what had happened. He ignored the woman who was sobbing hysterically as he picked up the gun. He knew the table had caught fire, saw the damn thing blanketed with flames, but he barely glanced at it. His movements were slow and deliberate as he faced Dobbs.

The other man was watching him over Abigail's head, one of his arms fit snug beneath her neck as he held her against him.

"I could break her neck," Dobbs pointed out.

"I would suggest you not." Calvin did not point the pistol at the other man. He let his gaze drift between Dobbs's face and Abigail, who, all things considered, looked reasonably calm. Looking at her—hands holding loosely to Dobbs's coat sleeve, hair spilling down over her shoulders, her eyes patient and waiting—Calvin wondered what he would ever do without Abby.

Heat filled the room, he noted. In a brief glance he saw the fire was spreading more rapidly now. It had reached the damask curtains that bracketed the windows. Flames licked at the ceiling and closed in around Dobbs's ankles.

"Let her go, Dobbs"—Calvin kept his voice calm, hinting at none of the rage that boiled inside him—"and you'll come to no harm."

"An' if I don't?" Dobbs's voice shook.

"You'll not live to see another day."

The other man took a step backward, as if he feared he might be injured by Calvin's deadly tone, then screamed. He had stepped directly into the fire.

Abigail fell to the floor when he released her to bat at the flames crawling up his stockings. Calvin reached her less than a second later, catching her by the elbows and lifting her to her feet.

"My crutch!" Abigail grabbed hold of the back

of his shirt, scanned the floor. Her face fell when she spotted the walking stick's charred remains beneath the curtains. "Bloody hell. What shall we do now?"

"Run." Calvin's gaze was on the door.

"I cannot." Abigail shook her head, shoving at his chest. "You go."

"Like hell." The words came from the pit of his belly. In one fluid move he knelt, pressed his shoulder into Abigail's stomach, then lifted. She released a breathless shriek as he strode toward the open doorway.

"What about them?" Her words shook in time with her bouncing against his shoulder.

He looked back, saw Katrina dragging Raleigh to his feet. Dobbs was doubled over, breathless after his fight to keep the fire from eating him alive.

"They'll be fine." Calvin faced forward again. "Pity."

Smoke was already filling the hallway beyond the ballroom, following them as they found the front door.

He was waiting at the end of the front steps. In one hand he held the reins of Achilles and a mare from the stables; in the other, the hunting rifle Raleigh had left behind after allowing Dobbs to nearly kill Abigail with it.

"Timothy?" Abigail swung her head to the side to look at him. "I thought I saw you outside that window."

He nodded, eyes on the flames that burst through the window he did not shoot out. "Margot said you might need help." He focused on his employer. "Are you all right?"

"She's fine, Timothy," Calvin said. He swung Abigail back to her feet, steadying her when she wobbled.

Timothy went to Abigail once she was astride the horse, looked up at her with apology in his eyes. "I didn't steal it, Lady Abby. I found it in the field. I didn't think it was right the viscount should have it back after what he did."

"It's all right, Timothy. I'm glad you had it for safekeeping." Abigail smiled down at him as Calvin swung up behind her. "You may have saved our lives."

In the glow of the fire that was filling the Raleigh home, the young man smiled.

The shouting startled Abigail, who felt, quite honestly, she had been through enough for one evening. She looked up from the last tie on her robe as she heard the door slamming. Heavy stomping crossed the hall before her own door was thrown wide.

She lifted her brows. "Is something amiss, Mrs. Poole?"

The older woman strode into the room, the lines of her face even deeper as she glowered. "The man's as big as an ox and as strong as a bull, but can't take a little of my poultice for that bump on his head!"

"It does take some getting used to," Abigail tried on Calvin's behalf. Her nose wrinkled despite herself; the jar in which the cook kept it could not contain the herbal remedy's vile stench.

Mrs. Poole reached for her employer's hand. "You put it on him then. If not, the stubborn fool might get an infection." She slapped the jar into Abby's palm, releasing a string of irritated curses as she marched out of the room.

Abigail looked from the poultice to the door closed directly across from hers. She sighed.

Not without some effort, she managed to make it across the room and into the hall. She had forgotten how much she depended upon her wooden crutch until Calvin was obliged to carry her to her room and Margot had to aid her in removing her smoke-scented clothes for her clean nightgown. By the time she reached Calvin's bedchamber, Abigail was breathing heavily and forcing herself to ignore the pain awakening in her knee.

She rapped lightly on the door.

"Go away, I said!"

Abigail blinked then reached for the door handle. She had managed three steps inside the room by the time the man scrubbing vigorously at his shoulders in the bathtub noticed her. He scowled darkly before realizing who she was. Then his scowl went darker still.

"You should not be on that leg."

"Don't get up!" Abigail lifted a hand, diverting her eyes when he began to push himself out of the bath. "I'm fine, really." She moved quickly to the nearest chair, feeling her skin catch fire when she realized she could see directly into the water. Though such modesty was ridiculous given all they had been through, she scooted from the chair to the rug beside the tub.

Calvin's lips had begun to curl into a smile until he spotted the jar in Abigail's hand.

"I'm not putting that stuff on my head, Abby."

She had to bite down on her bottom lip to keep

from laughing at his expression. There was something about a man in a bathtub, water gleaming off the defined muscles in his shoulders and back, with a rather childish look of petulance upon his face.

"It's really not so bad, Calvin." She removed the lid.

"It smells like sh—"

"I heard that!" Mrs. Poole's shout penetrated the closed door and was punctuated by the slamming of hers.

Abigail returned the lid to the jar when her eyes began to water. "Perhaps later."

Calvin's frown was less than encouraging. "It sounds like all the commotion has died down." He twisted his rag; fat drops of water spilled down into the bath to make ripples.

Abigail watched his strong fingers wrap tightly about the cloth, trailed his arms to his naked chest. She swallowed. "Margot thinks that most of the servants from the viscount's came here after the fire."

"I was downstairs for a while"—Calvin nodded—"but decided it would be best to retire when everyone kept staring at me."

Gazing into Calvin's face, Abigail could understand the others' interest. The cheek where he had taken the broadside of Raleigh's pistol had swollen, and blood still marred his brow. When she reached for the washcloth, he did not resist. "You do too much. After having been knocked unconscious, you should have rested." Recalling what Margot had told her in between moving up and down the stairs, she chuckled.

"What is it?" He flinched a little at the tentative press of the washcloth to his brow.

"Sorry," Abigail offered with due sympathy, but continued to gently wipe away the remnants of blood from his hairline and temple. "Raleigh's servants were attempting to hash out what had happened. All had been taken off their posts and sent to their respective chambers earlier than usual tonight. Some said they saw the viscount and Mr. Dobbs dragging in a drunkard who could hardly walk between them. One young woman was certain she heard a gunshot before smoke filled the house."

"What of the viscount and his cohorts? Any news?" Calvin's eyes slipped closed as Abigail's ministrations moved down his cheek. He rested his head against the lip of the bathtub, the dark line of his neck arched.

"The last anyone saw of Raleigh and his cousin, they were loading up into a carriage with Mr. Dobbs at the reins. They were overheard talking of relatives in France." Abigail let the cloth drop back into the water; her fingertips traced a pattern across its surface then brushed the top of Calvin's knee. She remembered Calvin covering her badly scarred knee with the palm of his hand as if the puckered and red flesh did not exist. Then she remembered something else. . . .

"I should think you will be forever rid of them, Abby." His eyes remained closed as he spoke. "You succinctly ruined every attempt the man made to frighten you."

Her eyes moved down the sinew of his chest to where it disappeared under the water. Her hand moved forward. "Thank you." She took a deep breath. "Calvin, I am very glad you chose to come here. Especially after what I have been through with the viscount."

His eyelids slowly lifted. "Abigail, there is something you should know."

She ignored him, too afraid she would lose her nerve. "I have never told you, because it is hard for me after all the time I've spent trying to depend only upon myself, but I do not know what I would have done without you."

His knuckles were damp when they touched her cheek. Her gaze rose to meet his and her fingers drifted closed around him beneath the water.

His jaw went immediately taut, his eyes wide. She saw the muscles of Calvin's body go tense and felt the one in her hand go hard.

"Oh." She smiled because it was not only she that could be affected so easily at a touch.

Abigail released a startled cry when Calvin wrapped his arms around her waist and began abruptly dragging her into the water with him. The now-lukewarm stuff splashed over the sides of the bath and onto the floor as he positioned her knees on either side of him, completely unconcerned with the brace still fastened about one.

He released a low growl that rumbled against the core of her when he saw the material of her sheer robe and nightgown go translucent. Abigail wrapped her arms tightly around Calvin's bare shoulders as he bowed his head into her neck and opened his mouth against the flesh there. His hands came up to cup her breasts, and she released a contented sigh as his head lowered further still. Her head rocked back as his mouth closed over her nipple through the material of her gown, groaning when the scrap of fabric proved too much a barrier.

She heard the strap tear and smiled at Calvin's brief, murmured apology as he pressed kisses down her now-bare shoulder to the eagerly awaiting flesh below.

One of her hands moved from the burning skin of his back to the rim of the bathtub as Calvin brought one of his to her lower back, guiding her closer still. The breath hissed from between his clenched teeth, a near-inaudible gasp parted Abigail's lips, and then they were rocking back and forth beneath the water.

Calvin's forehead touched hers, and her lashes lifted so they were eye to eye. She felt his lips curl against hers before he was kissing her, holding her with both hands at her hips, driving himself deeper and deeper until he felt an indispensable part of her.

Abigail sobbed—both hands now clenching the bathtub as if for dear life—and the world shattered around her. She felt as if she were floating, Calvin's sound of release coming from far away as she settled back into an awareness of her surroundings.

She let her head fall forward against his chest. "Calvin," she breathed, "I love you." The last word hadn't slipped from her lips before she was frozen solid, eyes wide in the dim light and a single hand fisted over her mouth.

Dear God, she hadn't meant to say it. The feelings bursting inside her had forced the words out. She squeezed her eyes tightly shut, terrified of Calvin's response, certain she had made a fool of herself.

He sighed. Ran his hand down her back as he continued to stir inside her. "All right," he said against the part in her unbound hair. "I'll use the damn poultice."

Despite herself, Abby giggled.

Chapter 30

He did not sleep, but watched as—somewhere between the time when the stars shone at their brightest and the first brush of pink appeared across the horizon—Abigail drifted into slumber. Faint rays of sunlight glanced off her naked shoulder and across the exposed curve of her cheek. She moved only once while he stroked the line of her back and brushed his fingers through the soft tendrils of her hair, to smile and snuggle deeper into his chest.

"Calvin," she had said no more than two hours before, *"I love you."*

The three words may have been taken for granted by another, but to a man who had never had them spoken to him before they were a precious gift beyond compare. He held to Abigail's confession as tightly as he did the soft curves of her body throughout the night. More times than he could count, as he remembered her breathless whisper against the wall of his chest, he found himself grinning stupidly at the ceiling. As dawn broke across the horizon, however, the grim reality of his situation set in and he knew what he had to do.

Calvin only hoped Abigail's sudden love for him did not turn quickly to hate.

"Abby . . ." He trailed the tips of his fingers up her smooth spine, squeezed her shoulder. "Abby, love, wake up."

She moved only to press her face further into his chest.

"It's important, Abigail." He tugged on her shoulder, laying her back into the pillowcases until she was blinking blurrily up at the ceiling.

Her eyes gleamed like gemstones as they moved to meet his. Her brows drew together as she asked sleepily, "Are you all right, Calvin? Does your head hurt?"

Her concern squeezed at his heart, and his gaze dropped momentarily to where the bedclothes fit snug across her breasts. "My head is fine."

There was a smile in Abigail's voice. "I told you the poultice would work."

His eyes met hers again. "There's something I have to tell you."

"Oh?" Her lashes drew together slightly as she inspected the lines of his face. "What is it?"

He swallowed, finding it most difficult to look at her like this, with her hair fanned out on the pillow around her, lips and the upper curves of her breasts still flushed from his lovemaking. "Firstly, let me say that I would never do anything to intentionally hurt you. You . . . you are everything in the world to me, Abby. It is important you remember that. I've never met anyone like you in all my life.

As a matter of fact, you are the only woman I've ever—"

There was no warning, as if the woman had flown over the stairs and soared to the door, forgoing the delay of walking. The door crashed open, hitting the inside wall of the bedchamber, and Margot appeared—wild-eyed, her unbound hair sticking out around her.

"A carriage comes up the drive, Lady Abby!" The second came out a horrified whisper, "Your brother."

"Oh no." Abby's eyes went wide as she shot upright amidst the tangled bedclothes, peered down the length of herself and then the breadth of Calvin's bare chest.

"Bloody hell." Calvin acted quickly. He climbed out of bed and reached for his breeches.

"Her brace!" Margot looked away quickly, searching the room for the contraption.

"No time." Without bothering to button his pants, Calvin drew the sheets around Abigail and swung her into his arms. She released a startled squeak before linking her arms around his neck.

Margot led the way across the hall, throwing open Abigail's bedchamber door much the same way as she had Calvin's.

He took her to her own bed, not without noting the sound of knocking from downstairs. She bounced when he dropped her atop the mattress, eyes still wide.

Calvin paused only to press a brief kiss to the place between her brows before turning back to his own room, never imagining the kiss would be their last.

He was aware of Margot disappearing into her employer's bedchamber, closing the door after her. He left his own open as he fished out his boots. He was tucking the tails of the shirt he had worn the night before into his breeches when Thomas bounded up the stairs.

The other man was about to take his fist to his sister's door when he saw Calvin's open, as the latter had hoped.

"Good God, man!" Thomas Wolcott changed his direction to turn into his friend's chamber. "What is going on about here?"

"It's early, Thomas." Calvin shrugged casually into his jacket. "I'd have thought you had more decency than to barge into your sister's home before she even rises."

Thomas's mouth opened, closed, opened again. He looked a lot like Abigail when his eyes went round. "How the hell can you be so calm? How can you expect me to be the same?" He strode to the window, pointed out to where the viscount's estate once stood. "I came to make sure all is going well, and what do I come across but Edmund Raleigh's home charred to cinders! I find it difficult to believe you know nothing about it, Calvin, when you smell of smoke." Thomas frowned, sniffed the air. "And, oddly enough, dead fish."

Calvin scowled, touched the spot on his scalp that was a great deal less sore than he expected and still sticky with Mrs. Poole's poultice. "If you would be so good as to relax, Thomas, I can explain everything."

"You'll forgive me, my friend, but I am finding that very difficult, considering . . ." Thomas rested his freckled hands on his hips, dropping his chin.

His shaking head came to an abrupt halt when it was tilted toward the bed. He reached into the remaining bedclothes. "Well, what have we here?"

Calvin said nothing, staring at the scrap of silk that dangled from Thomas's hand: Abigail's nightgown.

When the other man faced him again, his lips had curved into a knowing smile. "I see."

"You do?" He went forward to snatch the nightgown from Thomas's grip.

"No wonder you are so relaxed. You found some female companionship for the night, eh? Took the edge off." Thomas's expression turned thoughtful. "Not one of the other servants?"

"No."

"Someone you recently met?"

Calvin considered that, and then shrugged. "One might say that."

"Now I understand why your eagerness to leave my sister's home has waned. I'd never thought a woman would get to you, Calvin."

The other man did not hesitate, his fingers cinching tightly around the silken material in his hands. "She's extraordinary."

Thomas released a heavy breath. He moved back toward Calvin, past the bathtub and its chilled contents and toward the door. "I am sorry I barged in. I was worried about Abby."

"Abby is doing quite well."

"Let's see if Mrs. Poole will be so kind as to make us some tea"—Thomas nodded—"and you can tell me what happened." He was waiting at the door, smiling, when the gleam of steel caught his eye.

Calvin watched his head slowly turn toward the bathtub and then Thomas's smile slowly disappear.

His brows furrowed abruptly and his face turned an unpleasant shade of red. He followed his friend's gaze to the bath and then the rug beneath it, atop of which rested Abigail's brace.

"You bastard."

Calvin hadn't realized the other man moved until a moment too late. His head turned in time for him to take the brunt of Thomas's punch against his already abused cheek.

"Thomas, wait—" The rest was cut off as Calvin was forced to dive from the other's next blow.

Thomas released a pained groan when his knuckles made contact with one of the bedposts.

"Don't do this." Calvin lifted his hands, ducking to escape another punch.

The other man, smaller in both height and width, continued to close in on him. His normally jovial gaze was filled with overwhelming hatred. "You lying, depraved, son of a—"

"Thomas, stop." The staunch order, not shouted but said with grim resolve, affected the man like Calvin's could not.

Both men slowly turned in the direction of the door where Abigail stood in a clean nightgown, relying heavily on Margot's shoulder to hold her. Her eyes moved from her brother, who was panting with rage, to her bleeding lover.

To Thomas she shook her head. "You do not understand."

"You're damned right, I don't understand." His gaze rolled back to Calvin as he said through his teeth. "I thought you were my friend."

"Thomas, don't say any more." Calvin made his voice insistent, trying to break through the cloud of fury that surrounded the other.

Thomas took a deep breath before whispering like a man who was lost, "You were supposed to take care of her."

Calvin felt everything inside him turn frigid, his gaze slowly moving to the woman in the doorway. He saw the moment understanding hit her, saw her features go slack and her eyes fill.

"Abby." He tried to speak, but the word came out a croak.

"How could you do such a thing?" Thomas was saying. "I depended on you to keep her from harm, save her from that monster who was trying to frighten her out of her home. I never imagined I was actually letting a monster in it."

Though his friend's words cut at him like a knife, his attention remained fixed on Abigail. Something broke inside him when he saw her blink and her tears disappear, her chin lift and her hands clench into fists.

"Get out," she said, looking at the floor between her bare feet. "Get out of my house."

"Abigail, dear . . ." Thomas opened his arms to her but froze when she focused on him.

"Both of you. I want you both out of my house." Her tone hinted at no emotion. Her gait was steady as she turned from the room.

Mrs. Poole appeared at the empty space Abigail left behind when the two men moved in unison to go after her. "You had best do as she said, lads. Let her be."

Calvin scowled darkly, glaring at Thomas before moving out of the room.

"Who do you think you are, looking at me as if I've done something wrong?" Thomas ran down the stairs after him, indignant.

"Because you did." Calvin peered back over his shoulder, past the other man.

Mrs. Poole had put herself at the end of the stairs, her face harder than granite—a living blockade.

Calvin strode to the front door, swung it wide. "You should have let me tell her."

"You?" Thomas laughed bitterly, squinting in the morning sunlight. "The man who has ruined my sister?"

"You have no idea what you are talking about, Thomas." Calvin turned on his friend, directing rage that he knew should be aimed at no one but himself toward the other man. "I suggest you back off."

"I have half a mind to call you out for this." Thomas made a grab for Calvin's sleeve. "I won't let you abuse Abigail in such a way."

Calvin spun around, seeing surprise register across his friend's face as he took hold of his lapels and then slammed him back into the closed door. "I would never harm Abby, you stupid son of a bitch!" Calvin stopped himself before he gave in to the urge to knock the other man into the door again and again. With effort, he released Thomas's coat lapels, his teeth clenching together as he turned away. "I love her."

The ruler skidded; the piece of charcoal Abigail was using followed suit. The entire diagram was ruined by the jagged black slash that was to have been a small line. Abby's fist shook as she restrained the urge to hurl the charcoal piece against the wall. She sighed, dropped the charcoal atop her desk. The fine drawing paper crumbled into a tight ball between her hands—days of hard work and concentration so easily destroyed.

Much, she inwardly reasoned, like her heart only a few hours before.

She didn't realize she was holding her breath until her lungs began to burn. When she exhaled, her breath came out shaking.

There was a light knock on the study door. Instead of moving inside after only that brief warning as she usually did, Mrs. Poole waited until Abigail bade her to enter.

The younger woman could hardly read the expression on the cook's face. It was neither bitter nor sullen, but patiently concerned.

"Mr. Garrett has returned."

Abigail's gaze dropped quickly to the top of her desk. She swallowed back the lump in her throat. "Send him away, please."

Mrs. Poole didn't move. "He doesn't look as if he's going to take one foot off the front stoop until he speaks with ye, lass."

"Tell him he can stand there as long as he likes." Abigail blinked rapidly. "I have no wish to see him."

The other woman sighed, staring down at the toes of her well-worn boots. Abigail could only guess at what was going through her mind, and never in her wildest dreams would she imagine Mrs. Poole was recounting what she had heard earlier while standing sentry on the stairs. Listening not without due interest to the shouting of the men beyond the front door and the declaration of love from one for her employer. When her chin lifted, her expression was hard. "Ye tell him."

Abigail stared at the doorway her cook quickly vacated.

"Margot?" she called.

"She went into the village to check on those servants ye put up at the inn!" Mrs. Poole's shout was her only response.

Abigail scowled, scanning the contents of her study as if there might be some help there. Her gaze fell upon the knotted walking stick Timothy had produced for her until she could have a new crutch made and, against the wall, the small valise that held all of Calvin's belongings. She remembered asking Margot to pack then toss the thing out the front door. After sharing a surreptitious conversation with Mrs. Poole, the maid had disregarded her employer's request.

It took some time, using the simple cane and bearing the valise, to reach the foyer. When she paused at the front door, Abigail found herself hoping Calvin had decided she was not going to come and departed the property. When she parted the door a crack to peer outside, however, midnight blue eyes met hers instantly.

She made herself look away as she opened the door wide and set Calvin's bag at his feet. Abigail refused to acknowledge the painful squeezing of her heart, refused to let her eyes drift back to where the skin had broken across Calvin's cheek after his encounter with her brother. If she made it through the next few minutes without her heart seizing up inside her, she would be surprised.

"Abby, I must talk to you." He made no move to take the valise.

Abigail gazed steadily at the bag that remained at his feet. "There's nothing to discuss, Mr. Garrett. Please, take your things and go."

"I never meant for things to happen as they did."

His words were directed at the top of her bowed head. "I wanted to explain what I did, why I was really here this morning. You remember I wanted to talk?"

She remembered believing Calvin was about to tell her he loved her as the morning sunlight gleamed in his black hair and made the skin across his broad shoulders golden. Her eyes moved from the valise to his boots. "You must go." She turned away.

"Dammit, Abigail!" She stumbled when he grabbed her, but was instantly steadied by his hold on both her arms when he spun her round to face him. "For once"—his shout dropped to a whisper as his gaze explored her face—"can't you try not to be so bloody stubborn?"

"How dare you?" She slapped at his hold, knowing it was a mistake even as she looked up into his beloved features. "At least I admit to what I am. I never pretended to be anything different."

"Abby, I never set out to deceive you as I did." Calvin shook his head. "You must understand." He reached out to touch the curve of her cheek. "You said you loved me."

Long ago, she had taught herself not to cry. The pain in her heart as she stood in the doorway of her home was a thing beyond that which she had felt with a broken leg, fighting off a strain of pneumonia. Abigail's eyes filled despite her efforts to hold steady. She jerked back from his touch.

"I told a man I believed to be my friend that I cared for him, but now I don't know who you are."

"Abigail, whatever you might believe because of your brother bringing me here, you must know that I am your friend." Calvin's hands had clenched into fists at his sides. He shook his head. "Something greater than that, I should think. If you weren't being so blasted obstinate—"

The sound that came from Abigail's throat was partially a laugh, partially a sob. "I'd rather be stubborn," she said, "than a liar." She flinched at Calvin's reaction to her words. He looked as if he had taken them as a physical blow. She took a breath, steeling her insides against the man who towered over her, the man she still loved.

"If you see my brother, sir"—she lifted her chin, not knowing a single tear was trickling down her cheek until she felt Calvin's gaze follow its journey—"do not hesitate to let him know you did not fail in your service to him." Her smile trembled. "You took excellent care of me."

Chapter 31

"My lord, you've a visitor."

Calvin continued to gaze steadily into the flames.

"My lord?"

He blinked, remembering where he was. Who he was.

"Who is it?" Calvin kept his voice neutral, not hinting at the hope that came to life inside him.

"Wolcott, sir." The young doorman, Nigel, shifted nervously in the drawing-room doorway. Most of the household staff had been ill at ease with the dourness that had settled around their employer like a fog since his return. "Lord Wolcott."

"Tell him I shall call on him later." Calvin hunched further into his wing chair, hands wrapping tightly about his brandy snifter. What the hell did he expect? The woman who loved him, to whom he had lied, to come running into his arms? "I am not in the mood for company."

"That is no way to treat a friend." Thomas stepped

around the doorman and moved confidently to the chair beside Calvin's.

Calvin glanced at Thomas's dark rose jacket and brown breeches from the corner of his eye. "A bit much for a friendly visit."

Thomas chose to ignore the other's tone. "Another soirée tonight, you know. For Jeanette." He eyed his friend's plain breeches and shirt. "Did you not get your invitation?"

"I received it."

"Then you forgot the party was tonight?"

"I did not forget."

"Plan on making a grand entrance later in the evening?"

"I'm not going."

Thomas sighed, following his friend's gaze to the hearth. "You've heard nothing from her?"

"No," Calvin returned grimly. "Have you?"

Thomas shook his head. "It's been barely two weeks though."

"How long should it take?"

"Perhaps three . . . or four"—Thomas shrugged— "months."

"She will never speak to me again."

Thomas laced his fingers in his lap, cleared his throat. "I'm sorry, Calvin. Sorry I got you into this mess in the first place."

"We've been through this already, Thomas. I care not to go into it again." He looked at his friend, who was gazing at the hands in his lap. "You should go. You'll miss your sister's party, and someone beneath her might ask for a dance."

Thomas chuckled at that, pushing up from his chair. He was halfway to the door before he halted. His chin lifted, though he did not look back at

Calvin. "You know, Jeanette always gets nervous dancing. She was never very good at it. It was Abigail who was teaching her how; before her accident, I mean. I think it helps Jeanette just to see her sister there in the ballroom when the dancing starts. It relaxes her, and Abby knows it. She never misses any of Jeanette's parties."

Calvin lost his focus on the flames in the hearth.

"Never," Thomas said again.

Abigail peered under the table in the hall, frowned, and straightened.

"I believe we already checked everywhere downstairs, Abby." Margot bustled out of the cloakroom, dark velvet draped across her arms.

"I know," the other woman sighed. "I just wanted to be certain."

"He'll turn up sooner or later. He always does." Margot paused to straighten the length of pale ribbon she had laced through Abigail's hair. "Here, now. Let's put this about your shoulders." She unfolded the cloak, moved around the smaller woman.

Abigail's eyes caught the gleam of the candlelight against the soft velvet. The material was dark, but not black: a painfully familiar shade of midnight blue. "I think I should like to wear something else, Margot."

"Nonsense." The maid shook her head. "This cloak matches your gown and will keep you nice and dry if it begins to rain."

"My black cape would suit." She jerked when the cloak was put about her shoulders, engulfing her body much the same way a gaze of a matching hue had wrapped around her heart.

"Abby, this cloak is just fine. We must make haste. Miss Paxton's carriage is waiting."

"I do not want to wear it." Abigail did not need to catch the shock that passed across the other woman's features to feel instantly contrite. She bowed her head as Margot took the garment from around her shoulders and returned to the cloakroom. She reappeared a moment later with a cloak of black satin, not meeting her employer's gaze as she put it in the other's place.

"I'm sorry." Abigail caught Margot's hand as the other was straightening the cape. "I shouldn't have snapped at you."

"No matter." The older woman was smiling again, her eyes filled with knowing sympathy as she moved to open the front door. "Had I known you hated the cloak so, I would have burned it."

Abigail had found a little of her own smile at that. It continued to curl her lips as she reached Emily's carriage.

"There was really no need of you to go to such trouble," she said by way of greeting. "It was very silly to come all the way from London just to take me back again."

The woman who had been waiting outside the coach with her driver waved a hand in dismissal. "I know Timothy dislikes the traffic in Town. Quite the opposite, Hildegard loves to travel."

The burly woman who had been holding Abigail steady as she moved up the carriage steps grunted her agreement.

"Good evening, Abby." Isabel smiled from where she sat inside.

"Isabel." Abigail nodded in turn as she sat across from the other woman. A moment later, Emily was sitting beside her and the door slammed closed. The inside lantern swayed to and fro as the vehicle moved forward, illuminating Isabel's anxious expression and Emily's closed one in turn.

"Well"—Isabel took a deep breath—"I hear you had an interview for the new opening in your household?"

"Yes." Abigail folded her hands in her lap. "A Mr. Jennings from the village."

"You hired him?"

Abigail looked down at her hands. "I did not."

"Did he come with no references?"

"Actually, his references were excellent."

"Then he was much too old for the position?"

"I wouldn't say he was old, no."

"He made you uncomfortable?"

"He was very polite."

"Oh." Isabel frowned. Her gaze moved to Emily and then the roof of the carriage.

Abigail bit her bottom lip. "I should have hired him," she said. Not for the first time, she acknowledged the fact that she had been treating the men who came to apply for the position in her home unfairly. Not only did they have Tuttleton to contend with, but also another man who had made an impact on her home and her heart.

"We do not have to go to the party, you know," Emily said. "You were already planning on staying with me. We can go to my home as soon as we reach Town, if you'd prefer."

"Thank you for the offer." Abigail shook her head. "But my sister will expect me."

"You can talk to us." Isabel peered at her over the rims of her spectacles. "You know that, Abby, don't you?"

She dropped her gaze to the hands she had folded in her lap. "There is nothing to talk about."

"We worry about how you might be feeling after what happened with Mr. Garrett."

"No need to worry about me." Abigail's laugh sounded ridiculous to her own ears. "I am doing fine." Her false smile died away quickly when she felt Emily's intent gaze remain on her. "Really," she lied.

Chapter 32

The whispers trailed after him like a mist as he moved through the crowded ballroom. He did not have to dodge the individuals who milled about the floor—they moved quickly out of his way. People to whom he had never spoken in his life waited until he passed before turning to whomever stood beside them to exchange their gossip. The open stares at his size and scarred face had once bothered him, the word being passed about him being a vile blackguard even more so. Now, however, the gossips had other stories to tell. The last the earl had heard, he had fought off a group of seven men intent upon doing his Bernice harm. In the process, his body had been riddled by bullets.

The truth was less remarkable—one man, one bullet. Neither of importance considering he had, in fact, kept Bernice from harm.

"Thank you, Sebastian." His wife barely glanced at him as he slipped a cup of cider into her chilled fingers. Her bronze gaze was distressed—clearly evident behind the spectacles that slightly enlarged it—and directed across the room.

"Black." Harriet nodded her thanks, downing her entire cup as her attention focused on the same point across the room.

Sebastian followed their gazes, seeing clearly above the heads of most of the other partygoers. "Tell me again why you cannot speak to her?"

"It's our fault, Sebastian." Bernice cast him another brief glance. "Had we never insisted she have a . . . relationship with that man, things would not be so difficult for her as they are now."

Harriet, standing on the opposite side of the earl, nodded her agreement. "It was bad enough that he was in her home under false pretenses. I cannot imagine how she must be feeling after having followed our encouragement to . . . well . . ." She eyed Sebastian from the corner of her eye before scowling. "It really is our fault."

"She must hate us," Bernice breathed.

Sebastian lifted a black-as-soot brow. He focused again across the room. Abigail looked up from her conversation with Emily and Isabel. She caught Sebastian's gaze, lifted a hand and smiled.

Sebastian waved back. "She appears to be overcome with wrath."

Bernice, the only person in the world bold enough to do so, glared up at the man towering over her. "It's not funny, Sebastian. I shall never forgive myself for what we made Abby do."

Harriet eyed one of the dancers moving across the floor. "Poor Augusta is going to have blisters by the end of the evening. I think she's partially afraid stopping will mean she must face Abby."

Bernice watched the other woman and her fiancé

move past them. "She was so certain it had the makings of a great romance. I was not much different." She sighed, glancing at her husband. "He reminded me of you, Sebastian."

"Forgive me, sweet"—Sebastian let one large hand rest against his wife's lower back—"but I think you overstep yourself in thinking you and your friends could have made Abigail do anything. She is a grown woman who has taken care of herself for a long time. I cannot imagine that anyone would make her do anything she did not want."

"We are friends, Sebastian. We listen to each other."

"I don't recall you listening to your friends when they told you I was a disreputable blackguard."

"No." Bernice almost smiled. "I did not."

"I would not go so far as to say we believed you to be a blackguard, my lord." Harriet cleared her throat. "We simply received some inaccurate information about your personal character." She smiled. "Once we knew how much Bernice cared for you and you her, we brought our confused meddling to a halt."

Sebastian looked down at her to inquire, "Was this before or after you knocked me unconscious?"

"After." Harriet nodded.

Sebastian inclined his head before he focused on Abigail's brother. He had positioned himself directly across the room from his sister. Lord Wolcott's distressed expression matched Bernice's exactly as he peeked at Abigail before turning back to the man with whom he had been speaking.

Sebastian's brows drew together. "What exactly does this Mr. Garrett look like?"

"Black hair," Bernice clarified. "Blue eyes."

"Large muscles," Harriet sighed.

"And he is a friend of Lord Wolcott?"

Harriet nodded. "That is all we really know of the man."

"So, Lord Wolcott could very likely have invited his friend here?"

"I couldn't imagine." Bernice shook her head. "Why ever should he force Abigail to be in the same room with the man again?"

"Why, indeed?" Sebastian wrapped his long fingers around his wife's much smaller hand, steadying her as she blinked and followed his nod.

Bernice gasped as she watched the black-haired, blue-eyed man leave Thomas Wolcott's side, walking directly toward Abigail.

He was aware that it was Emily Paxton who saw him first. Her unemotional features did not change, but her chin lifted as she reached for the wrist of the woman who stood between her and Isabel Scott. A moment after Emily turned to speak into her companion's ear, Abigail's lashes fluttered up and down, then lifted.

He had begun to think he had imagined it all; her peaceful bay gaze, the sprinkle of freckles across the bridge of her nose, her delicate features. Yet they were all there in the moment she met his gaze from across the room, and the realization that the pleasurable weeks he had spent with Abigail Wolcott had not been a dream almost brought him to a halt halfway across the ballroom floor. Instead of stopping in his tracks, the rush of emotion guided Calvin on.

He could not be certain it was his longing to see

her again that made her so lovely this night. She wore a gown he had never before seen; powder blue muslin clung to the faint slope of her shoulders and cinched just below the swell of her breasts before spilling toward the tops of her matching slippers. Most of her chestnut hair was pulled up into braids that circled her scalp, but a few of the downy locks had escaped the ribbon used to hold the braids in place and curled against the pale skin of her nape. She bore most of her weight on a new crutch, he saw, made of dark wood that was stark against her white elbow-length glove.

Calvin wondered as he closed the distance between them if Abigail was aware of the range of emotions that crossed her features as he drew near. She had frowned at first, as if not quite believing her own eyes. Then her eyes had gone round with understanding, and less than a heartbeat later her lovely gaze shimmered with a sadness that almost broke his heart. By the time Calvin stopped before her and her companions, Abigail's chin had lifted and her eyes taken on a stubborn gleam.

The look was so familiar to him that he could not help but smile. "Good evening, Abby. Miss Paxton, Miss Scott." Though he included the other women in his greeting, his gaze did not waver from the one who stood between them.

"Good evening, Mr. Garrett," Emily said.

"What are you doing here?" Abigail inquired frankly.

"Your brother has invited me to all Jeanette's parties since her coming out."

"I've never seen you at one before."

"I've never come before."

Abigail blinked.

Calvin had decided, upon arriving at Thomas's home, that he would carry Abigail away from the bustle of the crowd kicking and screaming if he had to. He needed her somewhere private where he could speak to her, explain himself. Standing at the edge of the dance floor watching her as she watched the dancers, a new thought occurred to him.

"I seem to recall you mentioning you loved to dance, Abby." He let his attention focus on her again, held out a hand. "Shall we?"

At first he thought it was Abigail who gasped, but it was the open-mouthed Isabel beside her. Abigail's lips pressed together for so long he wasn't sure she had heard his request.

Then she glared at him. "Have you lost your mind?"

"I thought I might," Calvin chuckled. "I find myself feeling better now." He glanced back over his shoulder again. "It looks as if the orchestra is about to begin a new tune. We had best find our place."

"What, exactly, are you trying to do, Mr. Garrett? Embarrass me by making a scene?"

"It is you who are making this difficult, Abby." He reached for her free hand. "I just want you to dance with me."

"I cannot." She tugged against his hold, but he would not relent.

"I think you can," Emily said, meeting her friend's horrified stare.

Abigail looked like a woman who had been betrayed. Her chin dropped, and her loud whisper was aimed at her feet. "I will like as not make a fool out of myself. Perhaps even fall before everyone."

"You will not let her fall"—Emily turned to Calvin—"will you, Mr. Garrett?"

"Never." Calvin took no pause to wonder at his new ally.

"Here, Abby." It was Isabel who reached for her crutch. "I'll hold that for you."

Abigail wobbled unsteadily, suddenly without the crutch, and Calvin moved forward. He caught her other hand in his as she watched in stunned silence while Isabel moved to stand behind Emily. The crutch she held carefully in both her hands well beyond the other woman's reach. She met Abigail's gaze with a brief, apologetic smile.

Abigail slowly turned back to Calvin. The breath that parted her lips was none too steady, and he thought he could feel the rapid beat of her heart through her hands.

The music came to a halt, and those who had been dancing erupted into breathless applause. Calvin stepped backward onto the floor, bringing Abigail along with him. He looked toward where the orchestra had positioned themselves in the balcony. Calvin nodded at Thomas, who, in turn, nodded toward the conductor.

"Ah." Calvin stepped closer to his less-than-ecstatic dance partner as the orchestra began. "A waltz. I am no expert on dancing, love, but are we not to hold tightly to each other?"

Abigail peered up at him, more flustered than he had ever seen her. "What did you say?"

Their noses almost touched he leaned in so close to whisper, "Hold on."

Her body remembered. As if the abuse years before were a thing to be surmounted, her limbs began to move of their own accord. One of her hands settled lightly atop Calvin's shoulder; the other shook only a little in his warm grip. The waltz was familiar; she had danced to it a dozen times at least. Mostly when she was younger and trying to teach Jeanette the steps. She could almost hear the sound of their mutual counting as her feet stepped in time to the melody.

Abigail was barely aware of her surroundings, looking over her partner's shoulder as he guided her unerringly about the floor. She saw the faces of her friends in passing: Harriet and Bernice with their mouths slightly agape, Isabel looking chagrined, and Emily as composed as ever save for an unusual gleam in her eye. Abby tried to direct a scowl toward the first two women, but couldn't manage a dirty look for their abrupt and perplexing abandonment. It was when she saw Augusta, standing to the side with her fiancé, Maxwell Darcy, that something inside her gave a lurch. When the two women's gazes met, Augusta's lips curved in a smile as brilliant as the moon shining outside.

Abigail finally looked at her partner. Her gaze started at the tips of his Hessians and traveled up over the breeches he wore, dark brown and tailored to fit across his legs. The shirt he wore was made of expensive lawn, his cravat tied in an elegant knot. Everything he wore rebuked any idea that he might be a servant, might have ever worn hand-me-down clothing. Everything except the jacket he wore.

Abigail's gift.

She was frowning over the black material when

the music came to an unexpected halt. Abigail stumbled a little, but no one but she and the man who put a securing arm around her waist noticed.

Calvin slipped into a bow, the light from the chandelier above gleaming across his dark hair and then reflecting in his eyes when he straightened. Gazing into the dark blue depths, everything came rushing back to Abigail: the love and the betrayal.

She steadied herself on her good leg and dropped her gloved hands to her sides so she wouldn't have to touch him as she said, "Would you be so kind as to take me back to my friends now?"

He was smiling, she noticed belatedly, but the smile slipped away. "Not yet." He linked his arm through hers and began to guide her off the dance floor.

She scowled when she realized they were headed not toward any of her friends, but to the opened French doors not far away. "Mr. Garrett," she hissed so those they passed would not hear, "what are you about?"

"You are going to listen to me," he said as he lifted her without warning down the steps into the moonlit garden, "whether you like it or not." He halted once to glare at her in the little light that remained from the ballroom. "And, if you will recall, it is Calvin."

She huffed as he took her hand, moving them so the strains of the orchestra's latest tune grew farther and farther away. "How do I know that is your real name, sir, and not another lie?"

Calvin rounded on her so abruptly she released a startled sound. Abigail took a shaky step backward and encountered the rough bark of a tree.

She used both hands behind her to hold herself upright.

"You go too far, Abigail."

She worried that she had pushed the man to his limits. His tone was enraged and his eyes gleamed like black fire in the muted starlight. He stepped closer, until the tree was biting into the skin of her back and she had to lift her chin even higher to hold his gaze.

"What I did, what brought me to your home in North Rutherford, I did for your brother. Thomas was worried about you. I believed I was going to play the role of servant, investigating Raleigh and his attempts to frighten you out of your land, to an aging spinster who needed protecting."

"And you found her, did you not?" Abigail's voice shook.

"No, Abby." Calvin shook his head, his voice suddenly dropping. "You were nothing like what I expected. You are damnably stubborn and independent, to the point you put your own life at risk."

"Is this supposed to be a compliment, sir?"

"And a quiet peace seems to surround you everywhere you go." Calvin went on as if she hadn't spoken. "You sit down for dinner with individuals others of your rank might never speak to and break the law to save an animal from ill treatment. The one physical flaw you have"—his hot breath beat against her cheek, and Abigail was certain she felt it steal around her nape and down along her spine—"only serves to further illustrate how perfect you are in every other way imaginable." He paused to take a breath, his gaze traveling her body like a caress. "Your inability to lie is amazing, as is your ability to make a man who has never been cared for in his life feel like he has finally found a home."

Abigail fought through the clouded awareness that filled her insides. She scowled. "You have a home, Calvin. A marquis does not simply appear out of thin air."

"The things I told you about my past were not lies." In the dim light, his jaw flexed. "My father was of rank and considerable wealth, but my mother was less socially accepted. Both my father and her penniless family abandoned her once she was with child, and she died shortly after my birth. I spent a few happy years with a kind parson and his wife, but when the lady of the house fell ill they had no choice but to send me to the workhouse. I left there when I was ten and seven and was beginning to make a considerable living aiding some other young men in stealing from the docks late at night, when the gentleman in charge of my father's estate found me. The marquis had died from a blow to the head while in one of London's less-than-charming brothels. He had never married, and as far as anyone knew, I was his only living heir."

Abigail was stunned into silence. Her fingers hurt where she was digging them into the bark of the tree.

"Your brother," Calvin went on, "was one of the first who befriended me. There are few in the ton who do not know I am a bastard son who a twist of fate made into a marquis. Thomas did not particularly care about my past; he did not judge me as others found it so easy to do. You and he have a lot in common."

"Our father came into his title after his two eldest

brothers died at sea. On the social scale," Abby explained, "we are somewhat lacking."

"Perhaps that is why you and I got on so well, Abby." His touch was light against her cheek. "We had more in common than we knew."

"Calvin." Abigail struggled against the rush to her heart at his touch. "You should have told me who you were. If not as soon as we met, at least before . . . before I . . ." Her gaze drifted into the darkness beyond his shoulder.

"Can you deny that you would have sent me away had I told you the truth after our first kiss?"

"That is not the point—"

"It is the point, Abby. You would have sent me away, just as you did two weeks ago. Then you would have been left alone to fend for yourself against that bastard Raleigh and his cohorts. I couldn't let that happen."

"So instead you let me make a fool out of myself"—her teeth clenched in an effort to hold back her tears—"by professing my love for a man I thought was my servant."

"I never thought you a fool." Calvin's warm palm wrapped about her nape; his thumb forced her chin to rise. "I believed you were the most wonderful woman I'd ever met."

Abigail's heart pounded in her ears. The words were nice, and they nearly broke her heart, because they were not the ones she so needed to hear. Not only did she give her heart to a man who was in her home only because her brother had asked him, but one who did not love her in turn. "I think I should like to be left alone now, Calvin."

"All right, Abigail." He released her, took a step away. "Remember, I may have lied to you about my station and reasons for coming into your life, but I never broke my promise."

She blinked at him. "Promise?"

"I never left you behind." Calvin turned away. "You are leaving me."

Her heart skipped a beat when, minutes later, she heard the approaching footsteps. She lifted her forehead from the tree trunk believing he had come back to tell her he had forgotten to tell her one thing. That he loved her.

When Abigail peered over her shoulder at the man who approached, her hope died fast and silent.

"Calvin asked me to bring this out to you." Thomas held out the crutch.

Abigail took a breath, slipped her arm into the wooden cup, and rested her hand upon the grip.

"You know it is not entirely his fault, Abby. We are both responsible," Thomas insisted. "You should be angry at me as well."

Abigail glared at him as she began to march back toward the house. "I am angry at you."

"Oh." Thomas paused before following. "Good, then."

She hoped that was the end of it, but her brother ran up behind her. "You know, I did it because I was worried about you, and you wouldn't tell me what was going on."

"I know, I know." Abigail waved her free hand, wishing she could maneuver her crutch and blasted braced leg faster. "I'm damnably stubborn."

"Then, when I found out about what Calvin had done . . . well, I was quite furious."

Abigail stopped, turned to scowl at her brother. "You know, Thomas, normal brothers do not bring up such personal things with their sisters. It is considered rude."

"Terribly sorry." He was breathless when they reached the steps going up into the ballroom. "I just wanted you to know I felt as betrayed as you, even more so."

Abigail rolled her eyes. "It appears you recovered well. You did bring him to the party, did you not?"

"Yes, well, that was after I realized why he"—Thomas cleared his throat—"did what he did." He ran his fingers through his hair, removed a handkerchief to blot first Abigail's tear-stained cheeks and then his damp brow. "I like to think I understand now. In fact, after what Garrett told me, I cannot say I would not have done the same."

Abigail's brows snapped together. She was unable to imagine what Calvin had told her brother about her. "What, pray tell, did he say?"

Pale green eyes locked with those of brown. "He told me he loves you."

Chapter 33

The raging storm beyond the windows of Emily Paxton's stone mansion brought with it nightmares. For the woman who tossed and turned upon a bed in one of the guest chambers, her dreams were not haunted with toppling carriages or the dying cries of horses. Instead, she stood in a place of cold shadows and watched as the only man she ever loved walked out of her life forever.

On a brutal crash of thunder, she woke.

Abigail paused only to put on her brace and slippers. The ends of her robe billowed out about her so she appeared a specter throwing open the door of the house to the torrential winds beyond. She squinted against the rain and kept moving, not realizing the carriage was in the drive until she almost ran into it.

"Let me help you inside, m'lady." The driver's voice was muffled behind the heavy coat she wore, her face indistinguishable beneath her floppy brimmed hat.

"Hildegard?" Abigail asked even as the other woman lifted her into the cab as if she weighed nothing.

"Aye." The driver hunched her large shoulders against a particularly fierce gust of wind. "Miss Paxton said you might have an emergency this evening. Told me to keep an eye out." Hildegard slammed the carriage door closed, and the vehicle creaked as she took her place behind the reins.

As the wheels began to move, Abigail leaned forward to peer out the conveyance's only window, set centered in the door. Even so far away, she met her friend's gaze from where she stood backed by candlelight at her bedchamber window.

Emily lifted a hand to wave.

He thought the pounding was coming from his skull. It was very possible he was feeling the after-effects of the gin he had consumed before collapsing into bed. Calvin lifted a hand to the back of his head, fully expecting to feel the vibrations from his throbbing brain.

The pounding came again.

"Bloody hell," he growled into his pillowcase and threw himself onto his back. He was almost fully clothed, had only doffed his cravat before dropping onto the mattress. His throat was dry, his skin hot, and a sense of overwhelming loss ate at his insides.

The knock came again from his bedchamber door.

He could easily imagine the cook with her weathered old face parted in a grin as she dragged him from his painless sleep.

"Damn it, Mrs. Poole!" he shouted at the ceiling, eyes still closed. "Can you not leave a man alone?"

"My lord?" The voice on the other side of the door was a little disoriented. "It is Nigel." He clarified. "Your servant."

Calvin's eyelids parted and he found himself staring at the ceiling of his bedchamber in London, not North Rutherford. His jaw clenched as he remembered why he had returned to Town, why he drank himself into oblivion.

"I know . . ." Nigel's voice was shaky. "I know you said you wanted no interruptions tonight, but you have a visitor."

Calvin glared out the nearby window and found the time indistinguishable in the turbulent gray sky. He knew he had not returned home until midnight; it had to have taken him two hours to finish the bottle of gin. God only knew what hour of the morning it was.

"Sir, I'm very sorry," the servant continued through the door, and his employer could almost sense him wringing his hands together, "but I thought it was important, what with it being so early. The lady, she is soaked through and only in her nightgown."

Calvin pushed himself into a sitting position, threw his booted feet over the bed.

"She's . . ." Nigel's voice lowered. "Sir, she is crippled."

"She is not a cripple, Nigel." The younger man released a surprised squeak when Calvin threw open the bedchamber door. "Do not ever refer to her as such again."

Nigel bowed his head in apology, his face going red. "I beg your pardon, my lord."

"Where is she?" Calvin scowled down at himself as he strode to the stairs; he reached for the buttons of his wrinkled shirt.

"The entryway." Nigel tripped down the stairs after his employer. "She refused to go any farther. Afraid she'd ruin the rugs, wet as she was." The young man released a muted grunt when he slammed into the broad back of his employer, immobile on the last step.

Abigail stood just inside the front door, barely illuminated by the taper left burning on a table nearby. She brushed ineffectually at the wet tendrils of hair that hung to her cheeks. Her teeth chattered until she looked up and met Calvin's gaze.

"Go get a blanket, Nigel," he said without looking back. "Hot tea."

"Yes, my lord." Nigel contorted his body to ease around the larger man, offering Abigail a slight bow before he passed her.

She had one hand fisted, pressed against her heart; the other held her crutch in a white-knuckled grip. "I'm sorry I woke you, Calvin. I never even stopped to think. . . ."

He parted the space between them in two great strides, shrugged out of the coat she had given him as a gift and swung it around her shoulders. The dark material engulfed her small frame as she clutched its lapels together.

"Come into the parlor." Calvin found his voice unsteady as he guided her down the hall. He positioned her before the fire, pushing a chair toward her, but she refused to sit.

Abigail licked her already-damp lips, her lovely

gaze shifting about the room nervously. "You have a nice home, Calvin."

He lifted a single brow, folding his arms across his chest as he propped a shoulder against the hearth. "You came here in the middle of the night to inspect my housing?"

"No." Abigail shook her head, her gaze dropping to his booted toes. "It's just"—she took a deep breath—"Timothy cannot recall where you put all the tools."

Both Calvin's brows lowered.

Abigail cast him a brief glance. "And Margot needs help with the upstairs rugs because Mrs. Poole has a bad back and I cannot carry them."

"The rugs?"

"Yes, sir. And Timothy can't stand to drive the carriage anymore and Harry has gone missing again."

"Again?"

"Again." Abigail sighed.

"You came here in the rain, in your nightgown, to ask where the tools are and obtain guidance on the best way to beat the rugs?"

"Yes." Abigail smiled, and then frowned just as quickly. "No." Her lashes slowly lifted and her bay eyes met his. "We need you to come back."

Calvin felt his heart shudder against his ribs. "Abby . . ."

A tear slipped down her pale cheek, then another. Her head lifted as he approached. "I miss you, Calvin. I want you to come home."

Fine china clattered, and both Abigail and Calvin turned to look at Nigel, weighed down with several blankets and a tea tray. He gaped at them in turn.

"Excuse us, Nigel."

"Of course, my lord." The young man disappeared as quickly as he had come.

As if they hadn't been interrupted, Calvin lifted his hand and rested his open palm against Abigail's chilled cheek. She pressed into his touch, just as she had the night she had first given herself to him. He put an arm around her, brushed his lips across her waiting mouth. He could feel her heart pound in time with his own.

"Abigail," he said against her lips, "I love you." He wrapped both arms around her when she pressed her face into his chest. Against the top of her head, he breathed, "I very much want to come home."

Her crutch hit the floor with a sharp crack as Abigail brought both her hands to his back and lifted herself for his kiss.

Epilogue

Abigail peered out the parlor window, her eyes going round as she watched a familiar phaeton begin up the drive. She spun back around to the clergyman.

"Can we not hurry this up a bit?" She interrupted his prattle about the joys of love. When the old man made a face, she smiled. "Please?"

"You'll have to forgive my Abby, Pastor Fine." Calvin put his hand to her waist and hugged her to his side. "She, like all females, is eager to be an obedient wife." He smiled, ignoring her scowl.

"Ah." The clergyman peered between the couple. "Well, let's skip to the vows, shall we?"

Calvin nodded.

"Oh," Abigail gasped, pushing away from him. "Oh!" She maneuvered herself rather gracefully around the two men and toward the window from which she had been gazing worriedly.

Calvin offered the clergyman a chuckle, eyeing

Abby from the corner of his eye. "Are you all right, love?"

She bit her bottom lip as she concentrated on the shifting of the curtain down where it touched the floor. The plump bulge pressing against the damask made its way to the end of the fabric before Abigail threw back the material. "Got you!" She scooped Harry easily into her free hand and turned back to the men who were staring at her.

"Are we finished?"

"Bloody hell." The pastor slapped his Bible closed, his neck turning red as he glared at Calvin, then Abigail, and then the rabbit that stared at him from within her arms. "You are man and wife."

"Very good." Abigail beamed.

There was a light knock from the front door.

"You know," Pastor Fine said to Calvin when the younger man reached to shake his hand, "most women prefer a long ceremony, complete with fancy dress and flowers."

"I believe I knew from the first, Abby was not like most women." He saw her tap a toe impatiently as she watched him from the parlor doorway. "I also learned that when she takes on a certain stubborn tilt to her chin, she will not be refused. Such was the case when she concocted the marriage arrangements."

"Why should there be a need for such a hasty wedding?" The old man's gaze rested on Abigail's stomach, not out of proportion beneath her plum-colored gown. "She's not in trouble, is she?"

"No, sir, nothing as exciting as that." Calvin lifted a brow as she stopped tapping to walk toward him. "She is just a woman who cannot bear to lie."

"I forgot, Calvin," Abigail said when she stopped before him.

"Yes?"

She pressed her lips to his, gently, only stopping to take a nip at his bottom lip as she drew away. "I love you," she said. Her forehead rested momentarily against his shoulder, and he gently squeezed her nape.

"Lord Garrett," Margot appeared in the doorway, smiling knowingly between Calvin and Abigail. "Lady Garrett—the Redmans have arrived."